W9-BDY-879

Date: 4/19/18

GRA WATARI V.4
Watari, Wataru,
My youth romantic comedy is wrong, as I expected.

PALM BEACH COUNTY
LIBRARY SYSTEM
3650 Summit Boulevard
West Palm Beach, FL 33406-4198

Yuigahama, you hold the knife steady and turn the pear.
Yukino Yukinoshita

Outdoor cooking
...
Wh-why?! But I watched my mom do it so many times!
Yui Yuigahama

Komachi
Hikigaya
Look!
Look, Bro!
I got
a new
swimsuit!
Shizuka
Hiratsuka

Swimming in the river
Yukino Yukinoshita
Yui Yuigahama

...I think it's quite nice. It suits you.
U-um...Yukino?
Komachi Hikigaya

Does a magician count as a monster...?
Spooky-forest trek
Saika Totsuka
Yukino Yukinoshita

Contents

MY YOUTH ROMANTIC COMEDY iS WRØNG, AS I EXPECTED

Wataru Watari
Illustration Ponkan⑧

VOLUME
4

YEN ON
NEW YORK

MY YOUTH ROMANTIC COMEDY IS WRONG, AS I EXPECTED Vol. 4
WATARU WATARI
Illustration by Ponkan⑧

Translation by Jennifer Ward
Cover art by Ponkan⑧

This book is a work of fiction. Names, characters, places, and incidents are the product of the author's imagination or are used fictitiously. Any resemblance to actual events, locales, or persons, living or dead, is coincidental.

YAHARI ORE NO SEISHUN LOVE COME WA MACHIGATTEIRU.
Vol. 4 by Wataru WATARI
© 2011 Wataru WATARI
Illustration by PONKAN⑧
All rights reserved.
Original Japanese edition published by SHOGAKUKAN.
English translation rights arranged with SHOGAKUKAN through Tuttle-Mori Agency, Inc., Tokyo.

English translation © 2018 by Yen Press, LLC

Yen Press, LLC supports the right to free expression and the value of copyright. The purpose of copyright is to encourage writers and artists to produce the creative works that enrich our culture.

The scanning, uploading, and distribution of this book without permission is a theft of the author's intellectual property. If you would like permission to use material from the book (other than for review purposes), please contact the publisher. Thank you for your support of the author's rights.

Yen On
1290 Avenue of the Americas
New York, NY 10104

Visit us at yenpress.com
facebook.com/yenpress
twitter.com/yenpress
yenpress.tumblr.com
instagram.com/yenpress

First Yen On Edition: January 2018

Yen On is an imprint of Yen Press, LLC.
The Yen On name and logo are trademarks of Yen Press, LLC.

The publisher is not responsible for websites (or their content) that are not owned by the publisher.

Library of Congress Cataloging-in-Publication Data
Names: Watari, Wataru, author. | Ponkan 8, illustrator.
Title: My youth romantic comedy is wrong, as I expected / Wataru Watari ; illustration by Ponkan 8.
Other titles: Yahari ore no seishun love come wa machigatteiru. English
Description: New York : Yen On, 2016–
Identifiers: LCCN 2016005816 | ISBN 9780316312295 (v. 1 : pbk.) | ISBN 9780316396011 (v. 2 : pbk.) | ISBN 9780316318068 (v. 3 : pbk.) | ISBN 9780316318075 (v. 4 : pbk.)
Subjects: | CYAC: Optimism—Fiction. | School—Fiction.
Classification: LCC PZ7.1.W396 My 2016 | DDC [Fic]—dc23
LC record available at http://lccn.loc.gov/2016005816

ISBN: 978-0-316-31807-5

10 9 8 7 6 5 4 3 2 1

LSC-C

Printed in the United States of America

MY YOUTH ROMANTIC COMEDY IS WRONG, AS I EXPECTED

four

Cast of Characters

Hachiman Hikigaya........... The main character. High school second-year. Twisted personality.

Yukino Yukinoshita...........Captain of the Service Club. Perfectionist.

Yui Yuigahama..................Hachiman's classmate. Tends to worry about what other people think.

Yoshiteru Zaimokuza.........Nerd. Dreams of becoming a light-novel author.

Saika Totsuka.................... Tennis club. Extremely cute. A boy, though.

Shizuka Hiratsuka.............Japanese teacher. Guidance counselor. Single.

Komachi Hikigaya.............Hachiman's little sister. In middle school.

Hayato Hayama..................Hachiman's classmate. Popular. In the soccer club.

Yumiko Miura....................Hachiman's classmate. Reigns over the girls as queen bee.

Hina Ebina.........................Hachiman's classmate. Friend of Miura and Yuigahama. Slash fangirl.

Rumi Tsurumi.....................Elementary schooler.

On Souseki Natsume's *Kokoro*
by Hachiman Hikigaya, Class 2-C

Souseki Natsume's *Kokoro* is the ultimate loner novel. The central theme of this work is most certainly not the romantic entanglements that compose the love triangle, but a rather more poignant story about distrust. This is a story that depicts individuals isolating themselves from the world, a story of the truth that there is nothing the world can do to help you.
You may set off all the right flags, but you will never get your happy ending. You may find someone who understands you, but that person will never be your friend. Neither love nor friendship will cure your isolation. Natsume calls this helpless feeling *loneliness*. But we, who live in the modern world, are already used to such loneliness. We accept it as very much a matter of course. Perhaps you could also describe this as the establishment of individualism.

Through this story, Souseki is communicating that humans are fundamentally lonely creatures and have no choice but to reflect on how they will live cast out

Summer Assignment: **Book Report**

from the collective, understood by no one. For example, take the narrator, Sensei, K, and Okusan. All of them are isolated. Though they have set off the right flags and won love, even so, their thirst cannot be quenched. Though they might live in the same place at the same time, they cannot share one heart, one *kokoro*.

It's been more than one hundred years since the Meiji period. The fact that this novel is still read, even after all that time, only proves this is a fundamental truth regarding human nature. I would like to close this essay with a quote from Sensei: "Nobody in this world fits the classic mold of the villain. Normally, everyone is good or at least ordinary. But in the right circumstances, they may change suddenly, and this is what makes them so frightening. One must always be on one's guard."

Trust no one. Source: Souseki Natsume.

1

This is how **Hachiman Hikigaya** spends his summer vacation.

"Wh-whoa..."

The whirring electric fan drowned out the tiny gasp, gently shaking its head side to side. Komachi slowly did the same. "Bro, you didn't have to go this far. Not this far..." She softly laid the sun-faded composition on the table. "I know what you're like, but this essay is too much... It's too much, man!"

"Shut up," I replied. "You're the one who wanted to copy my essay. If you don't like it, then don't look at it." I was saddened that Komachi had decried my essay and embarrassed that she had seen my writing from so long ago, and I snatched the paper from her hands.

"Hey, c'mon, I'm sorry. I'll just use the parts that look useful. So let me have it! ♪" Komachi pleaded. "...Well, most of it looks useless, though," she added, for no discernible reason, before she reclaimed the essay and started copying it down into her notebook.

This was about her summer homework. Apparently, in some elementary schools, they hand you a study workbook called the "Summer Vacation Companion," but once you hit middle school, you don't get that anymore. In other words, your summer vacation is devoid of companions. To express that in a cooler way: Friend/Zero. Not many characters in that one. I bet illustrations would be a cinch.

Komachi was working on her book report. My old middle school, the one she currently attends, doesn't assign much summer homework.

You get worksheets for English and math, a supplementary kanji workbook for Japanese, an independent research project, and an essay or a book report.

As Komachi moaned and groaned, writing in fits and starts, I watched her with an ice-cold MAX Coffee. There's a unique sweetness to the condensed milk that tightens your throat and percolates up into your head in a way that no café au lait can imitate. I also recommend pouring it over shaved ice.

Even adults need some sweetness in their lives. So when I need coffee, I make it MAX Coffee.

That's my idea for a stealth marketing campaign, since that's been so popular lately. Well, it's not like I'm getting paid for it, so it'll never actually happen.

The table was cluttered with a variety of textbooks. This mess had resulted from a vice characteristic of kids who don't know how to study: just open all the books at once. I pulled out a single sheet of paper from the pile and skimmed it briefly. The sheet had *middle school third-year summer homework* printed on it, and below the title were the specifics of Komachi's summer assignment. Said details were, well, what I previously explained. A single sentence on that page caught my eye.

"Hey," I said. "It doesn't have to be a book report, so why don't you just write a regular essay?"

"Huh?" Komachi raised her head, half rose from her chair, and peered at the paper in my hands.

"Look, here. It says, 'a book report or an essay on the subject of taxes.'"

Kids who don't like writing about books often don't enjoy reading them in the first place, and kids who hate reading inevitably end up being terrible writers. Komachi fit the model perfectly. She didn't generally read books, and aside from e-mails, she hardly composed anything. A regular essay with no required reading would probably be the easier assignment for a kid like her.

"Yeah, but taxes? I don't understand all that...," said Komachi.

"Hold on. I think I wrote about that in middle school." I began fishing through the cardboard box on the table. It was basically a case of memories. My mom had collected stuff I'd left lying around, like essays, class albums, and independent research projects, and stored them in that box. Komachi wanted to rip off one of my old book reports, so that was why it was out. As I rummaged around, I encountered a paper that appeared to be the right one. "I think this is it."

"Gimme, gimme!" Komachi jumped at me, twining around my arm, and yanked the paper away.

On Taxes

by Hachiman Hikigaya, Class 3-C

The institution of progressive taxation is evil. Those who earn more are taxed more, which is indistinguishable from receiving no reward for your labor. The more you earn, and the more you work, the more taxes are levied on you, and you receive nothing in return. In other words: Get a job and you lose.

If the purpose of progressive taxation is to make everyone equally happy, then I am forced to call the idea foolish. Equality in happiness is, in the first place, impossible. Most of all, the attempt to gauge the contentment of individuals through monetary means alone is shallow and thoughtless. At this point, we should explore introducing a progressive tax measure on normies, where people are taxed based on the number of friends and significant others they have.

Komachi read the first part of the essay and then immediately folded up the paper into a tiny square. "I'll write the book report…," she muttered with a short, subdued sigh.

"O-oh…um, sorry, I guess."

"No, *I'm* sorry…"

The fan shuddered and whirred with a low mechanical hum. A large brown cicada began chirping as if it had just remembered it should.

"…So, well…," I said, "I'll help you with your independent research project, 'kay?"

"Okay. I'll be here. I don't expect much, though," Komachi replied, returning to her notebook.

Homework and projects are essentially meaningless if the students don't do the work themselves. But I wasn't trying to help Komachi with this just because she was cute. If that were the reason, I'd only help her with the book report.

"Haah… I have to get this done fast. I'm supposed to be studying for entrance exams… I won't make it in time for the practice tests right after the holiday!"

"You're supposed to build up your knowledge over time."

"Hey, I've been building up plenty, okay?"

"Yeah, a pile of unread textbooks…" If this were Tetris, she'd be screwed. And yet she was gearing up to take entrance exams. "Just for my information, do you seriously intend to get into my high school?" I asked.

My sister was unquestionably an idiot. She embodied the sparkling, distilled essence of stupidity. "I'm serious," Komachi replied with utmost sincerity. "If I weren't, I wouldn't consider copying your work."

Not like I care, but that attitude doesn't generally make people want to help you. Well, if that was what she wanted, then all right. The problem was her grades. "You're setting a damn high bar for yourself, though," I told her. "You're hovering around one hundredth place."

"But I wanna go to *your* school."

"…"

My eyes suddenly watered. My sister, who usually didn't spare me an ounce of respect, had unexpectedly shown me a glimmer of warmth and love. My eyes burned. A single droplet of rain prepared to fall from the heavens.

"When we're going to the same school and I say I'm your sister, I look like a supergood girl by comparison! I started middle school when your reputation was at its worst, so everyone thought I was great! They all treated me like an angel! I'm *totally* an angel!"

That's a terrible source of motivation. "…Oh. Was it now?" I replied. *What part of that is angel-like? She's a devil. A fiend. Crush devils! Yeah, Komachi is totally a demon.* "Well, you know. Just do what you can."

"Yeah, I'll try my best," she replied, once again scribbling away with her mechanical pencil.

She was going for the book report, though, so I had no idea why she was suddenly writing her draft on that grid paper. *Read the book first! Wait. Are you one of those people who get all holier-than-thou every time they start a new anime? "It was crap, so I dropped it before the opening credits started," or "It was trash, so I dropped it before the ad break"?*

I marched toward the bookshelf in search of *Kokoro*. If I remembered correctly, I originally bought it because they got a famous manga artist to draw the cover for the special edition. They sold more copies just by giving it a face-lift. Light novels really are 90 percent appearance. Well, not that Souseki Natsume is a light-novel author.

My finger slid across the row of spines. A book called *Science Magic: Party Tricks You Can Try Out Right Now!* caught my eye. It was fairly old, and it led me to wonder about the worries my dad might have had back when he was a young salaryman at the bottom of the corporate ladder.

No life is more constrained than that of a free man thrust into a society of vertical hierarchies. I bet my dad got that book for year-end parties when his superiors would be like, "Hey, Hikigaya. Say something interesting," or "Show us your hidden talents, come on."

If it were me, I probably wouldn't have been invited in the first place, and even if I were, I wouldn't be able to say much at all, so I probably wouldn't be invited again and thus would have nothing to worry about. And what the hell is with calling year-end parties "forgetting-it-all parties" anyway? Don't just get rid of your memories. Also, please don't forget about me, either.

Anyway, the book appeared to have potential for Komachi's independent research project, so I decided to illicitly borrow it. Then I pulled out *Kokoro* from the shelf immediately below. "Here," I said, handing the volume to Komachi. "For now just read the book before you write anything."

Komachi accepted it with a reluctant groan and then began reading.

After I checked to see that she actually was, I turned my attention to the book of science magic something-or-other I'd just found. As I flipped through it, the pages were full of party tricks. Like sticking a toothpick in a cigarette so that no ash will fall when you light it, or like soaking a bill in alcohol so that if you set it on fire, only the alcohol burns and the bill remains untouched. When I thought about it, I realized that even if I memorized these tricks, I'd never have the opportunity to use them. But the scientific explanations between tricks were oddly fascinating, and before I knew it, I was completely engrossed. It was the same sort of phenomenon that would occur when I cleaned my room.

Suddenly, I came to my senses, and I heard the telltale even breathing of sleep. I looked over at Komachi and found her drifting through the Land of Nod. *Studying for exams is tough, huh?*

I set the fan to low, took the thin summer blanket from the sofa, and gently pulled it over my sister's shoulders. *Keep at it, Komachi.*

X X X

July was already over, and outside, the great brown cicadas were chirping in grand chorus. Figuring I should take care of the household errands for a while in order to lighten Komachi's workload, I left the house to do some shopping. While I was out, I'd go hunt down some reading material that could prove useful for her independent research project, like *Newton*, *Science*, or *Mu*.

In the heat, a shimmering haze was rising from the asphalt. The afternoon city buzzed with the din of cicada songs and cars whizzing by. Not many pedestrians were around. The people of this residential area were not fond of going out at such a hot time of day.

Damn, I should have waited for the sun to go down a little bit. It's been so long since I last left the house, I didn't even think of that.

My goal for the summer that year was to avoid going outside as much as possible. I mean, the original reason we had such a long vacation was because of the heat. This has always been the consistent and unshakable rationale for vacations. As proof, Hokkaido has an extremely short summer vacation and longer winter vacation; they have cool summers and frigid winters. This corroborates the idea that long vacations were established based on the weather. In other words, the purpose of this break is to protect people from the heat, and if we were preserving the original intent of the holiday, we wouldn't be permitted outside at all. Leaving to hang out and stuff during summer vacation is a legal gray zone, you see?

And I, of course, was an exemplary student who minded his manners and followed the rules, so I obediently spent the summer shutting myself away at home. No, don't call me a *hikki* for that. Well, I guess you could. I got plenty used to that malicious gossip back in middle school. But for my adorable little sister, I will occasionally venture out of the house. I *must* do it, for love.

When I arrived at the station, as you would expect, the people were more numerous. I waited for a while at the bus stop, took a bumpy ten-minute ride, and headed to Kaihin-Makuhari. The neighborhood supermarket was fine for groceries, but the new city center was more convenient for getting books.

The Kaihin-Makuhari area boasts considerable crowds during the summertime. There's the Summer Sonic, the pro baseball night games have fireworks, and most of all, it's near the ocean, so marine sports are a major draw. The problem is that none of these things have anything to do with me, and I find the swarms to be purely and fundamentally irritating.

I entered said irritating swarm and faded unobtrusively into the background. You could argue that I already was an unobtrusive element of the background. Still, I felt even more alone in large crowds like this than I did when I was by myself. Essentially, the designation *loner* does not indicate the density of population around oneself, but rather the spiritual nature of the individual. No matter how close people may be physically, if you do not acknowledge them as similar to yourself, your social thirst will not be quenched.

The cliques out walking with their friends, family, or significant others were moving incredibly slowly. Maybe it was because their attention never left their companions, or maybe it was because they were concentrating on conversation and ignoring their feet, or maybe they just wanted to spend just a moment longer together.

Gah! Don't walk all spread out! You there, that group of three! What's going on? Are you doing flat back three or what? How strong does your defense need to be?

I slipped past the trio as nimbly as a star soccer player. Next was a group of four uniformed high school girls blocking my way in catenaccio formation. But they were all so preoccupied with their hyperanimated laughter and cell phones as they talked, that whole group was unbelievably sluggish. I passed them, too, with no trouble at all.

Shall I tell you what's lacking? Just this! Passion, elegance, diligence, sophistication, insight, dignity!

And the most important thing of all…

You're far too slow!

I talked to myself in my head, though it was all worthless nonsense, and quickly threaded around the people as they cheerfully ambled through the city without a single care in the world. A loner like me, with no friends or girlfriend beside him, could fly alone on the wind and transform the world into an amusement park any time with sheer imagination. Boys who usually walk around alone are always thinking such thoughts. It's pretty fun. As I mentally trained myself for survival on the off chance I ever got embroiled in a war, my feet carried me to the shopping district that had an outlet mall, the various specialty shops of Plena Makuhari, and more.

As I wandered around, I caught sight of a familiar-looking bordered, fluorescent tracksuit. It was the same one I usually wore during gym class. *Someone from my school, huh? I'll do my best to keep them out of my line of sight*, I thought, but try as I might, my eyeballs just wouldn't listen to me. In the end, my whole body turned toward that tracksuit. To put it simply, yes—it was fate.

Silky, flowing, beautiful hair; white arms and legs reflecting the blinding, brilliant light of the sun… When he adjusted the racket on his back, he let out a soft sigh that dissipated into the air, summoning a gust of wind.

It was Saika Totsuka. He didn't notice me. Instead, he turned around as if he had just caught sight of something behind him. Oh man, talk about a beauty looking back.

He was like a momentary mirage of the heat waves rising from the asphalt. For just an instant, the throng that had once been such a hindrance had become a flat stage backdrop. It was as if Totsuka and I were the only ones in the world. My face relaxed into a smile at the notion. No matter where we were, I would be sure to find him. I knew it in my soul.

"Tot*snerkle.*" I tried to call his name, but it stuck firmly in my throat. Instead, I wheezed out a sort of weird huffing noise. People out with their families gave me a wide berth and weird looks as they hurried away.

I turned a quiet gaze toward Totsuka. This was because I had noticed someone running up behind him, waving his hands wildly. The boy's tracksuit was identical to Totsuka's, as was the racket case on his back. I guess he was late for their meet-up or something, as he pressed his hands together in a casual gesture of apology, and Totsuka shook his head. Even from afar, I could easily spot his shy smile. The two of them exchanged a few words and then strolled off together into Plena.

My mind was blank for a while, and my legs carried me automatically.

...I see. Totsuka has friends from his club, too. Mm-hmm. It's summer vacation, so of course he has club activities. It'd be normal for him to go hang out after practice. Yeah, it's not surprising he'd smile like that to a tennis buddy.

I wonder when I started thinking I was his only friend. In both elementary school and middle school, the kids who talked to me got along with everyone and had lots of friends... I might have thought we were friends, but they wouldn't, and even if they were my best friends, I wasn't theirs. I was already aware that this often happened to me.

Damn it, I can't believe I'm letting this shake me up. I'm mushier than tofu. I'd probably taste good with soy sauce.

Somehow, I reached the escalator and leaned against the handrail. I could zone out now and let it carry me upward automatically. But right in the middle of the ride, I saw a familiar face coming down in the opposite direction. Only one idiot in my circle of associates would wear a trench coat in the middle of summer. Though *associate* was an unnecessarily long word, in this case. He was just an ass.

Zaimokuza was engaged in a friendly chat with the two guys with him, who I figured were his so-called arcade buddies. The following is an excerpt from their conversation.

"Arcana chance." (Translation: Do you wanna play Arcana at the next arcade?)

"Take." (Translation: Sounds good.)

"Chance." (Translation: I'll go, too.)

"ACE chance." (Translation: Are you guys okay with the ACE arcade?)

"Sacrifice." (Translation: ACE is too far; we can't.)

"Admiral sleepy." (Translation: I'm tired, and I don't want to.)

"Garbage." (Translation: You guys aren't into that, are you?)

"Total sacrifice." (Translation: It's a total sacrifice.)

"Sacrifice chance." (🡐 I have no idea.)

I let their words wash over me. It sounded like they'd established a language understood by them alone. *You can't just converse using individual lexemes. You're relying too much on the inherent ambiguity of Japanese.*

I'd feel bad if I bothered them when they were enjoying themselves, and plus, it would be bad for my reputation if people thought we were friends, so I pretended not to notice. But the moment we passed by each other, his sharp eyes discovered me, and for a single moment, our gazes met.

"Oh?" he called out to me.

"...Fwaah." I immediately looked elsewhere and faked a yawn. In so doing, I was indirectly accentuating how I couldn't possibly have seen him. I'm an expert at such avoidance tactics.

Of course, the escalators were not about to stop. Zaimokuza and I continued to accelerate away from each other, and then he faded from view. The escalator carried me up to the third floor, and the current of people swept me into the bookstore. I didn't even have to look around; I knew where my shelf was. To the right of the entrance were manga, and beyond that were light novels. On the other side of the aisle were the medium-sized books, and the shelf behind that was for smaller books. *Phew,* perfect. *So...where are the cookbooks?* Usually, I didn't read those, so I had no idea. Well, people only pay attention to what interests them, so that's no surprise.

Of course, asking the staff wasn't an option, so I decided to just browse. But, like, I mean, it wasn't because it would take courage to talk to them or whatever. I was just a nice guy, and I would've felt bad bothering them over something so trivial. It wasn't a big store, so it wouldn't take much time to walk through the whole thing.

"..."

As I sauntered around, I felt eyes on me. *Oh, a security guard, huh? You've got it all wrong, sir! This book isn't too naughty, and it's, like, uh... It's for my summer independent research project! I know, it's bad!* ...Or so I prepared to defend myself, but when I turned around, I locked eyes with someone unexpected.

She wore a cardigan over her shoulders and leggings under her skirt, presumably to prevent the sun from darkening her skin. Her current attire suggested a more active personality than her uniform did, but still, her accessories, like her watch and bag, kept her modest charm intact and brought it all together elegantly.

It was Yukino Yukinoshita, the captain of the Service Club, of which I was a member. *If I recall correctly, she does live around here, right?* So she was here at the bookstore, too.

"..."

"..."

Neither of us said a thing. We just stared at each other for about two seconds, more than enough time for recognition. Then Yukinoshita deftly returned the book in her hand to the shelf and strode straight out of the store.

Ouch! ☆

She ignored me so hard I was actually impressed. *Come on, this has surpassed regular snubbing. This is outright silent contempt. She treated me like the Potsdam Declaration. This is one for the history books.* We had been standing less than a meter apart, eyes locked, and she had still refused to acknowledge me. *Compared with this, the way I usually get overlooked in class is nothing at all. I mean, they just ignore me because they don't even know I'm there. Wait, that's pretty hurtful, too...*

...Well, that was very like her, though. Cracking a vaguely bitter smile, I circled around to the shelf where Yukinoshita had just been standing. At a glance, this section appeared to be the photo books. *So she looks at albums of actors or pop idols she likes, too. How surprisingly girly of her*, I thought, skimming over the shelf, but every single one featured animals. A particular book caught my attention: a photo album of cats. *Just get a cat already.*

X X X

I picked out a number of volumes from the store, including both books that could be useful for Komachi's independent research project and purchases of my own. My shopping bag felt heavy... I guess I had used summer vacation as an excuse to splurge.

Before the summer holiday starts, I always come up with all these plans (about four months' worth), like how I should read all of Ryotaro Shiba or finish all the games I've dropped, or get a summer job, or go on a trip on my own. But when summer actually starts, I'm like, *It's still okay. I still have a month. Naw, just two more weeks is enough. Oh, I think a week is plenty of time to have some fun... Huh? Only three more days?* Time just flies by.

I left the building and emerged into the bright light of the sun. The day was ending, but it was still hot, and a sticky, lukewarm sea breeze was blowing by. Though it was the height of summer, the cicadas' chirps sounded far away from this patch of reclaimed land covered in skyscrapers. I began walking toward the bus stop. Sweat was oozing from my hands, so I adjusted my grip on the shopping bag.

But with my plentiful purchases, I would be able to live a comfortable lifestyle of reading for the next little while. The great thing about summer vacation is that you can read a long series all in one go. For instance, I'd recommend the Delfinian War, the Twelve Kingdoms, or the Moribito series.

Summer vacation isn't just partying and fooling around with friends.

I mean, everyone assumes that summer = the beach, pools, BBQ, summer festivals, and fireworks.

Reading alone and indoors where it's cool, getting out of the bath and yelling *Ahh!* as you eat ice cream alone and naked, catching a glimpse of the Summer Triangle in the sky alone in the middle of the night, lighting a mosquito coil, and dozing off alone to the sound of a wind chime—all wonderful summer memories. You can get by just fine on your own during the summer. Being alone is best. It's hot, y'know?

The world spun on as usual that day, even without me. It felt so real then, the way the world kept going 'round despite Hachiman Hikigaya's absence. That knowledge is a quiet relief to me. Isn't it terrifying, the idea of something irreplaceable? Knowing if that thing disappeared, it could never be undone. You could never fail. You'd never get it back again.

That's why I'm somewhat partial to the relationships I'm building now, the kind that barely even qualify in the first place. If something were to happen, I could cut them off easily, and nobody would get hurt. No contact, no intrusions, that's how I deal with her—

"Oh! Hikki?" A voice pierced right through the bustling noises of midsummer, though it was only a murmur. Maybe the reason I heard it was because she was on my mind. Yui Yuigahama was sliding by me sideways, almost automatically, with a friend of hers. Her hair was in its usual bun, and she was decked out in full summer mode: a black camisole, a loose-knit white cardigan, booty shorts, and gladiator sandals on her feet.

"Hey…," I casually greeted her in return.

Yuigahama grinned brightly at me. "Yeah, long time no see." I guess she was hanging out with the person behind her: Yumiko Miura. She was also in Class 2-F, as well as occupying the top of the Soubu High School caste. Nearly all the boys were terrified of this queen of hellfire. Her glamorous attire consisted of a little black dress with a plunging back and tall high-heeled mules, which were tapping in displeasure. She was glaring at me, and her eyes were painted pitch-black with mascara or eyeliner or eyeshadow or whatever, like Destrade. Is there a game this afternoon?

"Oh, it's Hikio," she said.

You only got the first two syllables right…

You may surmise from how she talked to me that she was attempting to insult me, but such was not the case. The boys and girls at the top of the social pile generally do not hold any animosity toward those of lower status. Forget animosity; they're not even concerned with us in the first place. It's exactly like how people are naturally apathetic toward things that don't interest them.

"Yui. I'm calling up Ebina," Miura said. Without waiting for Yuigahama's reply, she moved a few steps away into the shade. She's doesn't care about me, so she would never interact with me. Top dogs like her who make no effort to get involved are nice and easy to deal with. When you strictly adhere to a hierarchical system based on social status, you avoid conflict. Many quarrels originate in class conflict. Such clashes are born out of attempts to force people from different worlds into the same framework. If you segregate the classes entirely, they'll never encounter one another in the first place.

Miura leaned against the wall and began her call. After checking that Miura was occupied, Yuigahama spoke. "I thought I'd hang out with Yumiko and the girls today… What're you up to, Hikki?"

"…Uh, shopping?" I raised the bag in my hand to show it to her. It was the first time I'd spoken to anyone aside from my own family in a long while, so maybe that was why I could only manage one short phrase.

"Oh, really? You're not gonna hang out with anyone?"

"No."

"Huh? Why not? We're on break."

Why, she asks me. How terrifying that she so naturally concludes that vacation is equivalent to hanging out. Is she, like, one of those kids with that syndrome that gives them anxiety if their planner isn't packed to the gills with activities?

I had all kinds of replies in my head, but none of them reached my mouth. "It's summer break. It's for taking a break." Somehow or other, I managed to squeak out two sentences.

All right, I'm gradually becoming capable of holding a conversation again. If I rush things and try to do three sentences, I'll make some creepy, awkward laugh, so I gotta watch out for that.

"…Are you, like, in a bad mood?" Yuigahama asked rather uneasily. She was probably trying to be considerate because I was so taciturn. But her attempt was just a bit misguided. If she really wanted to be

understanding, then she would have avoided asking me the question in the first place.

"No, I'm fine," I said.

But Yuigahama was still examining me in a seeming attempt to diagnose what was wrong with me.

...Well, I was acting different from normal. I was being guarded with her. Or maybe it would be most accurate to say that, after we'd reset our relationship, I didn't know how to keep my distance from her anymore. In a bid to converse like I used to, I tried to be as casual as possible. "...I get like this when it's hot. You just kinda...slack off? Like how train rails get softer and stretchier in the heat, and, like, so do dogs. Do you know about thermal expansion?"

"What do dogs have to do with this?" she asked. "Oh, mine does like to stretch, though."

"Then dogs *do* have something to do with this, don't they? What was your dog called again? It was, like...something that made him sound like he'd be a good pinch hitter... Sabu... Saburo?"

"It's Sablé!"

Oh. Sablé, huh? Saburo is that guy, the baseball player. He came back to the Marines, and I had high hopes for him this year. Still, dogs sure do a lot of stretching and flopping, with both their bodies and tongue. And our local mascot Chiiba-kun's nose is too long all year round. Put that thing away; it'll dry out.

"But, like, you were born in summer. You don't like it?" Yuigahama questioned.

I quietly put a hand to my mouth and leaned away a hair, assuming a well-bred and proper tone as I replied, "...How did you know that I was born in summer? Are you stalking me?"

"Whaaat?! Is that an impression of Yukinon?! It actually kinda sounded like her!" Yuigahama burst out laughing, but if Yukinoshita were there, we would be dead.

So my impression was accurate, huh? Clearly, I was reaping the rewards of regular practice in front of the mirror before every bath. What am I doing with my life? "But, like, seriously, how do you know? You're scaring me," I said.

"Oh, you were bragging about it to everyone when we went to karaoke before, weren't you?"

"D-don't be a jerk! I wasn't bragging about it! Certainly wasn't trying to indirectly make sure Totsuka knew!"

"So you were after Sai-chan?!" Yuigahama yelped, astonished.

Hey, hey, who else would I be trying to point it out to? "Well, first of all, when you're born in summer, you're just a newborn, so they pamper you. They raise you indoors with the air-conditioning turned up so the heat doesn't get to you. That means you never build up a resistance."

"Ohhh. I get it." Yuigahama *mm-hmm*ed her understanding. For some reason, that convinced her. It was worrying how she just believed my random nonsense. But she continued, "Oh, so, like, it's almost your birthday, so let's have a party."

"It's fine. I don't need one. Forget it."

"You just instantly said no?! And three times over, too!"

"I mean, listen… It's different for girls. When you're a guy, having a birthday party when you're already in high school is embarrassing. No way." Most important, I had no idea how to behave during these events. Should I smile? In middle school, it had occurred to me that someone might throw me a surprise party, so I had practiced my exaggerated shock, but I stopped once I realized it was never gonna happen.

"Okay, so if you don't want a party, then why don't we all go hang out somewhere?" she suggested.

"Who's 'we'?" If I didn't ask this question, bad things would happen. In particular, right around the time I first started school, I had encountered problems. Like, someone I talked with fairly often would invite me to go hang out, but when I took them up on that invitation, it would be almost entirely people I didn't know. Plus, when it's the first social event of the school year, if you don't talk very much, you get immediately shunted down the road to lonerdom. When it comes from other kids at school, the question *Why don't we all hang out?* is actually a trial by fire. The invitation process itself is the first screening, and then you're all divided into ranks based on how you deal with it when you actually go hang out.

"Yukinon and Komachi and Sai-chan, I guess?" mused Yuigahama.

Oh dear. So good old Zaimokuza got screened out, huh? Well, it's the obvious choice. I'd cut him off first thing, too.

When I didn't reply, she tried again. "I-if you're against that idea… th-then the two of us could…" She touched her pointer fingers together, gazing up at me through her lashes.

At the sight of that plea, my heartbeat accelerated. Instantly, I ripped my eyes away from her and jerked my head up. "I'm not super against it, not at all. In fact, I love the idea, especially the Totsuka part!"

"Just how in love with Sai-chan are you?!"

"I-I'm not in love with him! I just like him a little!"

"That basically means the same thing!" Yuigahama cried, at wit's end.

Phew… The moment I let my guard down, Yuigahama has me right where she wants me. It's not easy, making a conscious effort to keep my distance so she doesn't get the wrong idea. Hanging out with Totsuka somewhere was a good plan, though. I had caught a glimpse of him that day, but I had failed to call out to him. *Agh! I'm such a spineless coward! I'm a maggot! Pond scum!* "So what're you doing?" I asked.

Yuigahama answered with enthusiasm. "Going to the fireworks! Come see them with us!"

"I can see the marine fireworks from my house. I don't want to bother going out."

"Wow, that logic just revolves around you!" Yuigahama pointed her finger straight at me, groaned, and deliberated for a minute. "Then a haunted house or something!"

"Ghosts are terrifying. No way."

"That's your reason?!"

Hey, Chiba's spiritual hotspots are no laughing matter. I saw some of that stuff online in the middle of the night this one time, and I couldn't even begin to fall asleep. There's Ojaga Pond, and, like, the statue of Kannon at Tokyo Bay, and Yahashira Cemetery. Around here, there's a former execution site in front of a certain university, and that old abandoned telecommunication place. Even if I lucked out when Totsuka leaped on me in fear, there was a high chance I'd be crapping myself, too.

Despite my refusal, Yuigahama soldiered on undeterred. "Th-then, so, so, the beach…or, like, a pool?"

"…Uh, well, those are, like… I just can't. It'd be too embarrassing."

"Yeah…I'd be sorta…embarrassed, too…" Yuigahama squirmed and bashfully lowered her eyes.

Wait, if it's so excruciating, then don't suggest it. You're making this awkward for me, too. "Don't you have any other ideas?"

"I know! We can go camping!"

"There's bugs, so no way in hell. Anything but bugs, seriously. I'm sorry."

"You're *so* selfish! And useless! Whatever! You're a stupid stupid-head!" Yuigahama mustered her full meager vocabulary to tell me off. She whirled around in an angry huff and started marching away.

"…But, like," I began, "we don't have to do anything summery. Just something normal would be fine."

Yuigahama's feet came to an abrupt halt. When she turned around, there was no hint of anger on her face, only a faint smile. "Okay… You're right. All right, I'll contact you later!"

"Yeah, whatever, sometime," I said.

Yuigahama spun around on her heel again and skipped up to Miura. The grumpy queen bee made the picture of boredom, but when Yuigahama put both her hands together and apologized fiercely, her mood seemed to improve somewhat. As Miura teasingly poked Yuigahama in the head, the two of them began strolling away.

The large columns of summer clouds stretching across the sky were dyed deep red. A crisp breeze picked up. It was the perfect way to alleviate the heat in my head. As the day cooled into evening, I decided to return home.

In the twilight, indigo bled into crimson, and it would take some time and effort to define the boundary.

2

No matter what you do, you can't escape **Shizuka Hiratsuka**.

The cicadas were so loud in the mornings.

Someone had left the TV on, and the news was heralding the biggest heat wave of the summer or whatever. Don't you guys say that every day? It's like those outstandingly talented people who you only encounter once a decade and yet somehow appear every year.

Grumpy from the heat, I switched off the TV, sank into the sofa, and turned on my handheld console. That day was another one frittered away lying around inside. Komachi was studying in her room, so I was alone in the living room. It had been less than two weeks since the start of summer vacation. I lived out each day the same way I did every summer. I'd sleep until noon, watch *Pet Encyclopedia*, watch *Summer Vacation Kids' Anime Festa*, go out to the bookstore when the urge struck me, and in the evening I'd read or play games and study. I liked this lifestyle.

Summer vacation. For a loner, this time is our sanctuary. No, not an angel sanctuary. I can laze around for the whole day without causing trouble for anyone. Well, now that I think about it, I never get involved with people in the first place, so I don't normally create inconveniences anyway. I'm such a good boy.

Anyway, during summer vacation, nobody can tie me down. Yes, I am free. In English, the word can also mean "freedom." Like the Gundam. I am…*we* are Gundam. I don't have to do anything. It's great. It means that the world I live in is content. I wonder why it felt so nasty when I was at a part-time job and they were like, *Agh, just don't do anything.* That stung. It hurt so much, I quit.

Now that I think of it, it's been a long time since I last had a job. Before I joined the Service Club, I'd worked part-time here and there, but…most of the time at those places, all the interpersonal relationships were already in place when I showed up, so I couldn't squeeze in, and then I ended up quitting within about three months. After last time, I was too embarrassed to go return the uniform, so I mailed it to them, cash on delivery. Anyway, come to think of it, I realized the Service Club was robbing me of considerable time. But they held no power over my summer vacation! *Fwa-ha-ha-ha!*

As I loudly cackled to myself, my phone chirped. Another delivery notice from Amazon? *Has my package been shipped from the warehouse in Ichikawa city, Chiba prefecture?* I wondered, picking up the phone from where I'd left it on the table. When I checked the screen, I had one e-mail. The sender was Miss Hiratsuka.

I turned off the screen.

Phew, that's that… Now all I had to do was send her a late-night reply to the tune of *Sorryyyy, my battery ran out* or *I think I was out of range!* She would be unable to respond. Source: me. When I was in middle school, every time I screwed up my courage and e-mailed a girl, about 40 percent of the time she'd answer with something similar. By the way, about 30 percent just didn't reply at all, and the remaining 30 percent were from some foreigner named Mailer Daemon. Nothing good comes of making an effort.

With a sense of accomplishment, I returned to the sofa and picked up the handheld that I'd put into sleep mode. It's nice; just about all handhelds can sleep these days, it seems. They allow you to make the best use of your time. The problem is that if you get one that's too newfangled, it'll have all these incomprehensible functions, and that's not even getting into the connectivity. And when they start talking about "playing with the rear touch panel," it doesn't even make sense. It just sounds dirty.

My phone rang again.

What, which burgers do they have a special deal on now? I thought, going to get my phone. But this time, the ring persisted for an oddly lengthy interval. Apparently, I was receiving a phone call. Considering when the e-mail arrived, it was probably Miss Hiratsuka. I doubt many people would be horribly pleased to get a call from their teacher. Of course, I wasn't, either. Plus, now that I had ignored her once, she could chew me out for that if I picked up now. I chose to disregard the call as well. Eventually, she gave up, as the ringing stopped short. But my relief was only momentary, and this time, I started getting a bunch of rapid-fire e-mails.

What the hell? I'm scared. Is she like this with her boyfriends, too? There were so many. I was filled with trepidation as I opened my phone. I read the e-mail at the top of the folder—that is to say, the newest one.

Sender: Shizuka Hiratsuka
Subject: This is Shizuka Hiratsuka. Once you've checked your mail, please reply.
Body: Hikigaya, I have an urgent message for you regarding Service Club activities during summer vacation. Please return my messages. Are you still sleeping? (haha) I've been texting and calling you over and over. You've actually read them, haven't you?
Hey, you've read them, right? Answer your phone

That's scary! You're scary! I'm slightly traumatized here! I felt like I'd just gotten a glimpse of one of the reasons Miss Hiratsuka couldn't get married. *Geez, woman, just how obsessed with me are you? You're scary. Also terrifying.*

When I reviewed the e-mails, all of them had the same content. In summary, they were instructing me to volunteer long-term during the holiday. This was no joke. It was time to feign total ignorance. With no hesitation, I switched off my cell phone. At times like these, it's convenient to be a loner. You won't get calls from anyone else anyway!

Right about when I had finally relaxed again, Komachi came down from her room on the second floor. By all appearances, she had spent the day in the clothes she'd slept in. All she was wearing besides her underwear was my hand-me-down T-shirt.

"Taking a break?" I asked.

"Yeah," she replied. "I've basically done everything but the essay and the independent research project."

"Nice work. Do you want a drink? There's coffee, barley tea, MAX Coffee…"

"Coffee and MAX Coffee are two different things…? I'll go with barley tea."

MAX Coffee does not count as coffee. That's common sense. MAX Coffee is categorized as condensed milk. The category error of the coffee world—that's MAX Coffee. By the way, the category error of the light-novel world is Gagaga Bunko. "Here," I said.

"Yoink." Komachi accepted the tea in both hands and gulped it down eagerly. With a satisfied *Ahh*, she set the cup on the table. "Now then, Bro." She suddenly adopted a grave expression. "I studied really hard."

"Yeah, that's true. You're not done with everything, though." She still had the book report and the independent research project. And with entrance exams, the end was that it was never-ending. It was Golden Experience Requiem. Still, she had finished most of her homework over the past few days, so you have to give her credit for applying herself.

"I did so much work, I think I deserve to treat myself," she said.

"Are you some big-city office lady?" Seriously, what is it about the phrase *treat yourself* that evokes the image of an unmarried woman? For an instant, Miss Hiratsuka's face flashed before my eyes.

"Anyway, I need a treat," said Komachi. "So you have to go out with me to Chiba."

"Your reasoning is something else. That leap of logic could win you the Japan International Birdman Rally," I replied.

Komachi pouted and huffed. Apparently, *no* wasn't an option.

"Well, I get what you're saying," I said. "You want something in particular? I can't buy you anything too expensive, though. I only have four hundred yen in my wallet."

"You can't even get something cheap with that… I don't really need anything, though. I just want to go out with you. Oh, that just scored some serious Komachi points!"

"You're so obnoxious…" She probably wasn't trying to pester me into purchasing anything, though, so she basically just wanted to go out and have some fun. I felt like she should call her friends for that, but, well, I didn't want her going to Chiba Station with her girlfriends and getting hit on by some guy. In fact, there's a place not far from the amusement district near Chiba Station that's called Pick-up Road. I've avoided it ever since that one time I was going by and someone mugged me out of my allowance, though.

Also, if she got mixed up with boys, I'd have to stain my hands with blood. Going along with Komachi now would be best. "I'm fine with going out, but get changed," I said. "If you go out dressed like that, I'll have to shine a laser pointer in the eyes of every boy on the street. Oh, that just scored some serious Hachiman points, you know?"

"Uh, that sister complex of yours is creepy, frankly. Also, that's a terrible thing to do." My little sister retreated a couple of steps.

...Is that so? I should have had about eighty thousand points, though. 'Cause I'm Hachiman. But I quietly kept my smug reply to myself. Komachi's grading system was strict.

Guys in Chiba with younger sisters have a high chance of developing a sister complex. And mine is actually this cute, so there's nothing I can do about it. Some guys are always like, *My little sister isn't cute at all*, but that's because she's *your* little sister. That's why she's not endearing to you. "I don't know what we'd do at Chiba," I said, "but if you want me to go with you, I will."

"Whoo! Thanks. Okay, I'm gonna go get ready. You change into something easy to move around in."

Something easy to move around in...which means... Are we going bowling? Well, at least it's not boring. I'm not much for punching holes in stuff.

When you tell me to dress for unhindered movement, going naked seems like the best option to me, I dunno... When we did the fifty-meter dash in elementary school, some guys thought that way. They'd say *I'm getting serious now!* and do it in their bare feet. Yeah, that was me.

I grabbed a random T-shirt and a button-down shirt, along with a pair of jeans. As I was putting on my socks, Komachi was dashing this way and that and ransacking the house. What was she doing, scurrying around like that? She was like a little squirrel. It was driving up her cuteness gauge, though. I zoned out (my special skill) and waited for her, and Komachi finished changing. She had undressed and redressed in front of me, as usual, but this process was so mundane, I don't think it even registered for me.

"There we go!" At last, she looked at herself in the mirror and posed.

Yeah, yeah, you're cute, you're cute. Could you hurry it up?

Komachi donned a newsboy cap and turned to me. "Okay, let's go!" she declared, holding her provisions in both arms. There were two bags, packed full of stuff and looking fairly heavy. I wordlessly reached out a hand, and Komachi passed me one, rather happily. *Don't get all gleeful over a little thing like this. Are you one of those easy-to-please heroines who're all the rage these days?*

Before we left, I checked that the door was properly locked, and then we set off for the station.

"So, like, what's with these bags?" I asked Komachi. "Are you trying to make me your mule? I'm not carrying anything illegal for you." I pointed to the bag in my hands as we walked.

Komachi quietly put a finger to her lips. "That's a secret! ♪" She shot a wink at me while she was at it.

"You're so obnoxious..."

"Heh. Secrets are what make a woman a woman, Bro."

"Are you Shelley or what? You learned that from *Conan*, didn't you...?"

One of the unique characteristics of guys with younger sisters is that we have this strong tendency to share manga communally, especially the ones bought back in elementary school. This tendency becomes especially noticeable when it's a series popular with both boys and girls. So we'll often get each other's references like that... Oh, it wasn't Shelley—it was Vermouth, wasn't it?

...Anyway, when I'm reading manga, Komachi will come to peek over my shoulder, and our mom will see it and be like, *Let Komachi see, too.* For a while, whenever I was listening to music with my earbuds in, Mom would tell me to share. How stupid. Are we a lovey-dovey couple? Or high school boys on the train home? Now there's something that'd give Ebina a nosebleed...

As I herded Komachi toward the sidewalk side and she fiddled with her phone, I casually surveyed the quiet city. The sun was beaming down brilliantly over the road to the station. The trees on the boulevard took the opportunity to rustle and stretch out their branches, and a stray cat lay on its side, fast asleep in the shade. The smell of a mosquito coil and the sounds of an afternoon TV show filtered out from someone's yard.

As we walked side by side, a group of elementary schoolers on mountain bikes passed by in a brief burst of animated chatter. Komachi and I paused, watching them absently, and then started again at a pace a little slower than I was used to. I matched my speed to Komachi's, and we wound our way to the station. When we arrived, I stepped toward the ticket gates, but my sister tugged my sleeve. "Bro, this way, this way."

"Huh? But if we're going to Chiba, the train's…," I began, turning around.

Komachi was going "Over there, over there!" as she pointed and tugged me along all the way to the bus loop, where we encountered a mysterious parked minivan with a black figure in front of the driver's-side door. From the curvy silhouette, I could easily tell that it belonged to a woman. She was sporting a black T-shirt with rolled-up sleeves, jean shorts, and hiking-boot-esque footwear. Her black hair was gathered up in a ponytail under a khaki baseball cap, and her sunglasses hid her eyes from view. When she turned to me, though, her mouth twisted sardonically.

I have a bad feeling about this.

"Now then…let's hear why you didn't answer your phone, Hachiman Hikigaya." She removed her sunglasses with a click and faced me with sharp, flashing eyes. Needless to say, it was Miss Hiratsuka. *Whoa, someone's mad…*

"Oh…my cell reception is unstable. I think there's a connection between the number of antennas they have and the number of hairs on their CEO's head. Sorta like Kitaro's antenna. Seriously. I always suspected there was something weak and flabby about a company with a name like that. What the hell is with calling themselves *soft*?! Get creative with your cell phone reception before you start creative publishing! I do like reading those books, though!"

"Bro, you're gonna die… You're gonna get punished in the name of justice…" Komachi, worried for my safety, stepped forward to stop me. But it would be fine. He was actually a pretty good guy. *…I'll be okay, right? Also, please do something about my reception.*

"Hmph, whatever. I didn't expect a decent excuse from you in the first place," Miss Hiratsuka said.

Then please don't ask…, I was about to say, but my teacher didn't give me the chance.

"Well, as long as you aren't involved in any accidents or other incidents, that's enough," she continued, smiling. "That's happened before, so I was a little worried."

"…Miss Hiratsuka." She was probably referring to the time I got hit by a car. Of course a teacher would hear about an accident involving a student of hers. *I guess…she's serious about her job. She's a good person.*

"Good thing I pulled some strings and got hold of your sister."

"…You're scaring me." *That storm of e-mails, the way you check up on my safety… You're freaking me out! That's basically stalker behavior!* I now know how terrifying it is to be loved…and I don't need love, summer.

"So, like, did you want something? I'm going to Chiba with my sister right now," I said.

Miss Hiratsuka blinked a few times in surprise. "Huh. So you haven't read my e-mails yet. We're going to Chiba, too, as part of a Service Club activity."

"What?" Did she send me a message about that? The first one I'd read had given me major creepy-girlfriend vibes, so I'd turned off my phone in terror. Figuring I should take another look, I pulled it out.

That was when I heard a voice behind me. "Hikki, you're late." When I turned around, I saw Yuigahama with a very full plastic bag from a convenience store in her hand. She wore a hot-pink sun visor with the kind of T-shirt and short shorts that make you want to go *Whoa, not enough cloth there*. It was like she was living for summer. These days, even elementary schoolers don't wear short sleeves with shorts like that.

Yukinoshita was standing behind Yuigahama, as if hiding in her shadow. Unusually for her, she was in jeans, paired with a shirt that had a stand-up collar. Though she wasn't showing much skin, she still looked breezy and cool.

"Huh? Why're you guys here?" I asked.

"What do you mean? This is for the Service Club. Aren't you here because Komachi told you about it?" Yuigahama said nonchalantly.

Agh, I'm starting to see what's going on here. Miss Hiratsuka tried to invite me to this club thing, but I totally stonewalled her, so she contacted Yuigahama, who in turn got in touch with Komachi. *Damn it! This isn't fair! I can't believe they would take advantage of my brotherly love, knowing full well I'd be excited to go out if Komachi was the one asking! And I fell for it and left the house!*

The cruelest one was Komachi, who had lured me here with lies by omission. The more you hate her, the cuter she gets. She was so cute now, I could hardly stand it.

When she saw the two older girls, she gave them a jubilant greeting. "Yui! Yahallo!"

"Yahallo, Komachi!"

Is that greeting in now? It sounds so dumb. Stop.

"Yukino, too! Yahallo!"

"Hey...hello, Komachi." Yukinoshita was almost tricked into saying it, but she came to her senses in the nick of time. She instantly blushed.

Komachi squeezed Yuigahama's hand. "I'm so glad you invited me!"

"Thank Yukinon," replied Yuigahama. "She's the one who called me. She told me the teacher had asked me to call you." Oh-ho. So in other words, the order went Miss Hiratsuka ➔ Yukinoshita ➔ Yuigahama ➔ Komachi ➔ me, huh?

Komachi responded by glomping Yukinoshita. "Really? Thank you so much! I love you, Yukino!"

Yukinoshita faltered for a moment in the face of Komachi's straightforward declaration. She averted her gaze slightly and cleared her throat with a cough. "...Oh, um...I just thought we would need someone to look after *that*."

Yes, hello. I'm "that."

"...Nothing I did was worthy of praise," she continued. "It was just because of how things normally are with you two."

Yuigahama and Komachi burst into affectionate grins as Yukinoshita blushed.

This was not good. At this rate, Yukinoshita would soon have Komachi in her clutches. It was already too late for Yuigahama, but I wanted Komachi to stay on the straight and narrow. I had to set her down the right path! "Komachi, you don't have to thank Yukinoshita. In fact, you should be thanking me instead for being such a loser. Otherwise, she never would have needed your intervention!" Heh, that was a good one. Now Komachi would most certainly show her brother gratitude, respect, and love.

"..."

"..."

"..."

...Or so I thought, but instead we all sank into immediate silence. All I could hear was the express train zooming away, a painful sound to my ears. Everyone was at a loss for words.

Yukinoshita chuckled. It had been a long time since I last saw her smile, or so it seemed. "It really was the right choice to invite you, Komachi. I'm glad you're here to take care of that thing."

"I really wish someone would take over for me, though." My own sister was about to forsake me.

In an effort to hide the tears threatening to fall, I raised my head toward the blazing sun. It was getting a little toasty. "It's hot, so can we finish this up quick?"

"Don't be so impatient. The last person is almost here."

Someone was indeed coming down the station stairs toward us. When I saw that figure glancing left and right, I instantly realized who it was. Before I even processed what I was doing, I'd raised my hand.

When he saw me wave, he dashed up to us. "Hachiman!" Panting, Totsuka gave me a bright and cheerful smile more radiant than the midsummer sun. But my chest squeezed at the thought that I wasn't the only recipient of such smiles. Something caught in the back of my throat, and that something gradually transformed into pain. The wounds in my soul festered and oozed.

But Totsuka's lovable expression was enough to heal it all in two sections. In English, you would say his *smile* could *cure* me with *pretty*. Totsuka's so cute. Abbreviated as: Totsucute.

Komachi, who had been standing beside me, hopped up to greet Totsuka. "Yahallo, Totsuka!"

"Yeah, Yahallo!" he replied.

What the heck. That's so cute. Let's make that greeting a thing. "They invited you, too, Totsuka?" I asked.

"Yes, Miss Hiratsuka said she didn't have enough people. But…is it okay for me to join you?"

"Of course it is!" I exclaimed. But, like, we were just going to Chiba Station. There was no cause for uncertainty.

If Miss Hiratsuka had invited Totsuka, though, I guess she kinda understood. Good job. Now everyone was here… Everyone?

I scanned our group. "Where's Zaimokuza?"

"…Who?" Yukinoshita tilted her head, perplexed.

Miss Hiratsuka *hmm*ed, apparently only just remembering, and explained. "I reached out to him, but he said something about a fierce battle or Comiket or deadlines or something and refused."

Seriously, Zaimokuza? I was jealous of him for getting the option of refusing. He must be having a blast right now with his arcade buddies… But why's the deadline last on his list? What about his ambitions to be a writer?

"Well then, let's get going," declared Miss Hiratsuka.

With that, we went to board the minivan. Upon opening the door, I saw the vehicle was a seven-seater. There was the driver's seat, the front passenger seat, room for three in the back, and another two in the middle.

"Yukinon, let's have some snacks, come on!" Yuigahama chirped.

"Those aren't for eating once we're there?" Yukinoshita questioned. The pair was already planning to sit together.

So that means…oh-ho. In other words, sandwiched between Totsuka and Komachi is the sword of promised victory. Now I can win!

But when I exultantly started climbing into the back, someone yanked at my collar. "You're sitting shotgun," ordered Miss Hiratsuka.

"Huh? Hey, why?!" I protested as she dragged me along.

She hid her bright-red face with a hand. "D-don't get the wrong idea, okay?! I-it's not because I want to sit by you!"

Oh-ho, how *tsundere* of her. If you could ignore her age, it'd be cute.

"It's because the passenger in that seat is most likely to die!" she continued.

"You suck!" I struggled, trying to escape.

But she let a smile slip. "...I'm joking. It's wise to keep me from getting bored while I drive, don't you think? I enjoy talking with you, you know."

"Oh, really...?" Faced with such a tranquil and soft expression, I couldn't defy her any longer. I sat calmly in the front seat, and Miss Hiratsuka nodded in satisfaction.

The teacher checked that everyone was in the van, and she and I fastened our seat belts. She turned the key in the ignition and pressed the gas, and we sped away from my familiar home station and down the road. If we were going to Chiba Station, it would probably be fastest to go from here out onto National Road 14. But for reasons unknown, Miss Hiratsuka was driving toward the interchange. The arrow on the navigation system was pointing toward the highway.

"Um, aren't we going to Chiba...?" I asked.

Miss Hiratsuka grinned. "Let me ask *you* something instead. How long have you been under the delusion...that we were headed to Chiba Station?"

"Uh, I'm not under any delusions or anything. You said we were going to Chiba, and usually, that means Chiba Station..."

"You thought our destination was Chiba Station? Too bad! It's Chiba Village!"

"Why are you so excited about this...?"

This often happens with those who lack social finesse. When they encounter a person for the first time in a long while, they sometimes get overenthusiastic. The next day, they reflect on their behavior and sink into self-loathing. I guess having some distance is the key. *I hope Miss Hiratsuka isn't depressed tomorrow, though.*

But still, Chiba Village... Chiba Village... That sounds familiar... I wonder why.

Chatting in the van

Driver

…Man, I really don't wanna get a job.

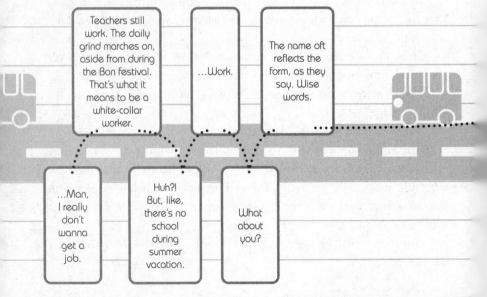

Teachers still work. The daily grind marches on, aside from during the Bon festival. That's what it means to be a white-collar worker.

Huh?! But, like, there's no school during summer vacation.

…Work.

What about you?

The name oft reflects the form, as they say. Wise words.

Hiratsuka's seat
How's summer vacation been?
Hachiman's seat
Sigh. The usual. Just chilling at home, watching anime, reading, gaming, studying.
Th-that's the usual?
Well, I don't have to go out and do anything, do I? Plus, you can get heatstroke, or drown, or get into trouble in the amusement district… The outside world is full of peril! Nothing beats the indoor life of the *hikikomori*!
Heading to CHIBA VILLAGE
Sitting shotgun

3

Hayato Hayama is socially adept with everyone.

The jagged contour of a far-off ridge suddenly appeared in my field of vision. "Whoa, mountains," I muttered.

"You're right, there they are. Mountains," Yukinoshita parroted with a nod.

Miss Hiratsuka followed suit. "Hmm. Indeed. Mountains."

Chiba natives live in the embrace of the vast Kanto Plains, so crags and peaks are a rare sight for us. On very clear days, you can see Mount Fuji along the coastline, but you don't get much of a chance to see any others, especially not lush green ones like these. That's why even a glimpse of a mountain will get us excited. You wouldn't expect Yukinoshita to be impressed, but even she let out a sigh of wonder.

After that, it was silent in the van. Yukinoshita and I watched the vistas roll by outside the windows.

Yuigahama's head lay on Yukinoshita's shoulder as she breathed gently in sleep. If I twisted around farther, I could see Komachi and Totsuka in the back row, also snoozing. At the beginning of our trip, they'd been bouncing around playing cards or Uno or something, but they must have gotten bored. As for me, I'd been obliged to converse with Miss Hiratsuka the whole time… Why did we have to recount our top ten anime to each other?

The sight of everyone sleeping gave rise to a few pangs of nostalgia, though. It was like the ride home on a bus after a field trip or a school camping trip. My classmates would expend all their energy and fall quiet with exhaustion after so much fun, but I would never really have an opportunity to tire myself out, so I would just stay fully alert and stare out the window the whole time.

The line of mountains loomed authoritatively over the high barriers to either side of the highway. The dark mouths of tunnels opened wide, illuminated with vivid orange lights. As I watched the scenery flowing past my window, I was assaulted by an intense sense of déjà vu.

...Now I remembered.

"Oh yeah," I said. "Chiba Village was the place I went for that nature program back in middle school."

"I believe it's a resort located in Gunma prefecture, belonging to Chiba city," Yukinoshita added.

"Oh, you've been there, too?"

"I returned here in ninth grade, so I didn't participate in the nature program," she explained. "I only know about the program at all because of the photos in the middle school graduation album."

"You 'returned'? From where? Actually, why *did* you come back?"

"My, you sound spiteful... Not that I care." I turned to find Yukinoshita gazing out the window. It was open a crack, and the resulting wind was mussing her hair and hiding her expression from view. "I was studying abroad. Did I not tell you before? Your memory has the storage capacity of a floppy disk."

"That's not much... Don't point any magnets at me, or I'll forget everything."

"Do kids your age know about floppy disks?" asked Miss Hiratsuka with considerable surprise.

Well, it wasn't that long ago that you could still find PCs equipped with floppy-disk drives. The last holdouts. "Oh, I think they still had them right around the time I was born," I said.

"I'm impressed you remember. Your memory is on par with an MO disk." Miss Hiratsuka joined the conversation, chuckling in gleeful pleasure at her own witticism. But her choice of *MO disk* as a synonym for high memory capacity only provided evidence for her age.

"Uh, most people wouldn't know about those...," I said.

"I know about MDs, but..." Yukinoshita trailed off.

"Ngh! I can't believe you don't know about MO... So this is what it means to be young..." Miss Hiratsuka raised a tragic cry.

I somewhat pitied her, so I decided to soften the blow. I'm so nice. "Well, you know. MOs were mostly used by businesses, so they weren't in common use in households. Just because she's not familiar with them doesn't necessarily mean you're old."

"Oh, so you do know about them!" Miss Hiratsuka reached out to punch me!

"Hey, hands on the wheel! The wheel!" I cried.

"Just remember, you'll pay for that once we're out of the van...," she muttered.

"Please don't have such high expectations for my MO-level storage banks," I retorted. An MO can hold way more than a floppy disk, though.

The car zoomed toward Chiba Village. Though it was a weekday, there were a fair number of cars on the road. We even hit a few congested stretches, about a kilometer each.

"It's surprisingly busy out, huh?" I commented.

"There's plenty of campgrounds around here, and it's also a popular spot for hot springs," Miss Hiratsuka replied. "I thought it was customary to make middle school students from Chiba city walk around the Sarugakyou springs?"

"Uh, you can't expect me to remember the names of every place..."

"I see. I suppose that's because it holds so many painful memories for you... It's understandable you would forget."

"Don't act like some old school outing is my dark past. I may not look it, but I'm an expert at field trips."

"So you're the type who comes out of his shell at parties, huh?" she said. "I know many students who are more outgoing during special events."

"Uh, no... I meant I'm good at switching off my mind to make it through...," I replied. When I had revisited the old photos in my middle school grad album, I had been startled by my dead expression. My classmates might have been even more alarmed. You know, like... *Wait, was this guy with us?*

"The plan is to stay two nights, just like that nature trip. Will you be okay?" asked Miss Hiratsuka.

"Two nights? Huh? We're staying overnight? I didn't pack anything!"

"It's okay," Yukinoshita cut in. "It looks like Komachi packed for him."

That was when it clicked. *Oh, so that's what those bags were. I guess there's two because one's mine and one's Komachi's.*

"Your little sister's character is even better than I'd imagined," Miss Hiratsuka marveled.

"Right?" I replied. "She's my pride and joy. She's delicate, dainty, and darling. All three *D*s."

"Functionally, that's only one..." Yukinoshita rolled her eyes.

After exiting the highway onto a side street, we turned off again onto a mountain road. The minivan smoothly ascended up the twists and turns of the slope.

X X X

When I stepped out of the van, I smelled the rich scent of grass. Somehow, the oxygen felt richer here. Maybe it was the lush green forest making me feel that way. A few buses were parked in a small open area: the Chiba Village parking lot. Miss Hiratsuka had stopped the van there.

"Hnnn! I feel great!" Yuigahama got out and stretched as wide as she could.

"...Yes, I'm sure you do, after using someone else's shoulder as a pillow for your lengthy nap," Yukinoshita sharply retorted.

Yuigahama put both her hands together and apologized. "Urk... I-I'm sorry, geez!"

"Wow...we really are in the mountains," Totsuka commented, filled with wonder as he stepped up behind the girls. Longing for the hills as one who lives on the plains—he was indeed a Chiba native.

"I came here just last year, though!" said Komachi, but she was taking in the mountain air and enjoying herself well enough.

Well, I was no Yuigahama, but the comfortable light filtering through the trees and the cool wind blowing over the plateau were indeed pleasant. Someday, I'd like to isolate myself in a place like this and become a hermit. I'd do all my shopping online.

"Yeah, the air's so sweet," Miss Hiratsuka remarked, just before lighting a cigarette. *How can you even tell if it's sweet or not?* "We'll go the rest of the way on foot. Unload your things from the van," she said, letting out a deep breath, as if the atmosphere was truly marvelous.

As instructed, we unloaded the van, and that was when another one drove up. Well, the place had a campground and stuff, too, so I shouldn't have been surprised that there were regular visitors. It was a public facility, so it was cheap. Maybe this was one of those great destinations not many people knew about. After the van unloaded its passengers, it returned along the same road. Apparently, it had only come to drop off a group of four young boys and girls. They looked like they would be at home in something called *Love Story of Four Boys and Girls*, the type of people you'd see biting into midsummer fruit. They were the kind who would have a barbecue or something on the sandbar of a river, get left behind, and end up having to call for rescue. Or go hiking in regular street clothes as if it were a picnic and get themselves stranded.

As my mind wandered, one member of the quartet turned to me with a casual wave. "Hey, Hikitani."

"...Hayama?" To my surprise, Hayama was among them. And he wasn't the only one there. Upon closer inspection, I recognized his whole posse. There was Miura; Tobe, the blonde party type; Ebina, the intense *fujoshi... Huh? Where's assimilating virgin Ooka?* "Why are you here?" I asked. "Did you come for a barbecue? If so, I recommend doing it on a river sandbar."

"Oh, we're not here for a barbecue." Hayama gave a wry smile. "I wouldn't have had my parents drive us all the way here for something like that."

Okay, so that's not it. Guess I should recommend hiking in street wear, I thought to myself.

Miss Hiratsuka crushed her cigarette. "Hmm. Looks like everyone's here."

Everyone's here? I guess that meant Hayama's crew was a part of the plan all along.

"Now then, do you know the reason I've called you all here today?" she asked.

We all exchanged glances. "I heard we were staying here two nights for a volunteer activity," Yukinoshita offered.

Totsuka nodded. "Yes, we're helping out, right?"

Beside them, Yuigahama responded with puzzlement. "Huh? It's not like a cabin thing?"

"I heard that we were gonna be camping," said Komachi.

"I never heard anything about this in the first place...," I added. Come on, which one is the right answer? This is like a bad game of telephone.

"I heard that this would give us extra community service points for our student record...," Hayama said with a smile that appeared rather strained.

"Huh? I came because I thought it was a free camping trip." Miura tugged and sproinged her tightly wound curls.

"Yeah, right?" Tobe chimed in, combing up the long hair at the nape of his neck. "I mean, if it's free, man, you gotta!"

"I heard that Hayama and Tobe would be camping, hnnnggg." Ebina's reason for being there was the only one that struck us as weird. And yes, she really did say that last part.

Miss Hiratsuka gave a mildly long-suffering sigh. "Hmm. Well, you're all more or less right, so I'll leave it at that. You're going to be engaging in some volunteer activities over the next few days."

"Um, what kind of volunteering...?"

"For some reason, the principal has ordered me to supervise service activities for the region...," she said. "That's why I've brought all of you here. You will be working as support staff for an elementary school camping trip, helping out the workers here at Chiba Village, the teachers, and the children. In short: You're doing odd jobs. More frankly: You're slaves."

I wanna go home... Even shady companies will sugarcoat the job description at first. Well, hiding their practices is precisely the reason they're called *shady*, though.

"This is also a camp for the Service Club, and as Hayama said, you may receive extra points in my unofficial scoring system depending on your performance," Miss Hiratsuka continued. "During your free time, you may go have fun."

Aha, I see. Everyone had basically grasped the situation, in their own ways. They had just absorbed only the parts that interested them.

"Well then, let's get going. Once you've dropped off your bags in the main building, you're going to work," she said, taking the lead.

We all plodded after her. Still, we didn't exactly form a unified group. Yukinoshita and I followed immediately behind, with Komachi and Totsuka behind us and Yuigahama trailing farther back. At the rear, Hayama and the others lagged after us. With Yuigahama in the middle, we somehow managed to pass for one single group.

The path from the parking lot to the main building was paved. As we trudged along a little gloomily, Yukinoshita said, "Um…may I ask why Hayama and his friends are here?"

"Hmm? Oh, are you talking to me?" Miss Hiratsuka turned around.

"Well, she's asking so politely, so she's got to be," I commented. Miss Hiratsuka was probably the only person Yukinoshita would speak to with such courtesy, I thought.

Yukinoshita gave me a disturbingly sunny smile. "Oh, that's not necessarily the case, good sir. It is my opinion that polite language can be employed not only when speaking to one's superiors, but also to distance oneself from another. Don't you agree, Mr. Hikigaya?"

"Oh, yes. You're quite right, Miss Yukinoshita," I replied, as both of us forced odd, haughty laughter.

Miss Hiratsuka cut off our exchange. "You two never change. Oh, and as for the reason I invited Hayama's group… It was looking like we wouldn't have enough people, so I posted a recruitment flyer on the school bulletin board. I suppose you didn't see it. I didn't think anyone would apply for this, though…"

"Then why did you go to the trouble of posting a flyer?" I asked.

"It was just a formality. It wouldn't be very interesting if it looked like I was only focusing on you guys. It was for the sake of appearances. I'm no good at dealing with normal kids and all their energy. The sight of them wounds me emotionally."

Listening to her was wounding *me* emotionally. Please! Someone marry this woman!

"Still, I'm a teacher. I have to treat you as impartially as possible," she continued.

"Uh-huh. Sounds rough, being a teacher." She can call it preferential behavior or special treatment or whatever she wants, but all she does is beat me up.

"Not just teachers. It would be more accurate to say that of all adults. Situations like this often occur out in the real world," Miss Hiratsuka said, her expression darkening.

To become a member of an organization also means to bear the burden of its flaws. And that's not even getting into how you're forced to consider your far-off future when you conduct yourself for long-term employment. You bow even when you don't want to, attend drinking parties you despise, and listen to things you'd rather not hear. You don't just run into people you hate every single day; you have to collaborate with them. If you want to avoid that, you have no choice but to become a househusband or a NEET. Not only do you have to do your job, you have to deal with all the social crap, too. It's like a sadistic game. Do they even properly compensate you for dealing with your coworkers? It's weird that there's no additional pay for that. I really have to avoid getting a job.

Miss Hiratsuka smiled gently back at me and Yukinoshita. "This is a good opportunity for you two. You need to learn the skills necessary to get along with another social circle."

"Uh, not gonna happen. We're not gonna be friends with them," I said.

"That's not what I mean, Hikigaya. You don't have to be friends. I'm saying you should *get along*. You need to gain the skills necessary to deal with them smoothly, with no trouble, in a professional manner, neither antagonizing them nor ignoring them. That's what it means to conform to society."

"I dunno..." If I'm not allowed to ignore them, then I've got no tactics left.

"..." Yukinoshita's response was silence. She did not reply or object, but neither did she acquiesce.

Miss Hiratsuka regarded us with a wry expression. "Well, you don't have to do it right now. Just keep it in mind." We continued walking in silence.

Getting along, huh...? It probably wouldn't be that hard. Becoming friends is a matter of feelings, but smooth interactions are simply a matter of skill. Starting new conversations, nodding in agreement, showing you sympathize with their concerns. In so doing, you narrow down your opponent's strike zone and indirectly reveal to them the range of your own defenses. I could probably squeak by. At first, I probably wouldn't be very good at striking up conversation, and the back-and-forth might grind to a halt. I might make the wrong replies. But just as with other skills, I would be able to learn it through repetition and practice. After all, the entire process of "getting along" is nothing more than a cycle of deception. You're lying to yourself and others. They acknowledge that they're being deceived, and you acknowledge that they're deceiving you.

It's no big deal. In the end, it's no different from what all those other kids learn and put into practice at school. This ability is necessary if you want to associate yourself with a group or an organization, and the only difference between how children and adults use it is scale.

In the end, it's nothing more than falsehood, suspicion, and deceit.

X X X

We left our bags in the main building and were subsequently hustled off to somewhere called the meeting plaza. Waiting there was a group of nearly a hundred elementary school kids. I thought they were all in sixth grade, but their wide range of sizes made for a motley crowd. When you look at high school students in uniform or salarymen in business suits, there's a uniformity that prevents even large crowds from looking disordered. But everyone in this teeming mass of kids was wearing whatever they wanted, and the brightly colored palette made for a chaotic picture.

Nearly everyone was talking at the same time, which was terribly loud. Their squawking was unbelievably obnoxious and overwhelming. Once you reach high school, you almost never see a group of elementary schoolers up close. The sheer power (to put it nicely) was startling. *Is this a zoo or what?*

Looking to the side, I saw Yuigahama slowly backing away, and Yukinoshita's face had blanched a little.

A teacher was standing right in front of the kids, but there was no indication that anything was getting started. The instructor was just intently studying a watch. After a few minutes had passed, the kids seemed to notice something was going on and began settling down. There was chatter…whispers…and then silence… "All right, it just took three minutes for everyone to quiet down," said the teacher.

Th-th-th-there it is! This was the legendary sentence that teachers always use to open a lecture during school assemblies and meetings. To think I would hear it again at my age…

As I had predicted, the teacher started with a reprimand. I guess this was the standard method for teachers to let their kids have it and quash their excitement at going on a trip. I remember the experience from my time in elementary school, too.

After the scolding, the teacher announced the plan for the day. The first activity for day one was apparently orienteering. I think you also call them stamp rallies. All the kids opened their school camping trip guidebooks as they listened to the explanation. On the cover was an anime-style illustration. *Oh, that must mean a girl drew it.* Probably some committee girl or one with artistic skills, like, *I—I could draw it if you want…* I could only pray that down the road, this would not become a skeleton in her closet.

"All right, and finally, let's introduce the boys and girls who will be helping us out. Let's give them a warm welcome! *Hello!*"

"Hello!" the students chorused. It was one of those formalities, those group chants like the drawn-out *Thanks for the fooood* everyone has to say before eating the school lunch. It's like the call-and-response at school graduation ceremonies. They're like, *The field triiiip!* and then we reply with *Left us with so many memories!* That sort of thing. I had to join the chant, too, and I was indeed left with many unpleasant recollections. It wasn't a lie.

Suddenly, all the children's eyes were on us. That was when Hayama took a soft step forward. "We're going to be helping out for the next three days," he said. "If you need anything, feel free to ask us any time. I hope this camping trip will be a wonderful experience for you all. I'm glad to meet you guys!"

The crowd broke out into applause. The elementary school girls were squeeing, and the teachers were clapping with gusto.

Whoa, Hayama's amazing. He's a natural at this. Not many people can make a speech appropriate for that age level without any prior planning. If it were a matter of mere skill, Yukinoshita could possibly pull it off, too, but… "You're the captain of the Service Club," I said to her. "Why don't you say something?"

"I don't really like standing in front of people."

No surprises there. She already drew attention without even trying. That reality had caused her certain hardships… Maybe she didn't like deliberately exposing herself like that.

"I do love standing above them, though…," she added.

Do you, now…?

"All right, let's begin the orienteering." At the teacher's signal, the students clumped into groups of five or six. They must have decided who was going with who beforehand, as the process finished quickly. They would probably be in the same groups for the whole trip.

Maybe for elementary school kids, dividing into groups isn't often a cause for upset. Everyone looked similarly cheerful anyway. I suppose at that age, the school castes hadn't yet become set in stone. Once they went on to middle school and high school, they would undergo a brutal and precise segregation. Their time in elementary school would be a brief and sheltered paradise. Man, elementary schoolers are the best! …Being one, I mean.

At loose ends during this process, us big kids ended up clustering together ourselves. As we surveyed the mass of children, Tobe ruffled his hair and commented, "Man, elementary school kids are so tiny! We're, like, totally old."

"Hey, could you not talk like that, Tobe? You're making me sound like an old bag." Miura shot him a threatening glare.

"Hey, I'm not being serious! That's not what I meant!" Tobe defended himself, flustered. For an instant, I thought I felt Miss Hiratsuka's eyes on us, but it was probably my imagination. I very much prayed that was the case.

"But when we were in elementary school, high school kids seemed so adult, huh?" Totsuka sounded nostalgic. I guess Tobe's comment struck a chord with him.

Komachi touched her pointer finger to her chin and tilted her head. "High schoolers seem adult to me, too, you know? Not counting my brother."

"...Hey," I protested. "I'm super grown-up, though. I make idle complaints, tell dirty lies, and do unfair things."

"You sound like 'A Night at Fifteen,' and that's not mature at all, Bro," Komachi retorted.

"Is that your mental image of adults, Hikki?!" Yuigahama joined in.

Giggling, Totsuka patted me on the back. "Maybe you don't see it much at home, Komachi, but at school, Hachiman seems very adult. He's so calm and composed. Right?"

"T-Totsuka..." I was so touched, I almost sobbed.

Suddenly, a cold voice interjected with an edge of scorn. "He only looks that way because he has no one to talk to. It would be more accurate to say that he is isolated and miserable." When I turned around, Yukinoshita's face was frozen in a chilly smile.

I faced her, returning her frigid expression with one of my own, and pitched my voice high as I haughtily replied, "...How would you know how I act in class? Are you stalking me? Are you aware of antiharassment laws? Would you like to have your life ruined?"

"That one was even better than last time...," said Yuigahama with an astonished grin.

Beside her, there came the snap of a foot breaking a dead twig. "...Was that...supposed to be an impression of someone?" Even though it was summer, I could have sworn I saw a blizzard blowing around behind Yukinoshita.

Your smile keeps twitching, and it's really freaking me out! I'm sorry!

Hayama, who had been listening to our exchange from the side, nodded as if he'd just figured something out. "Oh, I see. So that girl is *your* sister, Hikitani. She didn't look enough like Totsuka to be related to him," he said, moving to stand in front of Komachi.

Hey, not so close...

"I'm Hayato Hayama," he said. "I'm in Hikitani's class. It's nice to meet you, Komachi."

"Y-yeah, it's nice to meet you, too. Thanks for always being so kind to my brother." Komachi took a step back in mild alarm and then half hid behind Yuigahama to observe him from a greater distance.

"There's no way she could be Sai-chan's little sister, Hayato!" said Yuigahama. "She looks more like she'd be Yukinon's sister!"

You're just talking about her hair color…

Hayama shook his head. "No, Yukinoshita doesn't have a younger sister."

"Oh, reall— Wait. How do you know that, Hayato?" Yuigahama asked.

"Well, I…" Hayama glanced over in Yukinoshita's direction.

Yukinoshita did not engage with him and kept facing the elementary school kids. "I wonder what we're supposed to do?"

"Oh yeah," said Hayama. "I'll go call over Miss Hiratsuka." He withdrew from the group, probably sensing the awkwardness in the air.

Yukinoshita really seemed to have something against Hayama. She was always severe with me, too, but with him, her snippiness was more aggressive. Her attitude toward Hayama struck me as more of an attempt to exclude. *Maybe she's allergic to normies or something. Well, actually, I'm allergic to them, too. Can you use antihistamines for this?*

Once Hayama was gone, Komachi tiptoed up to me. "Oh no, Bro! What a disaster!"

"What?"

"You've got zero chance of winning against that hottie! That's a red light!"

"Shut up. Leave me alone." She came all the way over just to tell me that? What a dumb sister I have. I mean, I have no interest in competing with Hayama over anything in the first place. As long as he doesn't do anything to me, I don't give a damn about him.

But a follow-up attack came from an unexpected source. "She's right," Ebina added. "This could be rough. Your aura just screams 'bottom,' Hikitani, and not only that, you're especially weak. If Hayama makes his move, you'll go down immediately."

"I—I see… I'll watch out for that," I replied. Now that I think if it, this was the first time Ebina and I had ever spoken. I wanted to earnestly pray that there would never be a second, if possible. *What the heck is a bottom aura? I'm not emitting anything like that.*

Meanwhile Hayama had returned with Miss Hiratsuka in tow, and she explained our role. "So what we'll be asking you to do for this orienteering activity is to prepare the meals at the goal. You'll set out box lunches and drinks for the kids. I'll bring everything there first in the van."

"Are we riding in the van, too?" I asked.

"There's not enough room for that. Walk quickly. Oh, and be sure to get there before the kids do."

If we were supposed to be preparing their lunches, it would indeed be bad if we didn't reach the goal before the kids. Already a fair number of children had set off. We should probably hurry it up.

X X X

Orienteering is a sport where you pass through established checkpoints on the field of play in a fixed order, competing to reach the goal in a set amount of time. Yes, it's apparently a sport. It's supposed to be a fairly serious competition, rushing as fast as you can with a map and a compass. But what the elementary school kids were doing that day was not a real race. It was basically just for fun. They meandered around the mountain in small clusters, and when they reached the checkpoints on their maps, they would answer a quiz. They were scored based on the number of correct answers they had and the time it took to complete the course.

Upon reflection, I remembered doing an activity like this before, too. My group had been full of abysmal idiots, though, so our answers had been a disaster. I was the only one who knew the right answers, but the group hadn't listened to me when I mumbled them, so in the end, we'd had a pile of wrong answers, and everyone was moaning, like, *Aww maaaan…*

The plateau was cool even at the height of summer, and the leaves rustled softly with each gust. We weren't actually participating, so we headed straight for the goal. On the way, we caught sight of kids hunting around for signs, their heads all bunched together over their tiny pieces of paper as they solved the questions. Everyone appeared to be enjoying themselves, so that was good.

Every time Hayama or Miura noticed the kids, they would call out, "You can do it!" or "The goal's waiting for you!" just like proper camp volunteer types. It was only natural that Hayama would do that, but I was a little surprised to see Miura joining in.

"Hey, hey, Hayato," she said. "I actually kinda like these kids. Aren't they supercute?"

...She was just saying the word *cute* in an attempt to make herself look cute. I thought about trying to emphasize my own lovability, but as a guy, it would only result in accusations of having a Lolita complex, so I decided against it.

Once Hayama and Miura started calling out to the kids, Tobe, Ebina, Totsuka, and Yuigahama followed suit. What friendly boys and girls. And they were all attractive people, so the children would latch on to them immediately.

We ran into several little parties, some of them more than once, apparently. I wasn't watching all that closely, and I wasn't really engaging them, so I didn't remember much. Actually, I just couldn't tell them apart. They were uniformly loud and excited and radiating boundless energy. On one path that turned off to the side, we encountered a gang of five girls. They were especially energetic, active looking, and fairly fashionably dressed. Their interactions with each other made them sound like a giggling gaggle of gossips. I got the impression that this quintet would become central figures in their grade level once they went on to middle school. They were normie eggs, so to speak.

Apparently, such girls admired high schoolers, especially in-crowd types like Hayama and Miura. They went out of their way to come talk to us, in a mostly one-on-one fashion. And that meant none were approaching me nor poor little Yukinoshita. No *indeed*.

They would begin the conversation with the polite formalities and then go on to chat about fashion and sports and middle school... As they walked along with us, we ended up hunting down their checkpoint with them.

"Okay, we'll help you with just this one. But you've got to keep it a secret from everyone else, okay?" said Hayama. The kids cheerfully agreed.

Sharing a secret, huh? I was rather impressed. So this was another one of those techniques for greasing the wheels with people.

I would generally describe these girls as a bunch of cheerful and openhearted types, but one thing about them bothered me. Most of these little clusters had a proper sense of unity, or else they would be divided into two mini-groups with a loose connection, creating a single unit. With this group alone, you could detect an irregularity. One of the five was walking about two steps behind the others.

Her limbs were long and slender, and her straight black hair gleamed purple. Her impression was somewhat more mature than the other girls', and her feminine attire also seemed more refined. Honestly, she was more than a bit cute. She drew considerable attention. But even so, nobody seemed concerned that she was falling behind.

Oh, they noticed. The other four girls occasionally looked back at her, conveying things only they understood with smiles and stifled giggles. There was less than one meter between the outlier and the rest. It would only be natural for an observer to group them together. But there was a screen between them that could not be seen, an invisible wall, a distinct break.

The girl had a digital camera hanging from her neck, and occasionally, she touched it as if she had nothing else to do. But she didn't take any pictures. *A camera, huh?* When I was in elementary school, digital cameras were not yet mainstream, and everyone was using those disposable ones, like QuickSnap or whatever. I would go buy a new one every time, but I didn't have any friends and I didn't take group pictures, so I couldn't use up all twenty-four. Instead, I'd go back home and end up finishing off the film roll with pictures of Komachi's dog. Digital cameras are nice because you can take—or not take—as many photos as you want.

At the very back of the group, the girl's eyes wandered toward things the rest of her party ignored. Just as Stand users are drawn to one another, loners also apparently excel at discovering their kind.

"..."

Yukinoshita let out a small sigh. Apparently, she had also noticed the uniqueness of this girl. Well, that wasn't necessarily a bad thing. There comes a time or two in life when you should face isolation. No, you *have* to. Constantly being accompanied, having someone by your side always and forever—*that* is far more abnormal and creepy. I'm positive you can only learn and feel certain things when you're alone. If there are lessons to gain from having friends, then so also are there lessons from *not* having friends. These two things are two sides of the same coin and should be treated as equally valuable. So this moment, too, will also have worth for that girl.

With that conviction in my heart, I decided to pretend that I hadn't noticed. *Leave it, leave it.* But, well, there are many people in this world who wouldn't agree.

"Have you found the checkpoint?" Hayama called out to the girl.

"...No," she replied, giving him an uncomfortable smile.

Hayama grinned back at her. "Okay. Then let's all look for it together. What's your name?"

"Rumi...Tsurumi."

"I'm Hayato Hayama. Nice to meet you. Don't you think it might be hidden over there?" he said, guiding Rumi with a hand to her back.

...OMG, Hayama!!

"Did you see that just now?" I said to Yukinoshita. "He was supernatural about inviting her to join in, *and* he casually asked her name."

"I saw it. It was a feat you'd never manage, even if you spent your whole life trying," she said with a disparaging sniff. Then, her expression immediately hardened. "But I can't say that's a very good way to go about it."

Hayama escorted Rumi right into the middle of the group. But she didn't look particularly happy about it. Just as before, she was looking away from the other girls, focusing on the gaps between the trees or the pebbles on the path.

Rumi wasn't the only one who wasn't enjoying herself. As she joined her companions, a flash of tension quieted their chatter for a moment. It didn't go so far as hate, but you could sense her presence was an intrusion. They didn't openly avoid her. They didn't reveal their feelings by clicking their tongues or kicking the ground in frustration. They didn't attack her. They communicated via atmosphere alone. Without even raising their voices, their accusation was clear. Their violence was nonverbal, nonphysical, and nonactive: just coercive.

Yukinoshita sighed as if to say this was just what she expected. "Of course..."

"So it even happens with elementary schoolers, huh?" I commented.

Yukinoshita looked at me. "There's no difference between children in elementary school or children in high school. They're all human."

Though Rumi was briefly allowed into the center of the group, before you knew it, she was ejected once again. She hadn't spoken to anyone or vice versa, so her exclusion was obviously a matter of course. From a distance, I saw her fingers brush her digital camera again.

The map said there was a signpost nearby that would be the checkpoint. With so many people looking for it, we'd find it soon enough.

Before long, we discovered the somewhat grimy signboard planted in the shade of the trees. It had probably been white originally, but wind and rain had turned it a brownish color. There was a sheet tacked to it, so now the kids just had to solve the problems on the paper.

"Thank you very much!" they chirped, and we parted ways. They were most likely going to go on to search for the next checkpoint, and we headed off to get to the end of the race before they did.

I looked back just in time to see Rumi, exactly one step behind the others, disappear into the shade of the trees.

X X X

We marched through the trees and emerged out into an open area. This point, situated halfway up the mountain, seemed to be the goal. I figured this was another plaza. Now it was time to make preparations to welcome the students at the finish line.

"Oh, you're late," said Miss Hiratsuka as she stepped out of the van. "We don't have time to chat, so can I ask you to unload this and set everything out?" There must have been another mountain road up here that didn't follow the orienteering course.

Miss Hiratsuka opened up the trunk of the van to reveal a pile of lunch boxes and assorted drinks in foldout containers. I was a little sweaty, so the cool air wafting out of the interior was pleasant. The boys did the manual labor and carried out the containers. "We've also chilled some pears for dessert," she said, jerking a thumb at something behind her.

I could hear the trickling burbles of a brook, so the fruit must have been soaking in the running water.

"I have some knives here, so get those peeled and cut, too." Miss

Hiratsuka patted a basket. It was packed with fruit knives and mini cutting boards, as well as serving implements such as paper plates and toothpicks.

But peeling enough pears for all those kids would be a ton of work. Plus, we also had to set out the box lunches.

"It looks like it would be best to divide up the labor," Hayama said, considering the intimidating amount of work before us.

Studying her fake nails, Miura said, "I'm not gonna be slicing any fruit."

"Yeah, I can't cook," added Tobe.

"I guess I'd be fine doing either," said Ebina.

Hayama thought for a moment. "Hmm… How should we do it, then? I doubt it'll take many people to set out the lunches, so… Okay, why don't the four of us take care of that, then?"

"Okay, then we'll do the pears," replied Yuigahama, and we split into two groups.

"…Are you okay not doing setup?" I asked her as we went down to retrieve the fruit from the brook.

"Huh? Why wouldn't I be? …Oh, I get it. You're saying that 'cause I'm bad at cooking, aren't you? I can peel pears, at least!"

"No, that's not what I mean." I meant that she was friends with Miura's clique, so wouldn't it bother her to be over here with us instead? But whatever. We took the pears back to the plaza, got out the knives and other utensils, and went straight to work. Yukinoshita and Yuigahama handled the peeling, and me, Totsuka, and Komachi laid the slices out on the plates and stuck toothpicks in them.

Yukinoshita began skillfully slicing off the skin. Beside her, Yuigahama was rolling up her sleeves, bursting with confidence. Although she was already wearing short sleeves. "Heh. I've gotten a lot better, you know," she said.

"Oh? I look forward to seeing your results. I suppose this is where I ask you to show me what you've got." Yukinoshita chuckled, but…her expression gradually clouded.

The pear that Yuigahama had peeled had developed an hourglass figure: voluptuous, sexy, and curvy. *Is this supposed to be some kind of hand-carved Buddha figure or what? Why is it so lumpy…? She's got unbelievable antiskill when it comes to cooking.*

"Wh-why?!" she cried. "But I watched my mom do it so many times!"

"Just watched, huh…?" I commented.

An aura of despair hung over us. Yukinoshita sighed and plucked the knife and pear from Yuigahama with an expression of determination. Her knife smoothly slid along the fruit with a satisfying *schloop*. "Yuigahama, you hold the knife steady and turn the pear."

"L-like this?"

"No. You cut level with the skin. If the angle of the blade is too deep, you'll shave off the flesh," she said. "You're too slow… No. If you don't do it quickly, your hands will warm up the pear, and it won't be chilled."

"Are you my mother-in-law?! Yukinon, you're scary when you've got a knife in your hands!"

"Sorry, but we don't have much time," I said. "Leave the cooking lesson for later." I took the pear and tossed it to Komachi. "Komachi."

"Gotcha!" She caught the pear and began effortlessly peeling it with a leftover paring knife.

"You can do the toothpicks instead," I said to Yuigahama.

"Aww…," Yuigahama groaned, not at all pleased, but she reluctantly relinquished the knife to me.

Now that we'd switched places, it wouldn't do for me to look incompetent, too, so I did my best to be even more careful than usual. As I rotated the pear, I stripped off the peel to expose the juicy, ripe flesh within, like an old movie villain pulling the obi off a naive girl as she spun around and around. *Come on, little miss, come on*, I mentally prodded it. *All right, all right, it seems I've still got the touch.* When I say I aspire to be a househusband, I'm not joking around. I'll spare no effort if it means not having to get a job.

Totsuka peeked at the pear in my hands, his eyes sparkling. "Wow, Hachiman. You're really good at this."

"Ugh! It's true! You're stupidly good," agreed Yuigahama. "It's creepy."

"'Ugh'? What's that supposed to mean? ...Wait, huh? It's creepy?" Privately, I was shocked.

"...It's true—you're quite good at it for a boy." A rare compliment from Yukinoshita.

Wait, wasn't this actually the first time? Reflexively, I turned to look at her.

"...However." Before her was a warren of pear rabbits. "You still have a long way to go." The triumphant smile on her face was stunning. She had made so many decorative slices in such a short period of time just to show off how much better she was... This girl was way too competitive...

"Pear skins are tough, so wouldn't it be easier to eat with no peel...? I get it; I lost, geez." I acknowledged my defeat.

"Oh dear, I wasn't intending to make it a competition, though," Yukinoshita replied. But she was clearly pleased...

I was a little annoyed, but Yukinoshita in high spirits meant that we could get the work done quickly, so I left it at that.

Apparently, Yukinoshita was cheerful enough to be talkative, as she struck up a conversation with Komachi beside her. "You're studying for exams right now, aren't you? Here's a question for you. Which prefecture produces the most pears?"

"Yamanashi, right?" Komachi replied.

"Hey, don't answer instantly when you actually have no idea," I said. "At least take a little time to think." Komachi's response made me sad. Was she actually studying for her exams? It might be a good idea to supervise her study quite closely once we got home.

Yukinoshita gave Komachi a vaguely strained smile. "Well, you can start learning about that now, and there's still time before your exams..." Next, she turned to Yuigahama. "Now then, Yuigahama, what's the correct answer?"

I suppose Yuigahama had been expecting this question, as she replied with full confidence. "Heh...it's Tottori!"

"Wrong. You need to repeat middle school," said Yukinoshita.

"You're being way meaner to me than you were with Komachi!"

Because you're older... Of course Yukinoshita would have different expectations. Tottori was actually close, though. About ten years ago, it would have been in first. Now it was around third.

Komachi listened to Yuigahama's response and suddenly burst into an ominous cackle. "...Heh-heh-heh. Now I know the answer. If Tottori is wrong, that means...the right answer is Shimane!"

"No, it is not. And I'm unclear as to how your first statement entails the next..."

"Well, Tottori and Shimane do kinda feel the same..." Chiba people are bad at geography when it comes to anywhere far away. And speaking of geography, all I care about is Chiba's ranking within our region. Tokyo and Kanagawa are obviously at the top, but I've got my hands full fiercely battling Saitama for third.

"So, what is it, Yukinoshita?" asked Totsuka.

"The correct answer is Chiba prefecture," she announced.

"I'd expect nothing less of the great Yukipedia," I said. "Can we just call you Chibapedia now?"

"That doesn't even have my name in it anymore...," Yukinoshita said, exasperated.

Odd. In my books, that title is the highest compliment.

"Wow, so Chiba's number one," Totsuka said, sounding impressed. "Are Chiba pears pretty famous?" Even Chiba natives vary widely in their knowledge of their home.

"In Chiba city, not really, but outside the city they're a big deal," I told him. "They're famous enough that at some schools, you'll get suspended if you take someone's pear. And if you eat it, you get expelled."

"Your Chiba knowledge is the kind that would never show up on entrance exams...," Yukinoshita commented. Apparently, not even the great Chibapedia was aware of that factoid. I guess that settled my victory in the Undisputed Championship Match of Chiba Trivia.

Despite all our chatting, we had been working briskly, and the job was soon done. When I looked up, I saw a stream of kids arriving.

After that, the task of handing out the lunch boxes and pears to the starving elementary schoolers commanded our full attention.

Chatting in the van

In the middle row

...O-oh.
I don't know...

Huh?
They put two of the same movie in a set? Why?

Don't worry. They have a set that includes both the DVD and Blu-ray.

Oh...yeah. We only watch DVDs at my house, though...

That was not a remake—it was a completely new work. It would be more accurate to call it a reimagining. While it has been thirty-five years since the original, the revival made use of state-of-the-art film techniques in addition to Destiny's traditional hand-drawn style, so there was no question that it would be beautiful. Have you seen it on Blu-ray?

Oh! Me too! Did you see the recent movie? It was like a remake? It was really pretty, and Grue-bear was cu—

...If I must say, then perhaps Grue-bear. If I must.

Th-that's news to me... Hey, so, who's your favorite Destiny character?

....

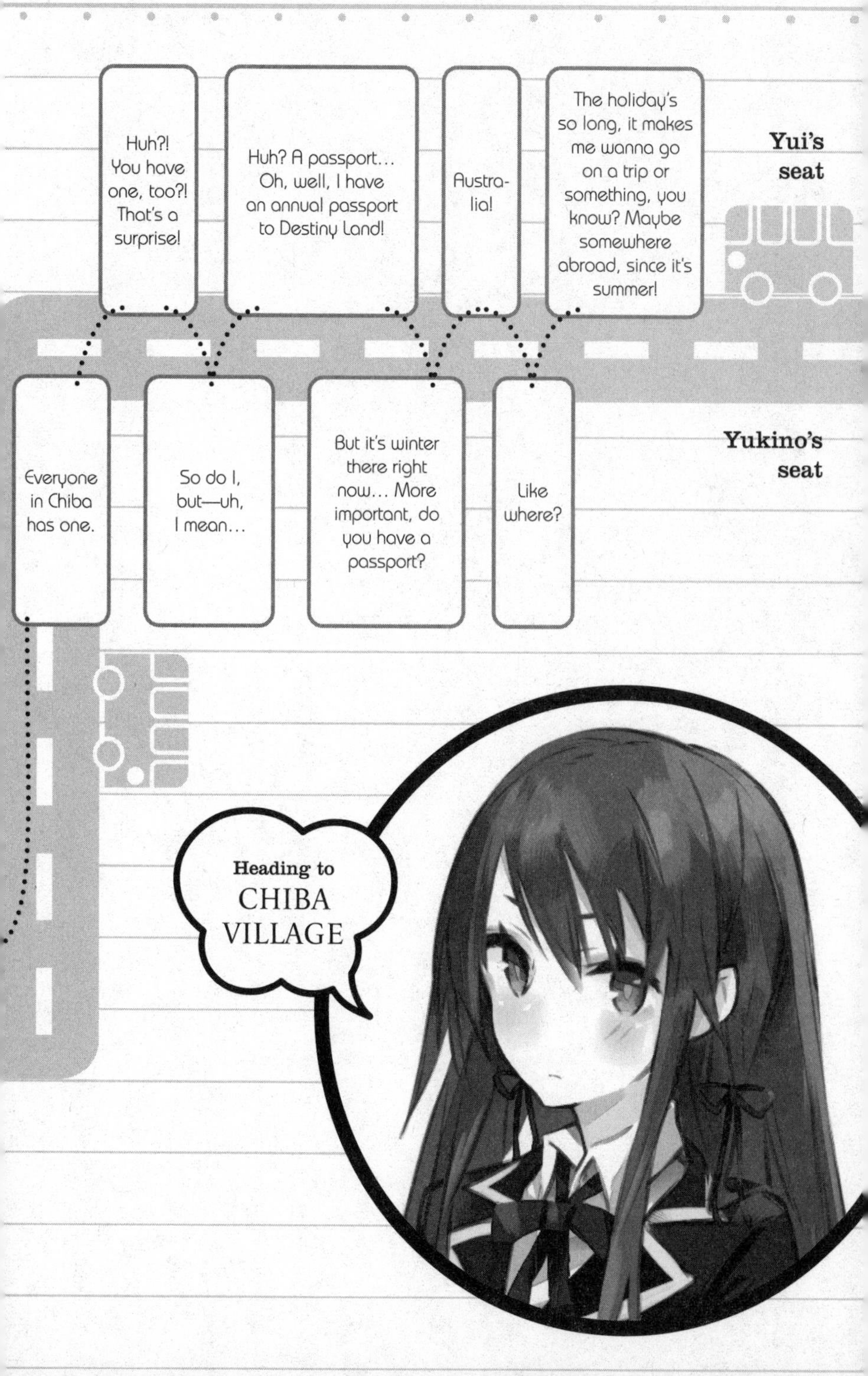
Yui's seat
Yukino's seat
The holiday's so long, it makes me wanna go on a trip or something, you know? Maybe somewhere abroad, since it's summer!
Like where?
Australia!
But it's winter there right now… More important, do you have a passport?
Huh? A passport… Oh, well, I have an annual passport to Destiny Land!
So do I, but—uh, I mean…
Huh?! You have one, too?! That's a surprise!
Everyone in Chiba has one.
Heading to CHIBA VILLAGE

4

Out of nowhere, **Hina Ebina** begins proselytizing.

When it comes to camping, you always think of curry.

Obviously, a proper househusband should be able to make a curry or two. In fact, I'm so good at it that no matter what I cook, it always ends up as curry. Honestly, as long as you put in the roux blocks, you can make it out of anything. It wouldn't even be an exaggeration to say that every kind of food is a potential ingredient.

If we're talking Chiba curry, Sitar is the most well-known restaurant, but of course, in Chiba Village it would be cooked with outdoor camping implements. Sitar is really good, though.

Anyway, dinner for the night was this camping staple. First, we started by lighting up the charcoal fires to show the kids how it was done. Miss Hiratsuka was the one who demonstrated by starting the fire for the teachers. "First, we'll give you an example," she said, and before she was even done speaking, she was stacking up charcoal and stuffing crumpled-up newspaper underneath to get the fire going. She ignited the newspaper, and it started burning.

She made a halfhearted attempt at fanning the flames with a plastic hand fan to help them reach the charcoal, but I guess it was taking too long for her tastes. After only a moment, she suddenly sloshed cooking oil over the fire. A pillar of flame immediately flared high before her.

This is dangerous stuff, so absolutely do not try this at home, kids. You could seriously get hurt.

The audience erupted into cries that were not quite cheers nor screams. But Miss Hiratsuka was unmoved—far from it. There was a cigarette pressed between her lips as she formed a cold and ominous smile. Leaning in toward the fire with the cigarette still in her mouth, she sucked in a breath and then withdrew and exhaled. "Like that, basically."

"You seem disturbingly used to this," I commented. She'd been very precise about it, and she'd even introduced her secret cooking-oil trick.

With a faraway gaze, Miss Hiratsuka replied, "Heh, you might not think it to look at me, but when I was in university, I often held barbecues with my friends. While I was busy lighting the fire, all the couples would flirt and fool around together… Tsk, I'm starting to feel sick." With that recollection of her unpleasant past, Miss Hiratsuka retreated from the blaze. "Boys, you light the fires. Girls, come with me to get the supplies for cooking," she said, leaving with half of the children.

Segregating the boys and girls right now makes me think you've still got some lingering resentment, Miss Hiratsuka… Are you okay?

So Totsuka, Hayama, Tobe, and I were left behind. "All right, let's get this set up," Hayama said. He and Tobe tugged on the work gloves and piled the charcoal, while Totsuka set up the newspaper kindling.

…Whoops. Looks like I waited too long for a job.

The prep went along smoothly, and eventually, the only part left to do was the simple task of fanning and fanning. I didn't have the fortitude to just sit there doing nothing. To tell the truth, if it were just Hayama and Tobe there, I'd have no problem being like, *All right, you guys can handle this*, but obviously, I couldn't bring myself to do that in front of Totsuka. Left with no other choice, I slipped on the work gloves, took up a plastic hand fan, and vigorously whipped up the fire, just like they always do with barbecued eel.

"You must be hot…," Totsuka commented with concern.

"I guess…" Though we were on the plateau, it was still the middle of summer. If you're working hard right next to an open flame, you're gonna be dripping sweat.

"I'll go get something to drink. For everyone," said Totsuka, and he left.

Tobe followed him, going, "If you're getting some for all of us, I'll help!"

Maybe he actually was a decent guy, contrary to my expectations. Or maybe he was the kind of manly guy who didn't want to force Totsuka to carry all those heavy things with his slender arms. Yes, you do that, young man.

After they left, it was just me and Hayama.

"..."

Fwap, fwap.

"..."

Fwap, fwap.

I switched off my brain and focused entirely on fanning with an empty mind. As the pitch-black charcoal gradually tinged with red, I started to enjoy myself. But the heat from the sun and fire made sweat run into my eyes. When I raised my head to take off the gloves, my gaze met Hayama's. The eye contact meant that he had been watching me and that if Ebina had been here, things would have gotten weird.

"...What?" I asked.

"Oh, nothing," Hayama replied evasively.

"..."

Still flapping at the fire, I gave Hayama a long, hard look.

"It's nothing, really," he repeated, continuing to dodge the question.

"It's nothing, it's nothing." Are you the opening song of Azuki-chan*?* I've never seen anyone say *It's nothing* when it was actually nothing. I employed the exceedingly annoying tactic of glancing over at Hayama every five seconds.

He finally slumped in resignation and spoke. "...Hikitani, Yu–"

"Sorry to keep you waiting, Hachiman." Totsuka cut him off as he pressed a cool paper cup against my cheek. The chilly sensation made my heart skip a beat. Looking up, I saw his pure and innocent smile of delight in the success of his mischief. I guess he had hurried back, as he was panting a little. His flushed cheeks were adorable. What a trooper. It only added to his cuteness, bumping up his angel score.

My heart was, as usual, pounding along with an emotion that wasn't quite surprise, but neither was it butterflies. I made a conscious effort to suppress that anxious patter and sound calm. "Hey. *Thank you,*" I said in English, and I was so shaken, my voice cracked and improved my pronunciation.

Tobe was not far behind Totsuka, holding a few plastic bottles. When he heard my remark, he shot me an odd look.

"...I'll switch with you," Hayama suggested with a quick smile, so I took him up on the offer.

I handed over the fan, removed the work gloves, and accepted the paper cup of barley tea from Totsuka. "Okay, you can handle the rest," I said to Hayama. "...What were you gonna say just now, though?"

"We can talk about it later." Hayama grinned brightly at me, showing no sign of distress, and returned to the charcoal fire and fanned it vigorously.

Phew, I'm tired. Sipping at my barley tea, I watched Hayama's back as he squatted before the fire. Huh... So what had Hayama been about to say, then? Well, I could imagine two possibilities, but not why Hayama would ask me about either of those. I took a seat on a bench in the sun and sipped my tea, like the ideal old-man-style break. That was when the girls came back.

When Miura saw the fire was all ready, she cried out in excitement. "That's amazing, Hayato! ♪"

"Oh yeah! You're pretty outdoorsy, huh, Hayato?" Ebina joined in to praise his achievements. And they glanced over at me. I keenly heard the unspoken *Why is Hikitani slacking off?*

"Hikitani did most of it," said Hayama.

Oh-ho, and he casually comes to my defense. Hayama really is a good guy. The problem was that it backfired, and now everyone was thinking, *Hayama's so nice for covering for him... Eek!* ☆ Well, that's how it goes in this world.

"Nice work, Hikki. Here." Yuigahama, who had returned with Miura and the other girls, held out a facial wipe for me. She wasn't being sarcastic or anything.

"Oh, Hachiman worked hard! He really did, really!" Totsuka asserted, clenching his fists tight. It was true that without context, the situation would look like I had done nothing.

"I know. Hikki gets serious over weird things." Yuigahama laughed.

From behind her, Yukinoshita was eyeing me. "We can tell. Don't wipe your face with work gloves. You're a disgrace," she said as if she had seen me do it.

Oh, so my face is dirty, huh? Now that I finally understood why Yuigahama was handing me a wipe, I accepted it gratefully. "...Thanks," I said.

But I don't think my gratitude was directed toward any one specific person.

X X X

Komachi was approaching me with Miss Hiratsuka, carrying a basket piled high with vegetables. The two of them were giggling over something together with a suspicious level of enjoyment. Somehow, I had a good guess as to the topic of their conversation.

In all probability, it was me. I'm so self-conscious that generally, whenever someone in our class giggles, I assume they're laughing at me, and it's a source of pride. This sort of prediction is a simple task for me.

Man, it's tough being popular! ...It really sucks.

As I wondered what Miss Hiratsuka was saying and what was in store for me next, it took all the wind out of my sails.

"What's wrong, Hikigaya?" she asked me. "You don't look well. Do book boys not like the outdoors?"

"What the heck is a book boy...?" It's true that I do like books, but it's not like I eat them or anything. "Hey, Komachi. What're you two talking about?"

"Huh? Just talking business. I was saying that you let me read your old essays and helped me with my book report like the superreliable and kind big brother you are. Oh, that was a freebie for all those Komachi points. ♪"

"Okay. I think I get what's going on. I'm gonna make you cry." Since when does the point system work that way? And she had definitely blabbed the content of my book report and that essay.

"I only did it for your sake, Bro! I don't think I was wrong!" Komachi whined.

I readied a flick for my sister's forehead, but Miss Hiratsuka interrupted our quarrel. "Come on, that's enough of that. We were actually mostly just gushing about how much we love you. She told me so many things, like her memories of when you were young."

"Waugh!" Komachi yelped. "Hey, you're not allowed to tell him that! That gets…a pretty low Komachi score…" My sister flushed bright red before my eyes, forced a cough to distract from her blushing, and then looked at me. "Ah…ah-ha, kidding… That reaction just now was worth a lot of Komachi points, don't you think?"

"You're an idiot…" I couldn't even be mad anymore. I was too busy being exasperated, and she was too cute. "Stop with the stupid chatter and start on the curry. We have rice to cook." If I played along with her nonsense, we'd never get to eat. I snatched the basket away from her and briskly carried it to the counter.

Komachi stood stunned for a minute, but then she nodded to herself and trotted after me.

I called it a counter, but it was basically just a big washstand. We would wash the rice and do the prep work there. The variety of ingredients wasn't exactly satisfying, but still, it was more satisfying than my life. There was pork rib, carrots, onions, and potatoes. The list immediately brought to mind your average Japanese household curry with rice.

"Well, this is about what you would expect for outdoor cooking for children." Yukinoshita expressed the most normal of opinions. I guess she meant that it was nothing special, but it was a safe choice you couldn't majorly screw up.

"Yeah, I guess," I replied. "When you make curry at home, though, there actually is a degree of individuality in it, depending on who does the cooking. The curry my mom makes has a lot of stuff in it. Like fried tofu."

"Hmm. I suppose so." Yukinoshita's reply was curt. Well, she was always curt, but this time her reply was more of a reflex. Her tone of voice was distinctly flat.

"No, seriously," I replied. "You can do, like, konjak noodles and daikon and stuff… I'm like, is this hot pot or what?"

"Yeah, yeah, you can put *chikuwa* or whatever in it, right?" Tobe suddenly jumped into the conversation.

"Y-yeah." I was so startled, I couldn't come up with a decent reply. *Hey, man, don't act so buddy-buddy with me. I'll start wondering if we're friends or something.*

But Tobe didn't seem particularly troubled as he muttered, "*Chikuwa*'s like seafood. Seriously?" I didn't really get what he was on about.

But if he was making an attempt to connect with me, maybe he was a good guy, too. But if that was the case, then I felt terrible about my inability to keep the conversation going. So terrible that I decided to never speak with him again so as to not bother him.

Off to the side, Yuigahama was humming as she peeled potatoes. Since she was using a peeler, I figured she'd given up on knives after that first go. "That does happen with the curry your mom makes, you know," she said. "Like just a little while ago there was this weird leaf in mine. She can be such a space case sometimes."

You're the space case here. It has to be hereditary. Please, cut out the potato eyes. You're gonna kill us with solanine.

"Oh, hey, look! It was just like this one," she said, leaving her peeling half-done as she trotted up to a twig on a tree, plucked a leaf off, and showed it to us. There was nothing special about it, just, like, *This is indeed a leaf!*

...Oh, wait, is she talking about bay leaves? I thought that was a pretty common spice, though.

"Perhaps the leaf in your curry was that of the *laurier*...?" Yukinoshita suggested.

"Huh? Lolie?" I said. Yukinoshita's choice of vocabulary set off my imagination.

"Waaah... There's a leaf in my curry..." —Little Miss Lolie (six years old)

Gotta go search that up on Pixiv when I get home...

Yukinoshita gave me a dirty look. "Just so you know, *laurier* is the name of the tree bay leaves come from. The term comes from the French. In English, it would be a *bay laurel*. Is that clear, Mr. Lolicon?"

Erk! Are you psychic?! But who's she accusing of a Lolita complex anyway? I'm a sister-complex kind of guy... "I know what a bay laurel is, too," I said. Hikki knows all about that. I know that bay leaves come from bay laurels.

But of course, Yuigahama had had no idea and looked a little shocked. "Laurier...doesn't mean pads..."

Those genes didn't just get passed down. They've evolved. Warp digivolved.

X X X

Not much thought had gone into the division of labor, but nevertheless, we got all the vegetable chopping and rice washing done. Now we were ready to get cooking. We laid out our utensils and then sauteed the meat and vegetables in the pot. As this was going on, I heard Ebina mutter, "Carrots are such a lewd vegetable...," but Miura whacked her over the head. Maybe Miura was actually the nice one here. No one else was willing to be the straight man in this routine, but she stepped up to the plate. Although, main heroines who smack people around aren't as popular these days, so I would recommend she actively ignore Ebina from now on.

We poured water into the pot and, once it came to a boil, dropped in two kinds of curry cubes. The fat of the pork rib would bring out the flavor, and the cubes would make it nice and spicy. Next, all that was left to do was slowly let it stew. Of course, we were big kids, and a few of us even cooked on a daily basis, so we finished the process without any serious hitches.

When I scanned the area, I could see smoke from assorted nearby fires. This would be the first outdoor cooking experience for the elementary school kids. From what I could see, a few groups were having a rough time of it. "If you don't have anything to do, you could look around and help them out," said Miss Hiratsuka. Implicit in her statement was *I don't wanna do it, though.* I felt much the same. I wonder why normies enjoy all that social interchange. Isn't that how you get off the highway?

Hayama seemed on board with the idea, though. "We don't get many chances to talk with elementary school kids, after all."

"Uh, but we've got a pot on the fire."

"Yeah. So I guess we can only go check on maybe one nearby group."

That's not what I meant when I said that... For some reason, he was acting under the assumption that I had agreed to this. Normally, you'd think, *There's a pot on the fire, so I can't go.* Right? That was what I meant. Why was he taking it like advice on how to pull this off? "I'll watch the pot...," I declared, quickly withdrawing, but my U-turn was immediately intercepted.

"Don't worry about it, Hikigaya. I'll watch the pot." A smirking Miss Hiratsuka was blocking my path.

I see. So this is part of my training in the art of "getting along," huh...?

Hayama took the lead, and we approached the nearest group. Not that I cared, but he was more like a Service Club captain than Yukinoshita was. It looked like the kids were treating the arrival of us high schoolers as a special event, and we received an enthusiastic welcome. They divulged the contents of their curry, and even though it wasn't done yet, they kept prodding us to *come on, have some, eat up* like a bunch of country grannies. Well, with Japanese curry, you always reach a certain threshold of flavor, no matter your skill. I doubted they'd come up with anything too weird.

Hayama and the others were surrounded by children, and the whole gang had really hit it off. I wish I could just chalk it up to his social prowess, like, *I'd expect nothing less of a normie.* But in truth, he wasn't the only reason the kids were being like this. Kids of that age bracket are the least intimidated by grown-ups. They don't know what makes an adult an adult, so they think older people are no big deal. Source: past me. They don't know the value of money, the significance of studying, or the meaning of love. They take for granted what they are given, and they have no clue as to where it all comes from. It's the age of certainty as to the workings of the world, even though you're only barely scratching the surface. Once you hit middle school, you come to know failure, regret, and despair; you come to appreciate that the world is a hard place to live in. Or if you're a clever child, you might have figured that out already.

For example, the one girl who had been excluded from the group and was trying to become invisible all by herself. The rest of the kids probably saw her alone every day, so they didn't think much of it. But from an outsider's perspective, it was an arresting sight.

"Do you like curry?" Hayama tried approaching Rumi.

When Yukinoshita saw his attempt, she let out a sigh so small you would probably miss it. I was with her there. That was a poor move.

If you're gonna try chatting with a loner, you should always do it secretly, out of sight. You have to take the utmost precaution to ensure they aren't publicly humiliated. A high schooler talking to Rumi, especially a prominent figure like Hayama, would only further highlight her uniqueness and cast her distinct loneliness in even sharper relief. To draw a simple analogy, it's like how it's more embarrassing to get paired up with the teacher than to end up alone. The sympathy and pity is the worst part. I'd be like, *Stop being so nice to me; I'd rather you just ignore me.* When you're alone, you're invisible, and you escape unscathed. But when you have to partner up with the teacher, you're less "veiled by a discreet curtain" and more "failed like a NEET virgin." That was why it was a bad idea.

When Hayama did anything, the people around him would follow suit. The high schoolers were celebrities, and the kids would go along with anything their objects of admiration did. Rumi was being herded into the spotlight all at once. She was now the center of attention, a mere loner shot up to stardom all at once. How nice, huh? What a Cinderella story. A Super Dimensional Cinderella. And they all lived happily ever after.

Of course not.

If I had to guess at what was running through their minds, it was not *Eek! That high schooler is talking to Rumi! She's so cool! Come be friends with me, too!* It was probably like, *Huh? Why her?* Rumi was now under fire—curious looks from the big kids and jealousy and hate from her classmates.

She was trapped. No matter how she replied to Hayama's question, people were bound to hate her for it. If she gave him a friendly reply, they'd be like, *She thinks she's good enough to be talking to him, huh?* And if she were cold to him: *Who does she think she is? Wow, so full of herself.* It was damned if you do, damned if you don't.

Rumi looked surprised to see Hayama speaking to her. "...Not really. I don't really care about curry," she replied coldly, feigning composure, and then quietly walked away. In a situation like this, there was no choice but to make a tactical retreat. There were no other cards available to play.

Rumi withdrew to the most private location she could, removed from the social circle. In other words, toward me. By the way, though Yukinoshita had distanced herself from me, she was also nearby. An aloof-style loner has a wide circle of personal space and emits a strong negative aura that keeps people at bay. The effect is so powerful that you could even call it a Reality Marble. To put it in simple terms, they just distance people. Whoa, that was blunt of me.

Anyway, Rumi approached a spot about a meter away, right between Yukinoshita and myself, and then stopped. She was close enough that we could just barely see each other in our periphery.

At a loss, Hayama smiled sadly at Rumi and immediately went back to engaging the other kids. "All right, it's a special occasion, so let's add in a secret ingredient! How about it? Does anyone want to put in a little something extra?" he said cheerfully, charming the people around him and drawing their attention. The hostile glares quickly broke away from Rumi. The kids raised their hands, shouting *Me! Me!* as they suggested all sorts of ideas, like coffee and hot pepper and chocolate.

"Oh! I think fruit would be nice! Like peaches or something!"

By the way, that one was Yuigahama. Why was she participating...? Even Hayama's face stiffened up a bit. She wasn't just coming down to the kids' level. Her proposal was clearly the product of the worst cooking ability among them.

Hayama promptly adopted his usual gentle expression and said something to Yuigahama. Her shoulders drooped, and she trudged toward us. By all appearances, he had gently requested her to buzz off.

"What an idiot...," I muttered thoughtlessly to myself.

A soft, whisper-like voice echoed mine. "They really are a bunch of fools...," said Rumi Tsurumi icily. Well, that settles it. Her nickname from now on is Rumi-Rumi. Is this *Nadesico*?

"Well, that's what most of the world is like. It's a good thing you recognized it early," I said.

Rumi gave me a curious appraisal that made me slightly uncomfortable.

Yukinoshita cut between us. "And you're part of that majority."

"Hey, don't underestimate me," I retorted. "I'm so outstandingly talented, I can end up alone even when I'm in the mainstream."

"I don't know anyone else who can say something like that with such pride," she replied. "I'm not even exasperated anymore. I'm contemptuous."

"Once you go past exasperation, don't you generally end up at respect...?"

Rumi listened to our exchange without smiling, in silence. She shifted just the tiniest bit closer to us and then spoke to me. "Name."

"Huh? Name what?" I asked back, unsure of what she meant by the lone word.

Rumi imperiously restated with profound displeasure, "I'm asking your name. Most people would have figured that out already."

"...You offer your own name first before you ask someone else's," Yukinoshita retorted with a dangerously sharp look. It might have been her scariest one yet. You couldn't even call it a glare; it was more like death by visual stabbing. Yukinoshita had no intention of going easy on Rumi despite her youth. In fact, she was acting even more severe than she usually did. Maybe she doesn't much like children.

Yukinoshita's glowering scared Rumi, too, as she awkwardly looked away. "...Rumi Tsurumi," she muttered in a sullen tone, though just audible enough that I could catch it.

Yukinoshita nodded, apparently having heard as well. "I'm Yukino Yukinoshita. And over there is...Hiki... Hikiga... Hikiguana, was it?"

"Hey, how do you know my fourth-grade nickname? By the end, they were just calling me 'Iguana'..." At some point or another, the connection with my surname had disappeared, and I was just a lizard to them. Words sure do have a life of their own. "I'm Hachiman Hikigaya." If I didn't say something, people would be calling me Hikiguana again, so I did a proper self-introduction.

"And this is Yui Yuigahama." I pointed at the girl in question, who was approaching us.

"Huh? What is it?" Yuigahama looked at the three of us and put the pieces together, more or less. "Oh, yeah, yeah. I'm Yui Yuigahama. Rumi Tsurumi, huh? Nice to meet you."

But Rumi only nodded in reply to Yuigahama. She didn't even spare a glance at the older girl. With her gaze on the ground by her feet, she spoke hesitantly. "Like, you two seem different. Different from those people." Her referents were vague, so it was hard to grasp what she meant, but I figured she was trying to say that Yukinoshita and I weren't like "those people"—in other words, Hayama and the rest.

Well, we were indeed different. Looking at the aforementioned group, they seemed to be enjoying their attempts to make their "special curry."

"I'm different, too," Rumi said slowly, as if taking the time to chew on her words. Perhaps she was confirming the idea to herself by declaring it aloud.

Yuigahama's expression turned serious. "Different how?"

"They're all just kids. Well, I got along with them fine for a while.

But it was a waste of time, so I dropped them. I think I'm fine on my own."

"B-but…I think the memories of your elementary school friendships are pretty important."

"You don't need them, though. Once I get into middle school, I can just make friends with the kids who come in from other schools." She quietly raised her head, her eyes on the sky. The sun had finally sunk past the horizon, and the sky was indigo, as if someone had spilled watered-down ink across it. Here and there, stars began to twinkle. Rumi had a sad, faraway look in her eyes, but at the same time, a beautiful hope dwelled within them. Rumi Tsurumi still believed and still had faith. She was sure that in a new environment, things could change.

But that hope wasn't real.

"Sorry to say, but that isn't going to happen," Yukino Yukinoshita bluntly asserted. Rumi shot her a reproachful look. But Yukinoshita gazed straight back into her eyes and calmly laid it out in no uncertain terms. "The kids in your elementary school will all go on to the same middle school, won't they? Then it will all be the same. And the 'kids from other schools' will be with them."

When you're going from a local public elementary school to a public middle school, all your relationships up until then just continue on as before. When you start middle school, you still hold the same negative score you racked up during your younger years. You may presume you can make new friends, but the liabilities of your past will sneak their way in somehow. Like it or not, your personal history becomes public domain in the form of funny stories and anecdotes. They have their fun, use it as a convenient communication tool, and then it's all over.

"…"

No objections were raised. I wasn't gonna argue, and Yuigahama had fallen into an uncomfortable silence. Rumi didn't reply.

"Don't tell me you didn't already know?" Yukinoshita landed the finishing blow.

Rumi was unable to reply. Yukinoshita watched her as if she was refraining from saying more, her mouth pressed into a tight line. Perhaps she saw a trace of her own past in the younger girl.

"I knew it..." Rumi was quiet and resigned. "I was really so stupid."

"What happened?"

As Rumi murmured to herself in self-condemnation, Yuigahama gently pressed for more information.

"It's happened a few times. Someone would be it, and then we'd stop talking to them. Eventually, it'd always end, though, and after it was over, we'd talk again. It was just a phase. Someone would always start it, and then everyone would be doing it." Rumi said it matter-of-factly, but the story gave me goose bumps.

What the hell. That's really scary.

"And then it happened to a girl I was friends with and talked to a lot, and I sorta stayed away from her, but... But then suddenly, it was me. Even though I didn't do anything."

I'm sure any reason would have worked. No, they don't need to have a defined justification. Just an odd sense that this was how it had to be.

"And I had told her a lot of stuff..." Someone who was your friend one day would spill your secrets on the next, just to make someone else laugh. She was a sixth grader, so she'd probably had a crush. You don't know how to deal with these unfamiliar romantic feelings, so you want to express them. But they're embarrassing, after all, so you open your heart and confide in a person you trust.

Why is it that the more you say *absolutely do not tell anyone*, the more they spread it around? It's like, are you Ostrich Club? I can laugh about it now, but at the time, it was a painful, difficult, and agonizing experience. You think you're trusting someone by sharing your secrets with them, but then those personal details just serve as ammunition.

Nobody in this world fits the classic mold of the villain. Normally, everyone is good or at least ordinary. But in the right circumstances, they may change suddenly, and this is what makes them so frightening. One must always be on one's guard.

The passage suddenly flickered through my mind. No one is born evil. Everyone believes that, including myself. You have no doubt that you yourself are a good person. But once something you stand to benefit from is threatened, that's when the claws come out.

You tell yourself that you're not evil, so when you do something bad, you search for reasons to justify your actions. In order to avoid cognitive dissonance after you've changed, you flip the world on its head to fit your new identity. People who were cool only a day ago are now full of themselves, and the ones whose wisdom and intellect you once respected you now hold in contempt, since they have to be sneering at less academic types. People you once described as energetic and active are now dubbed annoying and overexcited.

And so you wield your sword of justice, bringing down your judgment on the upside-down world. But you can't validate your beliefs all on your own. That's why you gather coconspirators. You band together and circle-jerk about how unscrupulous and immoral the rest of them are, as if it were an established fact. You cultivate your sense of justice in that echo chamber, taking that tiny, minuscule seed of dissatisfaction and growing it into a great tree. If that's not a lie, then what is it?

Caught within your own bubble, you tremble in anxiety, thinking it might be your turn next. That's why you seek out a new sacrifice before it happens to you. And thus the cycle continues. There's no end. What meaning is there in a friendship built upon the sacrifice of someone else's dignity?

"Maybe it'll end up like this again…even in middle school." Her voice was trembling with the beginnings of a sob.

Cheers erupted from the large group, drowning her out. Though less than ten meters separated us, the goings-on over there might well have been happening in a distant foreign land.

X X X

I could hear the noise of tableware and spoons clacking. We saw off a silent Rumi as she returned to her group with a half-resigned expression, and then we returned straight back to our own base camp.

As Miss Hiratsuka had been keeping an eye on the pot for us, the potatoes had softened up nicely, and the rice appeared to be done, too. There was a wooden table and a pair of benches near the cooking area. Each person served a plate of food, and the search for a place to sit began.

The first one to sit down was Yukinoshita. She snatched up a corner seat on the bench with zero hesitation. Komachi followed, plopping down right beside Yukinoshita, of course, and Yuigahama maintained the pattern. As I wondered who would be next, surprisingly enough, it was Ebina, and then Miura took the edge on the opposite side. I had thought for sure that Miura would want to plant herself right in the middle, but I guess not.

As for the boys, Tobe took the seat opposite Miura. *Ahh, looks like he's into her, huh?* Beside him sat Hayama. I'm the kind of guy who doesn't care where I sit, so I intended to go with whichever seat was left over at the end. In fact, I end up last every time in such group decisions. It's like, you know, I'm the kind of openhearted guy who will oh-so-generously let others go first. Most likely, either Totsuka, Miss Hiratsuka, or I would end up sitting beside Hayama.

"Um..." Totsuka was contemplating what to do, looking back and forth between me and Miss Hiratsuka. "Wh-where do you want to sit, Hachiman?"

"I'm fine anywhere. I'll go for wherever is left over."

"Like that saying, 'There's fortune in what's left behind'?"

"No, that's not really why," I replied. Somehow, things just end up that way. My free will or personal beliefs have little to do with it... Nothing at all, really.

"There's fortune in what's left behind, huh...? I see!" Miss Hiratsuka suddenly muttered to herself. "That's it... Yes...that must be true." She had this expression like she'd just received a divine revelation.

That's a rather extreme reaction to the phrase *left behind*... Seriously, someone get this woman some fortune. "Well, let's just sit wherever," I said. "Where do you wanna sit, Totsuka?"

"Anywhere's fine, as long as I'm beside you."

"..."

I was dumbstruck. Totsuka had said it like it was absolutely nothing at all. That's why I was so slow to react. He must have realized what he'd blurted out, too, as he quietly put a hand to his mouth in recognition. "Th-that was a weird way to put it, but, um, we were so busy preparing the lunches and helping out the kids, we didn't get much chance to talk, so..." His attempts to explain himself didn't really change the meaning of what he had said, though. It just made my chest a little tighter.

"Well, whatever. Let's sit down." Now thoroughly embarrassed and bashful, I prodded Totsuka in the back to hurry him along. Geez, why was his back so thin and slender? He must not have been very heavy, because there was no resistance at all.

"All right. Then I'll sit here, 'kay?" Totsuka beckoned me with little flicks of his hand underneath the table, so no one else could see.

"...Okay." He didn't have to check with me like that; I'd have sat there anyway. I worried my face would relax into a smile if I wasn't careful. I pretended to yawn, covering my mouth with one hand to hide it.

"All right then, let's eat." Finally, Miss Hiratsuka sat beside me at the very edge. At her signal, everyone at the table put their hands together and said a brief thanks. Thinking back, I realized it had been a while since I'd last shared a meal with a large group like this. The last time had been only two years ago, but that felt like ancient history now.

"This is like when we had school lunches," Totsuka whispered into my ear. I guess the same thing had crossed his mind.

Agitated due to his unusual proximity, I wound up giving him a straightforward and honest answer. "Yeah, and the menu's curry, too."

"Boys sure like curry, huh? They used to get so excited on curry days," said Yuigahama in a wistful tone. Apparently, school lunches, curry, and loud boys were a universal memory. It had been like that at my school, too.

"Yeah, yeah," I replied. "And then the kid whose turn it is to serve knocks over the whole pot, and everyone gives him crap for it."

Tobe cackled in his distant seat as he scarfed down his food. "Oh man, I remember that! Dude!"

"And so the entire class is chewing out this kid," I continued, "and he's still wearing the white serving uniform with curry all over it. He goes around to all the other classes, trying to get them to share, but they don't want him taking away their curry, so they immediately start raging at him, and he ends up so miserable that he goes into the hallway to cry. But the worst part is that the stains on the white uniform don't come out, and when he passes it on to the next kid in charge of serving, the guy says to him, 'This uniform stinks like curry, LOL,' and everyone starts calling him 'Curry Stink.'"

Yuigahama's spoon stopped. "Uh, I don't remember that..."

So did Yukinoshita's. "Why was that story so detailed...? Were you speaking from personal experience?"

"That stain really wouldn't come out," said Komachi. "I didn't know what to do..."

Suddenly, a cloud of pity toward me was hanging over the table. Thanks to the total silence, I got to hear the chirping of an early bell cricket.

Hayama casually cleared his throat and attempted to smooth over the awkward moment. "Well, boys do love curry, so they get really worked up about it. They get like that on malt jelly days, too."

Oh man, I miss those. That mysterious gelatin had a unique taste that was a lot like Milo. It was really good. On no other days did I wish so badly for everyone else to skip school.

Hayama continued, "I asked some friends from other prefectures about it, and apparently, Chiba is the only prefecture where they serve that in school lunches."

"Huh?!" Yuigahama gasped.

"Seriously?!" Miura echoed.

"I-is that true...?" said Komachi. Nobody could suppress their shock.

"Damn, everyone in all the other forty-six prefectures must live such unfortunate lives..." I was so shocked, I almost wondered if this would bring down Japan's rating for quality of life.

Ebina was speechless, too. An agitated stir ran through everyone. Hayama's Chiba knowledge had found its moment. But still, I couldn't let him declare himself Chibapedia over one mere factoid. I don't care if I come out behind in any other area, but when it comes to Chiba, I don't want to lose! "Did you know that miso peanuts are only served in Chiba school lunches?"

"Yeah, I know," Hayama replied.

"Why would we ever think otherwise?" added Yukinoshita.

"And, like, here in Chiba's the only place we eat them at home, so," said Miura.

You're all reacting way too coldly to this. Also, it appears they eat miso peanuts like normal in the Miura household. Even I don't eat them that much at home. I don't have any friends in other prefectures, so I don't actually know if they're served outside Chiba.

X X X

The whistle-topped kettle began rattling. The pot didn't qualify for large, but its whistle was piercing and loud. Komachi quickly stood and began pouring out the tea into cups with teabags.

The nights on the plateau were a little chilly, and once the elementary school kids began to withdraw and it quieted down, the night cooled even further. The treetops rustled in the wind, and I could hear a faraway brook babbling. It was about time for the kids to go to sleep. This night would be spent with their friends, though, so there was no way it would be a peaceful one. They'd probably throw pillows, pull out bedtime snacks, and talk to each other all through the night.

But one subsection of the children would fall asleep quickly. The kids who were not allowed into the social circle would try their best to go to bed just a little earlier, and not just because they couldn't handle their own isolation. They were also trying to be considerate, so that the other children wouldn't notice them and could easily pretend they weren't there and enjoy the night. Well, not that anyone would notice their efforts.

Listen up, guys, that's why I want you to stop with the pranks. Don't mess with me when I'm asleep and then giggle to yourselves about it or play around taking photos of me, okay? All right? I'm actually trying to be considerate here.

Hayama's paper cup landed on the table with a soft tap. "Maybe they're having those nighttime conversations everyone always has on field trips right about now," he said. Something in his tone sounded wistful for times long ago.

We hadn't yet gone on our high school field trip. That was scheduled for the second semester of second year. The simple task of walking three steps behind my classmates and then going straight to sleep awaited me yet again.

But the only reason it was easy for me now was because I'd overcome all those hardships in the past. For those still caught up in that whirling vortex, it was nothing less than mortifying.

"I wonder if she's okay…," Yuigahama said to me, sounding a little worried.

I didn't have to ask who she was referring to. It was Rumi Tsurumi. Only I, Yukinoshita, and Yuigahama had listened to her directly, but we weren't the only ones who had noticed her exclusion. Everyone had. And not just the people at this table—anyone would have.

A match scratched and burst into flame. Miss Hiratsuka's aloof profile was illuminated for a brief moment in the darkness under the trees. She took a shallow puff of her cigarette, the fumes wafting upward. She uncrossed and recrossed her legs as the smoke drifted in the air. "Hmm. Something you're concerned about?" she asked.

Hayama was the one to reply. "Well, there's this one little girl who has no friends…"

"Yeah, the poor thing." Miura's reply was probably just a reflexive attempt at conversation. She said it as if it were the obvious response.

That bothered me a little bit. "…You've got it wrong, Hayama. You don't understand the real problem here. Having no friends and being alone is just fine, if that's all it is. The problem is that the other kids are maliciously driving her away."

"Huh? How is that any different?" I had been talking to Hayama, but Miura was the one who replied. Scary.

"Some people are alone because they want to be, and some people don't want to be alone, but still end up that way… Is that what you mean?" Hayama asked.

"Yeah, that's the idea." That was why the problem to be solved was not her isolation, but rather the environment that was forcing isolation upon her.

"So what do you kids want to do about it?" Miss Hiratsuka asked.

"Well…" I trailed off. We all went silent. *What do I want to do? I don't really want to do anything.* I just wanted to say my piece. Basically, it's no different from when you watch a TV documentary about war or poverty, and you say, *Oh, the poor things, that must be so hard, we should do what we can about this*, as you eat good food in a comfortable house. *Eventually, that'll lead to something being done*, you say, but that's a lie. You start making it all about yourself and think, *Now I realize how fortunate I am*, and then that's it. Maybe you'll end up donating ten or a hundred yen. But that's as far as it goes.

Of course, some people are conscious of these problems and genuinely try to change them. That's truly noble, and I respect and admire that. Even those donations will probably help people who are in trouble in some way. But not us. Me, Hayama, Miura—none of us are going to seriously do anything, not that we necessarily even can. You know that, and you use the fact that it's not in your power as an excuse because you still want to believe you're kind at heart.

Once you've seen something that's got nothing to do with you, you can't claim ignorance. But you're still powerless. So at the very least, you want to let yourself feel pity and leave it at that. Those emotions are beautiful and noble, but they're also a cruel and ugly excuse. It's nothing more than an extension of the deceitful youth ideology that I loathe so much.

"I…" Hayama opened his mouth after a period of grave silence. "I'd like to do what I can for her, if it's possible."

It was a very Hayama-like turn of phrase. His words were kind. They were sympathetic not only to Rumi, but also to the people here listening to him. It was a benevolent lie that would hurt no one. He was dangling hope in front of us, but still his roundabout manner of expressing it connoted despair. He implied that perhaps it could not be done and left room for everyone else to interpret.

"That's impossible for you. You've already made your attempt, haven't you?"

Yukinoshita came in and ripped apart his equivocal, comfortable platitude. In the darkness of the night, illuminated by the lantern, she swept her hair back and pierced Hayama with a cold stare. She stated her perspective like it was an established truth, so axiomatic that there was no need to ask her to explain or justify herself. I figured she was referring to earlier, when Hayama had tried to talk to Rumi.

For a moment, Hayama's face flickered with an expression like he was burning on the inside. "Yeah, maybe you're right…but it'll be different this time," he replied.

"Hmm. I'm sure," Yukinoshita replied icily, shrugging.

At the unexpected exchange between the two, a heavy silence descended over the table. I kept my mouth shut, too, observing them. I'd noticed it before, when Hayama came into the Service Club room that other time. Yukinoshita acted differently around Hayama, more stiffly than usual. Her usual frigid exterior was simply an expression of her isolation, but there was something deliberate in the way she'd just spoken to him. It was evident there was something between the two of them that I wasn't aware of. Well then, so what? It wasn't like I cared about their issues, but they were making things superawkward and freaking me out.

"Good grief…," said Miss Hiratsuka. As if to give herself a certain presence, she lit another cigarette, slowly smoking the whole thing over the course of five minutes, crushing it in the ashtray before she attempted to get further input. "What about you, Yukinoshita?" she asked.

Yukinoshita put a hand to her chin. "…Let me ask one thing first."

"And that is?"

"You said this camp is also a Service Club activity, Miss Hiratsuka. Is this matter included as a part of those activities?" she asked.

Miss Hiratsuka thought for a while and then quietly answered in the affirmative. "…Hmm. Yes. Since I've designated helping out with this trip as volunteering, that does make it part of your club's activities. Strictly speaking, it should fall under that category," she replied.

"I see…" Yukinoshita closed her eyes. The wind that had been murmuring through the leaves in the trees fell still. It was as if the forest were straining to hear what she had to say. Nobody spoke a word as we waited. "I… If she wants help, I will use every means available to find a solution," Yukino Yukinoshita declared firmly and resolutely. Her assertion carried an elegant dignity, an unwavering determination.

You're so cool, Yukinoshita. If I were a girl, I'd totally be in love with her right now. I mean, check out Yuigahama and Komachi. They're both practically swooning.

I guess that answer must have been enough for Miss Hiratsuka, as she gave a firm nod. "So does she want your help then?"

"...I don't know," Yukinoshita replied. Well, it was true that Rumi hadn't exactly asked anything of us. We hadn't confirmed what she wanted in a concrete way.

Yuigahama gave Yukinoshita's shirt a few light tugs. "Yukinon. Maybe she wants to ask, but she can't."

"Because no one would believe her or something?" I asked.

Yuigahama hesitated just a little in her reply. "Yeah, there's that, too, but also...like, what Rumi said. This has happened before. And when it was other people, she joined in on it, too. That's why I think, maybe, she won't let us save just her. And I don't think she's the only one at fault, either. I think all the others are, too... Sometimes, it's like, even if you want to talk with someone and be their friend, you just can't because of the atmosphere. But you still feel guilty..." Yuigahama trailed off. She took a few steady breaths and then giggled *ta-ha-ha* as if to downplay the gravity of what she had said. "Well, it's sort of...really embarrassing to talk about, but, like...it really does take a lot of courage to talk to someone when no one around you is."

Yukinoshita was apparently bowled over, and her eyes were riveted on the other girl's smile.

Yuigahama was right. Usually, it probably would take courage to talk to a loner. At first, she had been nervous about entering the clubroom. But she had overcome that and struck up a conversation with Yukinoshita and me. I suppose that would be overwhelming.

"But in Rumi's class, like, that's just not something you can do, you know? When you think, like, 'If I talk to her, then they'll snub me, too,' you just settle for ignoring her for now. Like, you just need the time to feel ready, but then you might end up just not doing anything... Ahhh! Has all this sounded really mean?!" Flustered and flailing, Yuigahama checked everyone around to see how they were reacting. But not a single person present was showing her any ill will. Everyone reacted in slightly different ways—some bitter, some amazed, and others moved—but everyone was smiling.

You really are amazing, Yuigahama. If I were a girl, I'm sure I'd want to be your friend.

"It's okay. I think it's very like you to feel that way," Yukinoshita replied in a gentle whisper. Though her voice was terribly quiet and small, it contained a wealth of emotion. Yuigahama looked embarrassed to hear that, blushing and falling silent.

Miss Hiratsuka smiled at the two girls. "Are there any objections to Yukinoshita's conclusion?" She paused for a moment and slowly turned her head to see how each person would react. But there was not a single dissenting voice among us. If I had to put my finger on it, though, it would be more accurate to say that no one *could* dissent. If I tried saying, *No way am I helping anyone! I'm going back to my room!* it would only lead to my imminent demise.

"All right. Well then, you kids think about the best course of action. I'm going to sleep." Miss Hiratsuka stifled a yawn and stood from her seat.

X X X

Only a few minutes after it was unanimously decided that we would deal with this problem, the discussion was already turning chaotic. The topic: What should be done to ensure that Rumi Tsurumi could get along with the rest of the kids?

The one to kick off the debate was Miura. "She's cute, so, like, she should just hang out with the other pretty girls, y'know? So, she just goes and talks to them, and, like, they become friends. Easy, am I right?"

"That's it! Man, you're smart, Yumiko!" said Tobe.

She snorted. "Duh."

Wow, Miura. That's impressive. That was the kind of theory only the strong would come up with. And if that made sense to Tobe, he was just as impressive as her. I had to respect that.

"Y-you can only do that because you're Yumiko...," stuttered Yuigahama. As expected, she did not support the idea.

But I get it now. One of the reasons Miura wants to hang out with Yuigahama is her appearance, huh? Well, she is good-looking. She's a worthy person on the inside, too. She's also a naive idiot, though, so she's bound to get burned one day.

"Yumiko didn't really put it in the best way," said Hayama, "but her idea of creating an in for Rumi is a good one. The way things are right now, though, getting her to talk to someone may be too much to ask." Hayama both backed Miura up and simultaneously gently contradicted her. What a mature means of handling disagreement.

Miura looked a little dissatisfied, but she withdrew with a brief "I see."

This time Ebina raised her hand, brimming with confidence.

"Go ahead, Hina." Hayama called for her to speak.

Who the hell is Hina? I thought.

That was when Totsuka tugged at my shirt. "Hina is Ebina's first name," he said. "You write it with the character for *princess* and the *na* part of the *nanohana* flower," he covertly whispered in my ear. I guess my confusion was obvious. His breath really tickled where it brushed my ear, and he smelled nice. *Damn it! He's a guy! Why is he so floral?* So Ebina's full name was Hina Ebina. Chii is learning. I was learning, but I'd never use the information. Seriously.

Ebina spoke calmly. "It'll be okay. She just has to throw herself into a hobby. When you get devoted to something, you go to conventions and stuff and expand your social network, you know? I'm sure she'll find somewhere she really fits in that way. She'll realize that school isn't everything, and it makes lots of things more enjoyable."

That was a more normal response than I had predicted, and frankly, I was surprised. The part about school not being everything was especially on the nose. For kids of elementary or middle school age, their schools and families are their entire lives. That's why when you're rejected in those settings, it feels like a dismissal from the whole world. But Ebina was saying that wasn't the whole picture, that Rumi should seek out a place where she could feel good and walk with her head held high.

Huh, that made sense. If she could find a different social group, she would have a place to fit in, and other stuff could most likely grow from that, too. Besides, from the way Ebina described it, she was probably speaking from experience.

"I made friends through BL! There's no such thing as a girl who hates *yaoi*! So, Yukinoshita, you and I should—"

"Yumiko, you and Hina go get us some tea." Hayama swiftly cut her off.

Miura stood up and took her arm. "Okay, come on, let's go, Ebina."

"Ahh! But I'm still not done converting you!" Ebina struggled, but Miura whacked her over the head and dragged her away, and the two of them disappeared.

Yukinoshita watched them go with an expression of horror. "I wonder what she was going to recommend I do..."

"You don't want to know, Yukinon...," Yuigahama replied wearily.

I see. So she tried to convert you, too, huh?

Besides, even if you do make friends through BL, then you just get into ship wars, or you make friends with someone on the assumption that they're into BL, but it turns out they're not, and it tears your relationship apart... Anything can happen. The world of hobbies has its own unique set of complications, and much difficulty would await her there.

After Ebina and Miura's exit, we tossed out a few suggestions here and there, but no one came up with any great practical plans. And when a discussion doesn't get going, naturally, people stop proposing more ideas. Source: class meetings where no one really gives a damn.

Why is it that they can only come up with tons of opinions when they're all trying to gang up on me over some supposed wrongdoing? They raise their hands more then than when we're actually in class.

During a dead-silent lull, Hayama spoke up as if he'd just realized something: "...I guess we can't reach a fundamental resolution unless we find a way for everyone to be friends."

A dry laugh spontaneously erupted from me, and Hayama gave me

a hard stare. But I wasn't going to look away or put on a serious facade and yes-man him, not for something like this. I snickered in Hayama's face with absolute confidence.

He really failed to understand the issue at a basic level. He couldn't comprehend that the very concept that everyone has to be friends was the root of the problem. It was insincere, and it behaved like a curse. That claim is a form of coercion. It's a *geas*, an evil law.

So many teachers impose these constraints on the tiny worlds that are their classrooms. They enforce the law that *everyone must get along*, which gives rise to discord, but then they so often ignore the problem and just let it take root. Some people will never click, no matter what you do. There will be individuals you just can't stand. If you could just unambiguously say *I hate him* or *I don't want to be involved with him*, then things could still grow from there. There would be a chance you could improve the situation and start a discussion. But by stifling it all and pouring your effort into the appearance of classroom harmony, you make all that impossible. The problem is the unspoken implication of that lazy lie: If you tuck it under the rug, then it's not a problem. That was why I disagreed with Hayama.

And I wasn't the only one.

"That is not going to happen. Not in a million years." Yukinoshita's icy words, far more biting than my snigger, destroyed both his argument and his ability to maintain eye contact.

Hayama let out a short sigh and looked away.

Witnessing the scene, Miura howled. "Hey, Yukinoshita? What's your problem?"

"What do you mean?" Yukinoshita replied to the aggressive demand with cool composure.

But Miura's flames only burned hotter. "I'm talking about that attitude of yours. We're *trying* to help everyone get along here, so why d'you have to act like that? I don't even like you, like, at all, and I'm just putting up with you for the sake of having a fun trip."

"H-hey, come on, Yumiko…" Yuigahama tried to pacify Miura as she tactlessly, violently vented her emotions.

But Yukinoshita had no intention of backing down, either. "Oh?

I'm surprised you have such a favorable impression of me. I despise you, though."

"Y-you too, Yukinon, don't be so harsh!" Yuigahama, forced to stand between the two girls, was now struggling to extinguish Yukinoshita's anger.

You've got guts, kid! You're a little firefighter.

But water isn't always the right way to douse a fire. If you've got a chemical blaze, pouring water on it can just make it burn even hotter. This was exactly what was happening.

"Hey. Yui?" said Miura.

"...Whose side are you on here?" demanded Yukinoshita.

The flame queen's eyes were flaring wide, and the ice witch's tone of voice could freeze you solid. Together, they were indomitable. Is this Medoroa? This is so bad, even the Great Demon Lord Vearn would be in trouble.

"Eek!" Yuigahama shrank in terror, trembling like a leaf.

Oh dear. How frightening. "This tea sure is good, huh, Totsuka?" I commented. "Which reminds me, I wonder how Zaimokuza's doing right about now. I wonder if he's well."

"Don't ignore reality, Hachiman..."

Nope. Too scary, not gonna.

Yukinoshita and Miura glared at each other. But fortunately, there were three people between them, so it didn't look like the conflict would escalate any further than that. All you can do with kids who don't get along is keep them apart, it's true. If you put them on opposite ends of the same row, they wouldn't even see each other's faces.

Komachi, who was in the buffer zone, piped up like she'd just had a flash of brilliance. "At first glance, Rumi has a pretty strong personality, so it might be hard for her to fit in with the elementary school girls, but once she gets a little older, I think she might be able to make friends with the A-group types, you know?"

Komachi was right. If you considered Rumi's future prospects, she was probably the type who would go on to enjoy school. Even if she didn't connect well with the other girls, the boys would be sure to fawn over her, and some girls might befriend her in anticipation of that. Ugh, how stupid.

Hayama nodded in agreement. "That's true. She's a little cold…or I suppose you could say she's rather chilly."

"Cold?" replied Miura. "More like condescending. She's all up on her high horse, don't you think? She's got this attitude like she thinks she's better than everyone, and that's why they're ostracizing her. Just like a certain someone we know." Miura giggled as if trying to provoke Yukinoshita.

But Yukinoshita's reply was indifferent. "That's just your persecution complex talking. Maybe you feel like I'm looking down on you because you're simply conscious of your own inferiority?"

Miura stood from the bench with a thump. "Ngh! Listen, it's because you say crap like that—"

"Stop it, Yumiko." Hayama's low request held Miura in check. Somehow, it was different from the flippant tone he'd used up until now; his voice was powerful and intense. Frankly, it was a little scary…

"Hayato… Hmph!" Miura seemed momentarily surprised by his attitude, but she backed off without protest. Not another word left her mouth after that.

A heavy silence fell over the rest of the table as well. In the end, nobody was in the mood for further conversation, and all that really got decided was that the matter would be put off for the next day. Well, that's politics.

But you know…if not even us high schoolers can get along, there's no way we can tell the elementary schoolers to.

Yumiko Miura

Birthday

December 12

Special skills:

Tennis, nail art

Hobbies:

Shopping, karaoke

How I spend my weekends:

Shopping, part-time job,
hanging out and doing whatever

Hina Ebina

Birthday

July 14

Special skills:

Illustration,
waiting in very long lines

Hobbies:

Reading (historical novels,
mainly Three Kingdoms or
shogunate era), drawing

How I spend my weekends:

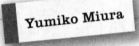

Conventions,
shopping in Ikebukuro,
hanging out with friends

5

All alone, **Yukino Yukinoshita** gazes up at the night sky.

From the washing area came the classic *kapon* sound of the bath. I've always wondered what that noise was supposed to mean. The sound of a water bucket hitting the tile? I quickly washed my head, body, and face and then slipped all the way into the water.

This was a hot spring, they'd said. I was all refreshed after rinsing off the sweat, and I felt like the water was saturating me.

There was a big bathhouse in the visitor lodge. As is often the case for most field trips, camping trips, and other school events, when students stay overnight, they allot separate times for the boys and girls. This time, though, I was soaking in the regular bathroom in the manager's building.

Since our discussion earlier had gone on so long, there was only time for one group to use the big bathhouse, even though they clearly needed time for three: the boys, the girls, and Totsuka. After some negotiations, they let the boys use the regular bathroom. But, well, this tub wasn't much bigger than the one in a normal home, so we were going in one at a time. Most of the guys probably wouldn't be keen to share a bath with other guys anyway, so it all worked out.

Maybe if Totsuka and I bathed together, we could have both fit in at once, but in that case… Well, it'd be kinda like, you know, sorta… I mean, if on the off chance that Totsuka was actually a girl, my Gae Bolg would be sure to activate, and if he's a guy and my Gae Bolg went off, one thing might lead to another, and I'd have to remove the *Bolg* part…

So this was for the best.

When a guy has a bath, he finishes up as quickly as a crow in a birdbath. If Totsuka had bathed right before me, I'd be taking a slow soak, but it was Tobe and then Hayama, so I finished up quick. I toweled myself nice and dry in the small changing room and then groped around in my clothes basket. "Underwear, underwear…huh?" My hand encountered my boxers just as the door opened. In other words, even if I did put it on right that instant, I wouldn't have made it in time. Hawawa! Master, the enemy is here! >.<

The door slid open, and Totsuka's face greeted me. "Oh, Hachi…"

"   "

And time resumes.

"Ah! Ah-ah-ah-ah! S-sorry!" Totsuka stammered.

"U-uhhhhh… U-uh, sorry, I guess!"

Flustered, Totsuka swiftly closed the door, and I swiftly got dressed. I got my underwear snugly Pilder-On and followed up with my T-shirt and shorts. All told, it probably took less than ten seconds.

"Y-you can come in now," I called.

The door opened slowly and extremely hesitantly, about three centimeters wide. Totsuka peeked through the gap, checking to see if it was safe. Letting out a sigh of relief, he entered the changing room. "S-sorry. I thought you were already done…" Totsuka apologized with a bow. But when he raised his head and his eyes met mine, his face flushed bright red, and he immediately looked away.

…Why is he blushing? Now I'm getting embarrassed.

"S-so…I'll be taking a bath now," he said.

"Y-yeah," I replied, and then we silently considered each other for a while more.

"Um… I'm going to…get undressed, so…"

Totsuka gazed up at me, eyes moist and almost accusatory as his

DING
DONG

hands grasped the hem of his shirt. "It bothers me a little…if you're watching the whole time."

"Oh, I see. Sorry, sorry. I'll go." Well, even if we were all guys here, it wouldn't be very pleasant to have someone stare at you while you change, I suppose. Closing the door behind me, I began to walk with the sound of running water behind me in my ears.

But man, that sure was nothing like the bath events I'm familiar with. Are the gods idiots? They wanna die?

If our positions had been reversed, at the very least… No, that would have been stupid, too.

X X X

Hayama and Tobe were already in the bungalow. It didn't look like they had much to do, seeing as they were mostly tapping away on their phones. Hayama was swiping along on some kind of tablet. Those cool, modern gestures make you look like you know what you're doing. People are so smug about those. I've said this before, and I don't know if anyone actually believes this, but they still need to wake up and realize it's the device that's amazing and not them.

There was a deck of cards lying at his feet, but they obviously weren't going to play with me. Occasionally, the two of them chatted between themselves. I made an autonomous decision to occupy the farthest corner of the room, laying out my futon and sliding under the covers. I rummaged around inside my bag, but there didn't seem to be anything in particular I could use to kill time. Even Komachi wasn't capable of preparing that much on such short notice.

Well, these days, you can do almost everything with just your cell phone. So I played around with mine off and on as I waited to get sleepy. Behind me, I overheard their conversation.

"Hey, hey, what're you looking at, Hayato? Porn?" asked Tobe.

"No, just books for studying. It's in a PDF," Hayama replied.

"Whoa, here comes the brainy vocabulary!"

I don't think there was a single brainy word in that whole exchange.

I suppose it is convenient to carry around schoolbooks as PDFs, huh? Lugging a pile of books all over gets really heavy, and then you end up forgetting one…

"You're so smart, Hayama," I said. I was talking to myself, and it didn't matter to me if anyone heard. Loners often make statements like that.

But of course, Hayama, incarnation of misplaced kindness that he was, had to respond. "I'm not really that smart."

"No way, man," said Tobe. "Your grades are, like, sick, Hayato! Like, you're up there in the humanities!"

I think *sick* generally carries a negative connotation, but I guess youngsters these days mean it as a good thing. It's just like saying, *I don't like you at all, Big Brother!*

"Well, I do have decent grades," Hayama replied with a vague smile, as if he was a little embarrassed.

Oh, is he one of those mildly obnoxious types who distinguish between test scores and intelligence?

"Decent?" said Tobe. "You're top of the class, aren't you?"

"Yukinoshita beats me, though," he replied.

…

Oh, I get it. It's all becoming clear. I understand now why I've been forced to accept my third-place ranking all this time. It was because first and second place were already permanently occupied. So he had the looks, the personality, *and* the brains, huh? A combination worthy of despair, like a Potara-fused Goku and Vegeta. Like, why are these guys alive? Can't you just let me win in Japanese, at least?

Right when I was ready to go to bed in a huff, I heard the clack of the door opening. "Phew… I'm out of the bath." Totsuka was back, closing the door behind him with one hand. As he dried off his damp hair with a towel, he passed by me, trailing the gentle scent of shampoo behind him. He sat down with a soft *thump* and began to blow-dry his hair with a dryer he pulled from his bag. The contrast between his damp hair and his flushed skin, fresh out of the bath, was oddly sensuous. Before I knew what I was doing, I was zoning out and staring at him.

After giving his hair one final ruffle to check it was dry, Totsuka let out a satisfied sigh. "I'm all done, so…"

"Let's get to sleep, then," Hayama replied.

Tobe and Totsuka both started getting ready for bed. I had already put down my futon, so I had nothing to do. What foresight I have.

With some effort, Totsuka hauled his bedding over and laid it out next to mine. He glanced over at me, giving his pillow a couple of thumps. "I can…sleep here, right?"

"…Sure." As we stared at each other, the awkwardness of our earlier encounter in the bathhouse came rushing back. That was a mortifying recollection. Totsuka had seen everything… *I believe at this point there may be no other option but for him to take responsibility and support me for life.*

Totsuka didn't seem to be bothered by it, though, and he snuggled into his futon without any evident suspicion toward me. *Hey, c'mon. From that position, if you roll around in your sleep, we'll end up kissing.*

Hayama, done with his bed, reached out to the light switch. "I'm turning off the lights," he said, and with a click, the naked bulb hanging from the ceiling flickered out.

"Hey, Hayato," said Tobe. "Kinda feels like we're on a field trip, huh?"

"Yeah, sure does." Hayama gave a lukewarm reply. Maybe he was tired.

"…Let's talk about our crushes."

"Let's not." Surprisingly enough, Hayama shut that down stat.

Totsuka laughed a little uncomfortably. "Ah-ha-ha… I'd be kinda embarrassed," he said.

"Why not?!" Tobe demanded. "Come on, let's talk! Fine, I get it! I'll go first!"

He had undeniably brought up the subject because he wanted to talk about his.

A pair of rather tired sighs suggested that Hayama and Totsuka had reached the same conclusion.

"The truth is, I…," Tobe began. There wasn't much point in listening. He was going to say that he was into Miura. "…I think Ebina's kinda okay…"

"…Seriously?" I blurted out. *That* had been unexpected.

I think Tobe couldn't tell for a moment who had spoken, as his response was hesitant. "Huh? ...Y-yeah. What, you were listening, Hikitani? You were just lying there, so I thought you were asleep!"

"Hmm. I'm surprised, though. I thought you liked Miura," I replied.

"Aw, I can't make a move on Yumiko... She's too scary."

So you're scared of her, too, huh? That meant that by my reckoning, practically all the guys were afraid of her. Come on, I mean, even with ghosts or something, not *everyone* believes in them. In other words, Miura is natural-disaster level on the scale of terror. "For being scared of her, you sure do talk to her a lot. More than Ebina."

"Y-yeah...that's just 'cause, like, you know that saying? Like, if you wanna shoot the general, first shoot the horse."

"Uh, I think Miura is clearly the general in this situation," I replied. But I had a surprising amount of empathy for him. The more you like a girl, the less you can converse with her. As a guy, I get that.

"Yui is pretty nice, too, but she's kinda dumb, you know?" he continued.

Ah, that's true. She is dumb. But I don't think it's quite so bad that it gives you the right to say that.

"Plus, she's kinda popular, so there's a lot of competition."

......Well, I'm sure that's true.

Guys like nice girls. Loser guys interpret their kindness as interest—they fall for that horrifyingly often—so Yuigahama was sure to catch plenty of fish. No other lure could even compete. Even Grander Musashi would blanch at such a huge catch. I'm not really surprised or bothered, so I don't think it's unusual or startling, and it doesn't bother me at all.

What the hell, this is really getting to me.

Tobe ignored my sighs and went on. "Ebina is, like, well, lots of people are weirded out, and guys, too, so I guess it sorta made me wanna go for her instead?"

He had a point—as you would expect of a member of the upper caste, Ebina was cute. But guys tended to avoid her because of her special interests. Actually, I got the feeling that advertising her interests so openly was her own attempt at a defense strategy. I think if she were the real deal, she would hide it. Well, I may be analyzing it too deeply, though.

Tobe must have realized that he was the only one sharing, as he turned the question on us. "What about you guys?"

"Do I like any girls? ...Girls, huh... Mmm, not really," said Totsuka.

He doesn't like any girls. S-so what about boys? For some reason, my heart was pounding.

Tobe skipped over me, though, and moved on to Hayama. "What about you, Hayato?"

"I... No, forget it."

"Hey, hey, hey, Hayato, come on! You've got a crush, don't you? 'Fess up."

"..."

"Even just her first initial!"

Hayama gave a resigned sigh. "...*Y.*"

"*Y*? Wait, so then do you mean—?"

"That's enough. Let's go to sleep." Hayama refused any further probing. He sounded angry, for once. Hayama's the kind of good guy who's nice to everyone, so I doubt he shows irritation often. To take a different perspective, perhaps that means he's willing to share another side of himself with Tobe.

"Now this is bugging me so much I can't sleep! If I die from insomnia, it'll be your fault, Hayato." Tobe casually deflected Hayato's anger with humor. It was a social technique often employed to prevent things from getting serious, a conventional method used to avoid turning relationships sour or making things awkward.

I stared blankly into the quiet darkness. Who was that *Y* that Hayama had been referring to? A number of options flashed through my mind.

The room felt oddly tense, so despite the silence, I couldn't fall asleep. I rolled over and found Totsuka's face right there in front of me. His slow, even breathing told me he was asleep.

"...Nhn." He sighed. A ray of moonlight pouring in through the window softly illuminated his face. His glistening lips were moving very slightly, as if murmuring someone's name. He looked happy, smiling softly and gently.

The restlessness I'd been feeling transformed into a coil around my chest. Now that I had noticed Totsuka's lips, I couldn't stop thinking about them. I was hyperaware of every sound he made as he stirred in his sleep, every light breath he took. "I'm not gonna get to sleep here…" Peeking at the cell phone by my hand, I was surprised to find it wasn't even eleven. I guess once you get away from the city, time passes more slowly. There was no clatter of trains or brilliant streetlights. It was a quiet night.

Going outside to get some night air would probably calm me down. I stood up quietly, so as not to wake the other three, and left the bungalow. A night in the highlands. The tranquil cool gradually stilled my heart…

Or so I thought. It was actually just terrifying. Like, there was something hooting, and just a few leaves rustling was enough to make me squeak. Trembling on this inside, I scanned the area. I thought I could see a figure among the trees… Something incorporeal… Or maybe just arboreal. Yeah. The alternative would have been too scary.

Anyway, the point is that it was not a tree spirit, or a *dryad,* as they say in English. I don't even know if *dryad* is English in the first place. Among the trees stood a girl with long, flowing hair. Something about the scene was removed from reality, like a vision of a spirit or fairy of some sort. Under the gentle rays of moonlight, her white skin seemed to glow. With every puff of wind that blew past, her hair fluttered and danced. She looked like a fairy as she bathed in the silver light, singing quietly, oh-so-very quietly.

In the dark, chilly forest, her whisper-like melody sounded oddly pleasant in my ears. I only watched her. If I took even one step forward, I would shatter that little world that she had created all by herself. I was reluctant to make a sound. Figuring I should go back, I slowly turned around to return the way I had come. But when I stepped forward, my foot broke a twig with a snap.

The singing instantly ceased.

"…"

"…"

One second, two seconds, three seconds passed as we tried to identify each other in the darkness.

"…Who is it?" The voice belonged to a normal girl, Yukino Yukinoshita.

I could have tried meowing like a cat, and maybe she'd be like, *Oh, did a cat hear me sing?* but this is Yukinoshita, so she would probably actually have been like, *Oh, it's just that* thing.

So I resigned myself and approached her. "…It's me."

"…Who?"

"Why are you repeating the question? You know who I am." *Don't give me the quizzical head tilt. The cuteness factor just makes it even more aggravating, come on.*

"What are you doing up at this hour?" she asked. "You need to get your eternal sleep."

"Could you not pronounce my death by pretending to be concerned for me?"

Yukinoshita looked away as if to say she had no further interest in me, lifting her head toward the sky instead. Following her lead, I gazed up into a clear and starry sky.

"Were you looking at the stars?" I asked. You could see them so well out here compared with in the city. When there's no other lights around, the stars shine clearer. In that case, I bet loners shine extra hard, since there are so few others around them. Oh man, my future is *bright*.

"Not particularly," she replied.

Oh, so she wasn't doing the *At the Mercy of the Sky* thing? So was this the *Heaven's Lost Property* thing, then?

"Miura sort of came after me…" Yukinoshita's head drooped in despair.

Oh-ho, that's a rare sight. I was sure no one could talk her down. I'd expect nothing less of Miura. Confronting the queen of fire is a date with defeat indeed.

"I argued her into the ground for half an hour and made her cry. It was immature of me…"

Her Majesty of Ice is far too powerful. Never mind a *Date* with defeat, she's a *Nobunaga* with defeat. "So of course things got awkward, and you went outside, huh?"

"Yes. I didn't expect her to cry… Yuigahama is consoling her right now." Perhaps tears were too much, even for Yukinoshita. She seemed a tad remorseful.

Damn, I might as well cast my inhibitions aside about bawling my eyes out in front of her, too. Lame.

Yukinoshita smoothed down her hair, and as if that were some kind of signal, she changed the subject. "We should…do something about that girl."

"You seem awfully gung ho about helping some kid you don't know."

"The Service Club has done nothing but help people I don't know. I don't reach out just because I'm personally acquainted with someone. Plus…don't you think she's…somehow like Yuigahama?"

"Oh?" I didn't, not at all. She bore a far closer resemblance to a certain someone else.

Yukinoshita looked up at me, a trace of sorrow in her eyes. "I think she's probably…had an experience of that nature."

Oh, if that was her meaning, then I got that. Yuigahama was certainly more conscious of class politics than anyone else was. I don't really want to think much about it, but…I'm sure she's gotten sucked into the mob mentality once or twice.

And that was why she got it. She understood those feelings of guilt. Yuigahama's kindness was not blind benevolence. Her compassion was born of her awareness of the repulsive, ugly, and cowardly nature of humanity, and she nevertheless reached out without averting her eyes.

"And…" Yukinoshita hung her head, gently kicking a pebble at her feet. "…I'm sure Hayama has been concerned, too."

"Yeah, well, I wouldn't be surprised." I guess you could say he's got a certain disposition. Like some kind of legendary end-of-century leader. He might just have a predisposition to being a hero. He was probably raised on classic manga from *Shonen Jump* magazine. He wouldn't have had an easy and sheltered upbringing like me.

"That's not what I mean...," Yukinoshita hedged. But whatever she was going to say was overpowered by the rustling of the forest. After that, it was silent.

"Hey, is there something going on with you and Hayama?" I asked, a little curious. Yukinoshita had been giving him some serious attitude. I got the impression that she was especially cold to him. She'd been that way ever since the first time Hayama had come into the Service Club room, and this camping trip was just highlighting the issue.

"We just went to the same elementary school," Yukinoshita replied coolly, as if it were nothing to her. "His father is the legal advisor for my family's business. By the way, his mother is a doctor."

"Huh." Perfect grades, all-round athletic, elite family, good-looking, normie, *and* has a pretty girl as a childhood friend.

Hmm...I'm not sure how to put this, but maybe he won't slaughter me in this competition.

I've got an okay face, a knack for the humanities, a hatred of team sports, an extremely cute little sister, and that's about it.

...Okay, we're even! I want to know defeat.

If he had a little sister, I'd be in trouble. I was nearly destroyed there.

"It must suck, having your families push you together," I said.

"I suppose."

"You make it sound like it's not your problem..."

"It's my sister's job to handle those sorts of social obligations. I'm just a stand-in," she replied. The treetops murmured and swayed in the breeze. The sound of rustling leaves undulated out in the silent night, like ripples on the surface of water. But as the forest stirred, I could still hear Yukinoshita's voice. "Even so," she said, "...I'm glad I could come today. I wasn't sure I'd be able to."

"Huh? Why?" I turned toward her. I wasn't sure what she meant. She was still studying the stars, though. It was as if I had said nothing at all. Still, I waited for her reply. A particularly zealous insect gave a long, buzzing chirp. Maybe it was the late hour and the chilly air, but the ensuing gust of wind felt like autumn.

Maybe she had been waiting for that. Yukinoshita turned toward me. A hint of a smile was on her lips, and she said nothing. She gave me no replies and asked me no questions.

The quiet moment soon ended, though, and she stood upright. "I'm going back."

"...All right. See you, then."

"Yes, good night."

I never did probe further. I wasn't interested in trying to force her to say something she didn't want to. I think part of it was the comfortable relationship we'd built by not knowing each other very well.

Yukinoshita walked with sure steps down the unlit path, and I watched her gradually disappear into the darkness.

Now alone, I glanced at the stars above, the very same sky that Yukino Yukinoshita had been so closely watching. I've heard that the light of the stars is actually from the distant past. Through the eons, they've radiated the ancient light of an age gone by.

Everyone is caught up in the past. No matter how much you might intend to move on, with just one upward glance, those experiences rain down upon you just like the light of the stars. You can't laugh it all away or erase it. You just keep carrying it in one little corner of your heart, only to find it all flooding back when you least expect it.

It was like that for Yui Yuigahama, Hayato Hayama, and probably Yukino Yukinoshita, too.

Chatting in the van

In the back row

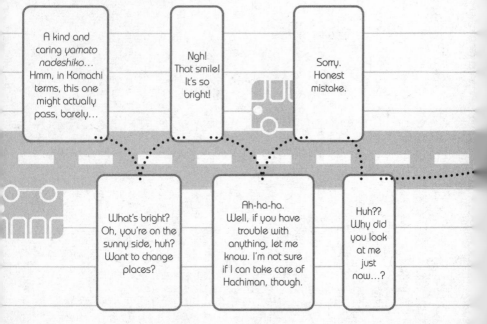

A kind and caring *yamato nadeshiko*… Hmm, in Komachi terms, this one might actually pass, barely…

What's bright? Oh, you're on the sunny side, huh? Want to change places?

Ngh! That smile! It's so bright!

Ah-ha-ha. Well, if you have trouble with anything, let me know. I'm not sure if I can take care of Hachiman, though.

Sorry. Honest mistake.

Huh?? Why did you look at me just now…?

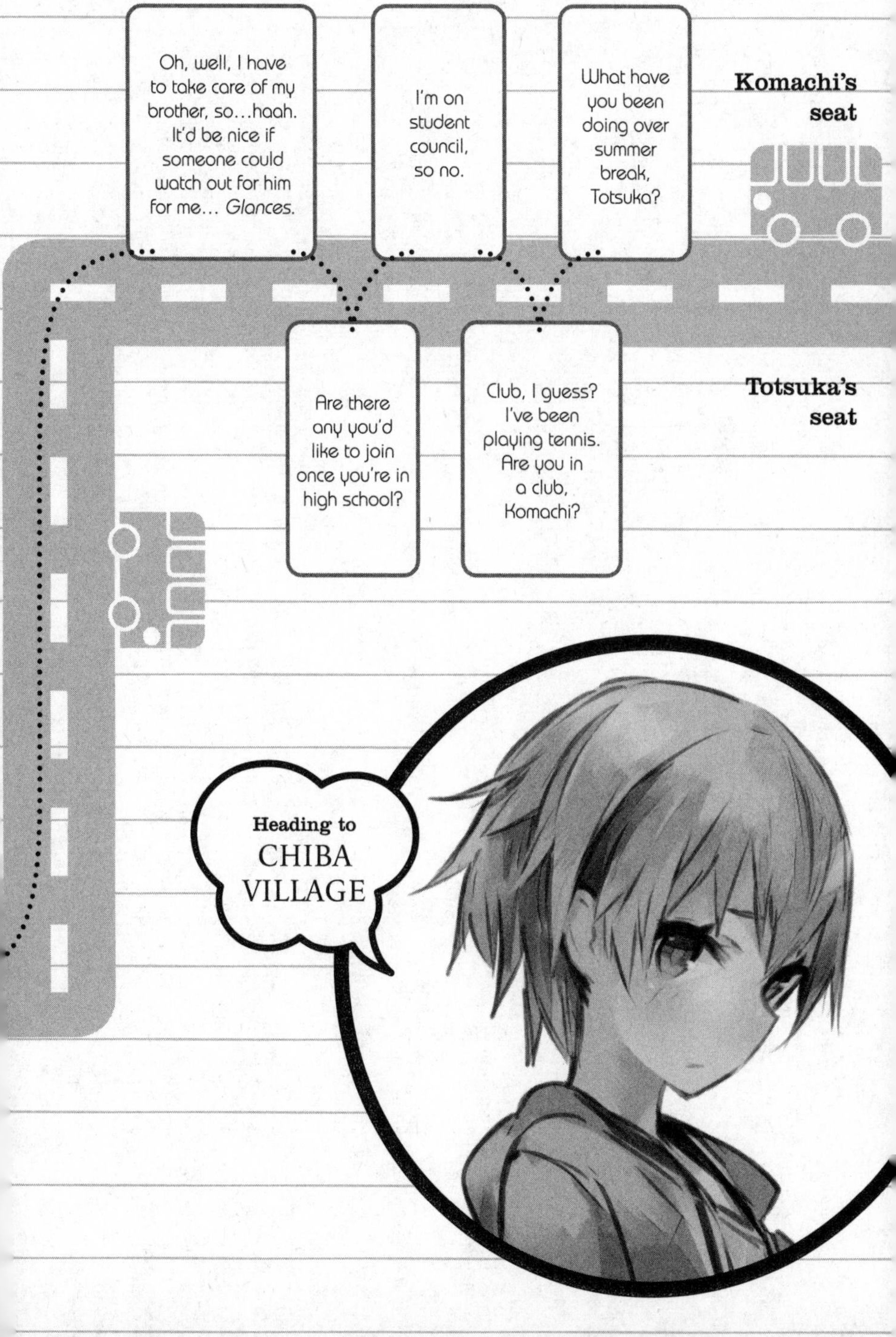

Komachi's seat
Totsuka's seat
What have you been doing over summer break, Totsuka?
Club, I guess? I've been playing tennis. Are you in a club, Komachi?
I'm on student council, so no.
Are there any you'd like to join once you're in high school?
Oh, well, I have to take care of my brother, so…haah. It'd be nice if someone could watch out for him for me… *Glances.*
Heading to CHIBA VILLAGE

6

Unfortunately, **Hachiman Hikigaya** did not bring a swimsuit.

I had a dream, a lovely dream.

Small, soft hands were gently rocking my body. Through them, I could feel the faint body heat of someone who had only just woken up themselves. A sweet voice called my name with some concern. It was terribly pleasant. But I knew it was all in my head. My sister doesn't usually come to wake me up, and my parents invariably leave the house while I'm still asleep. I am always awoken from my dreams by the inhuman, unforgiving alarm of my cell phone. Thus both my body and mind judged this to be a dream.

"Hachiman," the voice said. "It's morning. You have to get up..." The words repeated a few times as my body rocked, and finally, I opened my eyelids. The morning light was dazzling, and under the brilliant rays was Totsuka, smiling awkwardly. "You finally woke up," he said. "Good morning, Hachiman."

"......Hey," I replied, but the sight before me was so divorced from reality, my mind was totally blank. White sunlight was flowing in through the window, and outside, sparrows or skylarks or some unidentified birds were twittering. I saw one tousled, slept-in futon. And then, as I lay on the floor, there was Totsuka at my side.

"Uh..."

No way... Is this a morning-after scene?! Did I cross over that horizon in the middle of nowhere, that line that should never be crossed?!

While I was busy being lost and confused, Totsuka pulled the blanket off me and began folding it. "If we don't hurry up, we won't make it in time for breakfast," he said.

With this newfound information, I started to process what was going on. *Oh yeah, we were camping, weren't we?* I thought we'd suddenly moved in together or something.

I dragged myself into a sitting position and started folding up my futon like Totsuka. "Where are the other guys?" I asked.

"I told Hayama and Tobe to go ahead and leave without us. You just weren't waking up..." He gave me a stern, reproachful look.

Why do I feel so guilty now...? I've never once felt bad about being late for school or late for a job, but this time I feel like I've gone off the deep end and I'm about to start shouting nonsense. *Geisha! Hara-kiri! Fujiyama!* Huh, even *geisha* has the word *gay* in it... "Sorry...," I apologized, sincerely regretting my misdeed.

Totsuka was still pouting, though. "You haven't been keeping a proper sleep schedule during summer vacation, have you, Hachiman?"

"Y-yeah, well, I guess not."

"And you're not exercising at all, are you?"

"Oh yeah. I haven't really thought about doing anything. It's too hot."

"That's not good for you, you know? You have to get some exer— Oh, I know! Let's play tennis together sometime!" Totsuka proposed, clearly excited about the idea.

"Oh...yeah, whatever, sometime. Call me whenever." Reflexively, I provided my default response, the one I use whenever anyone invites me to do stuff. When you're hanging around the fringes of a group, people will make offers just to be polite. Sort of like, *Uh...you wanna come, too?* No, seriously, don't bother. I don't care. Whenever people say that to me, I have to give them a half-assed reply in the name of courtesy, too. Also, people who say *Yeah, whatever, sometime* usually don't get invited out again. There's a nugget of wisdom for you. Source: me.

But now I was getting flustered, worried that maybe I'd triggered that reaction in Totsuka. I looked at him.

"Okay, then!" he said. "I'll be sure to call you!" But I was probably in the clear, for once. Totsuka's cheerful reply set me at ease.

There's generally no reason to refuse an invitation from a guy. Though it's another story if it's Zaimokuza calling, or if you have some kind of plans, of course. But my schedule is practically nonexistent, aside from my time with Komachi. I've got so much free time that if there were a Hanging-Out Championship, I'd take the freestyle division, no sweat. I'm rarely invited to hang out, and more important, I never do the inviting. Ever since that time in middle school when I thought about hanging out with this guy Oiso, but when I called him up, he said he had to do some house chores, and then I went to the arcade by myself and saw him going into the karaoke parlor next door with Ninomiya, I've tried not to ask anyone to hang out. It's just because, like, I'd feel bad about forcing them into rejecting me. I'm just trying to be nice, you know?

"Okay, let's go get some breakfast," I said.

"Yeah. But, u-um… I—I don't know your e-mail address, Hachiman…"

Oh yeah. I usually treat my phone like an alarm clock / time-killing device, so I'd totally forgotten that Totsuka and I still hadn't exchanged contact info. *So his address will finally be within my grasp…* A flood of emotions surged through me as I took out my phone and immediately readied myself to input his information.

"Huh?! Hachiman, why are you crying?"

"Oh, my eyes are just watering 'cause I yawned." I was so moved, I had shed a few tears.

"I suppose you did just wake up," he said. "Okay, then what's your e-mail?"

"Here." I showed it to him.

"Um…" Totsuka wasn't very good with electronics, and he slowly checked both phones and pecked away, character by character. As he typed, he'd occasionally make quiet comments to himself, like "Wait, no. Huh? This one?" It was a little concerning. If he input my address wrong and my messages ended up not reaching him, the overwhelming regret could send me into convulsions. "Okay, done…I think. I'll try e-mailing you." Slowly, he began hunt-and-pecking away at an e-mail. At one point, he paused to tilt his head in thought. Finally, he nodded. "I sent it."

"Oh, thanks." A few seconds later, my phone rang. I caught a Totsuka! (Pi-Pikachu!)

Phew, that's a relief. *Now I just have to input his info into my phone*, I thought, opening up my inbox. That was when I saw it.

> **Subject:** It's Saika~!
> **Body:** Good morning, Hachiman! This is my first time e-mailing you. I hope we'll be sending each other lots more!

That string of characters was just too much for my heart to take. I spontaneously burst into a violent coughing fit.

"Hachiman?! Wh-what's wrong?! Are you okay?" Totsuka panicked and immediately started rubbing my back.

Ack. His hand is so small, but it feels so warm and soft… "I-I'm okay…"

"All right, then…," he replied.

I finally stood up straight again, but Totsuka shot me a questioning look. I put on a cheerful smile in an attempt to evade it. "Come on. We really should go get breakfast."

"Oh, of course."

I hurried Totsuka along, prodding his back as we walked. That tilted head just a moment ago had been him considering what to write. It was a no-frills message, but it was also dripping with cute. Totsuka's got some serious literary talent. Someone give the guy an award.

Anyway, I'd have to be sure to save his e-mail address. And also to set a special ringtone for him and make a special Totsuka folder. And just in case, I'd back it all up on my PC, too.

X X X

The elementary school kids had already left the lodge. The only ones there were the usual suspects, plus Miss Hiratsuka.

"Good morning," I greeted her.

"Yeah, morning," she replied, newspaper rustling. Somehow, this felt very old-fashioned. Nostalgia hit me like a truck.

Totsuka and I sat down together in a pair of open seats. Yuigahama was opposite us.

"Oh, morning, Hikki," she greeted me with the standard AM salutation. Apparently, *yahallo* was not for morning-time use. She probably started using it after noon.

"'Sup," I replied.

Beside Yuigahama was Yukinoshita, and beside her was Komachi. "Morning!" my sister chirped, but even as she spoke, she was scrambling to her feet to scuttle off somewhere.

Yukinoshita and Totsuka greeted each other, and then Yukinoshita turned her gaze to me. "Good morning. So you did wake up after all…"

"Hey, don't look so disappointed about it. Good morning." My conscientious greetings these days are indicative of my fine character, I feel.

I heard the *tump* of a tray being set down on the table in front of me. "Here ya go!" said Komachi. "Sorry for the wait. And one for you, too, Totsuka!" She had gone to get breakfast for me.

"Thank *youuu.* ♪" I thanked her in a singsong tone, like a part-timer at McDonald's. Let me explain. Whenever the burger patties are done, the timer on the grill goes off, like *McDooonald's, McDooonald's*, and when the fries are ready to come out of the deep fryer, the timer sounds like it's singing *friiiies, friiies.* So when the clerk tells the customer "Thank you" at the end of a transaction, they say it in the same singsong tone. That explanation was totally unnecessary.

"Th-thanks… I guess I'll eat, then," said Totsuka.

I put my hands together. I wasn't doing any alchemy or anything; it's just the polite thing to do before a meal. "Let's eat."

The breakfast before us was classic home cooking. White rice, miso soup, grilled fish and salad, omelettes, *natto*, flavored nori seaweed, pickled vegetables, and an orange for dessert. Imagine standard hotel fare, basically. As we ate in silence, I immediately ran short on the rice. By my calculations, the mere presence of *natto* and flavored nori entailed at least two bowls of rice for me. At a Japanese-style inn, they'd even serve you a raw egg, too, and then it's a real serious issue.

Noticing that my bowl was near empty, Komachi spoke up. "You want more rice, Bro?"

"Please." I held it out to her.

For some reason, Yuigahama was the one to take it. "I-I'll get it for you!" I guess she was feeling chipper for some reason. She hummed as she began digging up a large serving for me from the wooden serving bowl. "Here!" she said. The overflowing helping she handed me was like something out of *Manga Japanese Folk Tales*.

Not that I minded. I'd been intending to have a third bowl anyway, so I wasn't going to complain.

"Thanks…," I said, lifting the bowl high in the air in thanks and straining my wrists in the process. And then I went back to eating.

Free food sure does taste good.

We all had a proper breakfast, and when we were done, we sipped some tea. Totsuka took a bit longer than the rest of us, finally putting his hands together to say thanks and reaching out for his tea. The conversation wandered into a discussion of the trip so far and our plans for that day.

That was when Miss Hiratsuka began to fold up her newspaper. "Now, then," she said. "It seems you're done eating, so I'll let you in on the schedule for today." She took a sip of tea and then continued. "The kids have the entire day to spend as they please. In the evening, there are plans for a spooky-forest trek and a campfire afterward. I'm going to ask you to set those up."

"Huh. A *campfire*, huh?" I repeated the English word she'd used.

"Oh! The thing you dance around when you do *folk dances*!" Yuigahama's face had scrunched up at the unfamiliar vocabulary, but then her face lit up with recognition as she whipped out another English term.

Once Komachi heard that, the light bulb went on over her head, too. "Ohhh! Are they gonna make a circle and hold hands and go 'Bentora bentora'?" she asked.

"Did you mean to say 'Oklahoma Mixer'? …That's not even close…," Yukinoshita said, somewhere between astonished and exasperated.

Bentora bentora is like that thing, right? You get together in the park late at night and chant those words to communicate with aliens.

"It's not much different when the people you're dancing with already treat you like an alien, though," I said.

"Hachiman, that's a terrible thing to say…," Totsuka admonished me.

But I didn't think it was. I get to have my say, too! "No, really, that's what they think… The first girl I danced with was fine. But at around the fourth one, the girl was like, 'We don't actually have to hold hands, right?' and all the girls after that copied her. Then it was just the Air Oklahoma Mixer…"

"Hikigaya, your eyes are more rotten than ever," said Miss Hiratsuka. "…Well, they'll make you a great monster, though. You can help haunt the forest."

"So that means we're going to be doing the scaring?" I asked. Well, these things are standard for school camping trips. Still, being in the forest at night is distinctly more frightening than any jump scares.

"Yep. But they've already made up the course, and I've got a set of monster costumes for all of you, so all you kids need to do is follow instructions and get it over with. All right. I'll show you what you'll be doing. Let's go." Miss Hiratsuka stood up, and we cleaned up our dishes and followed after her.

X X X

We picked up Hayama's group on our way there and returned to the big plaza. The place was like a sports arena surrounded by forest. By one edge, there was something that looked like a toolshed.

Miss Hiratsuka explained to the boys what their tasks would be, and we began setting up the campfire. Totsuka and Tobe split the firewood and carried it over. Hayama piled it up, and I arranged it into a square.

"Quietly stacking up wood like this all by myself feels like Jenga," I said.

"Huh? You can play Jenga alone?" Hayama asked, in all sincerity.

What, you can't? I thought for sure Jenga was in the same category as card towers…

As for the girls, they were drawing a big white circle with the campfire in the center. I guess that line was for the folk dance.

We chopped the wood, piled it, and stacked it neatly. It wasn't long before we were done. The hard work was rough going, though, under the blazing sun. I wiped sweat off my dripping forehead. "...It's so hot," I moaned.

"Seriously...," Hayama agreed. He sounded like he wanted this to be over, too.

"Good work." Miss Hiratsuka, come to see how our work was progressing, held out two cans of juice. When I gratefully accepted one, she said, "The others are done, too. You're free to do as you please until it's time to get ready for the haunted trek this evening."

Everyone else had most likely been liberated after they completed their tasks, since only Hayama and I remained in the plaza. But now we were done, too. For the moment, I was a free man. As we started back the way we had come, I considered what I should do next.

"I'm going back to our room for now," said Hayama. "What about you, Hikitani?"

"Oh, me too—," I began to say, but suddenly a thought occurred to me. If I headed straight back, I'd have to walk there together with Hayama. It wasn't a big deal, but I was mildly averse to the idea.

To draw an analogy, it's like when you're on the way back from a class meeting, and you end up leaving in the same direction as someone you're not really friends with, and then you have to make awkward conversation. What can you do to avoid such incidents? There is only one answer. "Oh, I'm gonna drop by somewhere else first." Frankly, there's no reason to be stopping by anywhere; it's just a little white lie that you can use to avoid walking home with someone. Some people might fail to take a hint and be like, *Huh? Where are you going? I'll come with!* But well-mannered people won't butt in on your business unnecessarily. I think Hayama is one of those.

"All right. Well, I'm off, then," he said, raising a hand, and then went on back without me.

I gave him a noncommittal reply and saw him off.

Okay, then. What to do now...? If I just headed back to our room, then I'd run into Hayama, thus nullifying the point of splitting up with him in the first place. The correct thing to do would be to go kill time somewhere and then head back.

I mulled over my options as I meandered along the path wherever my whims took me. That's when I heard a trickling, babbling brook. *Come to think of it, I have gotten all sweaty...* The water in the area was clean, and there were no human habitations upstream. It was probably just fine for washing my face. I headed toward the sound, and the path eventually led me to a tiny trickle flowing along. It was shallow, small, and just about the size of an irrigation trench. I guess you'd call that a branch. So that meant if I were to follow this, I should come out at a slightly bigger flow of water. It would probably be the perfect spot to rinse off. As I walked, the dense foliage around me gradually began thinning out.

The rushing water got louder, and I emerged at a spot that was markedly more open. It was the river beach.

"Huh. This is nice." The remark just came out on its own. I'm good at talking to myself.

The river was about two meters wide, no more than thigh deep, and the current was calm—just the right place to splash some water on myself. I was gazing at the sparkling surface as I proceeded along the river for a while, when, out of the quiet forest, I heard the sound of feminine shrieks and cries. Sounded like someone was having fun.

"It's so cold!" It was Yuigahama's voice.

"It feels great, huh?" Komachi's voice followed. When I looked toward the voices, I saw the two of them splashing around in the river. Even from a distance, I could tell they were in their swimsuits. *What are they doing...?*

"Oh, it's my brother," said Komachi. "Heeey! Over here, over here!"

"...Huh? Hikki?"

While I was busy wondering if I should turn back, my sister had spotted me.

Now that Komachi was beckoning me over, I was forced to go. *Oh...well...I really didn't have any intention of going, and a gentleman like me can't just be randomly approaching girls in swimsuits...but now that she's called me over there, I really have no choice—and oh, right, I have to wash my face, don't I? Tsk, there's no helping it. I'll sprint straight over!*

"What're you guys doing?" I asked. "And why are you in swimsuits?" My pace had been just slow enough that I wasn't out of breath.

"*Wasseroi!*" cried Komachi, splashing a huge wave over my head. It ran down my hair and dripped all over me… It was freezing. I had been starting to get excited, but that fizzled out quick. *Come on, that's never happened to me in a bathroom stall…*

I glowered at Komachi for a moment, my eyes dull, but she didn't show the slightest smidgen of regret as she responded nonchalantly to my question. "We got hot from all that work, so we're going for a swim."

"We brought swimsuits 'cause Miss Hiratsuka said there'd be a river," added Yuigahama. "Wait…what're you doing here, Hikki?" She must have been embarrassed about her swimsuit, as she was using Komachi as a shield.

"Oh, I just came here to wash my face…," I began.

"More important, though!" Komachi cut in before I could finish. "Look! Look, Bro! I got a new swimsuit!" She did a nonsensical pose, like she was trying to show it off. Her pale-yellow bikini was decorated with a frilly border for a southern, tropical feel. The water sparkled in the light as she animatedly splashed around. Damn, is she a splash star or what? She spent a few moments in a variety of poses and then gave me a hard look. "So? Whaddaya think?"

"Hmm, oh…yeah. You're the cutest in the world," I told her.

"Wow, you sure don't sound enthusiastic," Komachi whined, discouraged and openly disappointed. She was evidently unsatisfied with my reaction.

But, like, you wear that sort of thing at home, too…

Then Komachi got a twinkle in her eye and reached around behind her. "Then…what about Yui?!" She yanked Yuigahama out from her hiding place and set her front and center.

The move had been so sudden, Yuigahama wasn't even able to react and staggered toward me. "Hey! Komachi—hyaa!" she squealed.

The first thing that caught my eye was a vivid blue. Yuigahama squirmed with embarrassment, and with each movement, her light skirt fluttered. The bikini was a rich color, quite pretty on her silky skin. Their horsing around earlier had left her wet, and the water-resistant swimsuit sent droplets sliding down her sleek skin. They traced the dainty curves of her face, down her neck, pooling for a minute in the hollow of her collarbone, and then sliding down into her rounded cleavage.

Damn. Frankly, I couldn't take my eyes off her. Somehow I managed to steel myself and tear my eyes away. If I didn't make a conscious effort to keep my gaze upward, they'd automatically be drawn toward a certain location. *So this is what they call the law of boobiversal gravitation, huh…? The resulting force is indeed proportional to the product of those two masses.*

"U-um…uh…," Yuigahama mumbled, blushing as she looked away. But when I didn't say anything, her eyes flickered toward me in a moment of uncertainty.

I can't have her asking me what I think of it. Why is this happening to me? Suddenly, I wanted to die. Trying my best not to be creepy, I maintained a calm tone of voice as I picked out the safest reply. "Um, well. It's nice. It looks good on you."

"O-oh… Thanks." Yuigahama smiled shyly.

I couldn't manage to look directly at her. I suspected that I was also blushing now, so I knelt down by the river and scooped up some water. It was cool, and the clear liquid felt good on my flushed skin. I splashed my face a few times, and that was when a familiar voice caught me by surprise.

"Oh my. You're groveling to the river?" The remark was cold and intended to provoke.

"Of course not," I retorted. "The holy land is in that direction. I do my worshipping five times a day…" My head snapped up. That's when I forgot to breathe for a moment.

Yukino Yukinoshita was, as her name suggested, the embodiment of snow. Her skin was white enough to be transparent, her slender legs formed an elegant contour from her calves to her torso, her waist was surprisingly tight, and her chest was, while modest, emphasized. But my glimpse of her was only momentary, and her body was immediately concealed by a sarong.

That was close! I almost suffocated.

"Don't you usually call yourself a Buddhist?" she asked.

"Y-yeah…" That's right, I'm a Buddhist. Which is why I won't let a petty temptation like this beat me! Don't underestimate ascetics, man. Still, even Gautama Buddha had kids. What's the deal with that?

"Oh, you came, too, Hikigaya?" A pat landed on my shoulder, and when I turned around, I saw Miss Hiratsuka with Miura and Ebina behind her. Miss Hiratsuka was clad in a glamorous white bikini that freely exposed her long legs and full breasts. Her toned limbs and shapely belly button was alluring in a fit, healthy way. Or maybe it'd be better to say she had a wild appeal.

"You can do it if you try, can't you, Miss Hiratsuka?!" I said. "You could even pass for thirtysomething!"

"…I *am* thirtysomething. Grit your teeth. I'll splatter your guts!"

"Gah!" An intense blow to my stomach sent me to my knees. Clenching my teeth didn't do a damn thing. As I moaned and groaned at the dull pain running through my body, Miura and Ebina proceeded right by me.

Miura wore a purple, somewhat fluorescent lamé bikini. It was painfully shiny, but the style was exactly what you'd expect from the queen and close to perfect. She probably put in special effort to achieve that kind of beauty. Her labors supported the confidence in her walk, and her pride made her all the more attractive.

As for Ebina, surprisingly enough, she was wearing a one-piece athletic swimsuit. The functional design of the navy-blue suit complemented her slender body and modestly sized chest. The shoulder straps crossed over her back, highlighting the beauty of her shoulder blades.

As Miura passed by Yukinoshita, she gave a satisfied smirk at the other girl's chest, chuckling. "Heh. I won…" There was a nearly emotional undertone to her voice.

Yukinoshita's gave her a quizzical look. "Hmm? At what?" Apparently, she didn't realize what Miura was smiling about.

I figured it out, though. "O-oh, I see…" This was probably where I should pat her on the shoulder and offer some encouragement, but, um, it'd be a little embarrassing to touch her bare shoulder, and my hands are sweaty. "Well, you know," I said, "your older sister's got it, so I think you've still got it, genetically speaking."

"My sister? What does she have to do with this?" Yukinoshita knit her eyebrows together in displeasure.

That was when Komachi cut in, giving a big thumbs-up. "It's okay, Yukino! A girl's value is more than that, and everyone has their own unique qualities! I'm here for you, Yukino!"

"O-okay… Thank you…," said Yukinoshita, confused, but also a little bashful. But once she had calmed down, that seemed to enable her to gradually put two and two together, repeating "Sister, genes, value, unique qualities…" over and over. "……Oh." She glared at me, her face bright red.

I panicked and looked away. *She's scaring the crap out of me; she's gonna kill me; I'm gonna die. Also, why am I the one she's glaring at? Miura's the one who said it!*

"I don't really care about that at all, really," Yukinoshita said. "Superficial features of that nature are not what decides victory or defeat, and even if we were going to compete over that, we should really be using relative evaluation, and generally speaking, the objective would be overall balance. So I don't mind at all, and in fact, the question we should be asking is: Who is the real victor here?" she railed. Her cheeks were a little flushed, probably with anger.

Miss Hiratsuka patted her on the shoulder. "Yukinoshita. It's not time to give up just yet."

"Yukinon, you're really pretty, so don't let it bother you!" Yuigahama immediately tried to comfort her.

"I just said it doesn't bother me…" Yukinoshita reacted to their consolation with indifference and repeated "It…doesn't" under her breath. As she did, her eyes flickered over Miss Hiratsuka's and Yuigahama's breasts, and she gave a particularly discreet sigh.

Before things could turn into even more of a pity party for Yukino Yukinoshita, the girls got into the river and began goofing around in the water. Around then was when a few newcomers appeared, late to the party.

"Man, I'm so stoked about this river!" Tobe cried.

"Oh, you came too, Hikitani," said Hayama.

"Hmm, yeah. Just happened to come by," I replied.

The pair were in their swim trunks, too. They were like, well, normal swimwear. I looked away, not like I gave a damn, and that's when I noticed Totsuka behind them.

He hopped up to me. "You didn't bring swim trunks, Hachiman?"

"T-Totsuka!" He was positively radiant—his skin was so pale, from his dainty toes and ankles and calves to his thighs. He wore a white zip-up short-sleeved hoodie that was a little large on him. The size and the blinding whiteness made him look like he was naked underneath a men's white dress shirt, which was a problem for me. The sight of such fragile forearms extending from his three-quarter sleeves made my heart feel fragile, too. Wearing clothing over his trunks only made him more captivating. It was like by concealing his body, he highlighted his charms.

"What's wrong?" he asked. Sometimes, blindness to your own allure can be sinful. When Totsuka tilted his head with a puzzled expression in that outfit, he only made my heart beat faster.

"Um, that hoodie..."

"Oh, this?" he said, tugging on the chest of the garment. "I tend to burn easily. I don't want to catch a chill, either."

I can't do it. I can't look straight at him. "I—I see... Take care not to catch a cold out there in the river."

"I won't. Thanks!" he said, dashing off to the water.

When I looked over toward the river, everyone had already begun playing around. The girls were splashing each other and grabbing some dolphin-shaped inflatable tube someone had brought, chattering and squealing and having a grand old time.

The boys were throwing themselves into some kind of special warrior training, like trying to grab fish with their bare hands.

If only I had brought swimwear, too... I wanted to splash Totsuka... All I had was the pair of trunks I had for swimming classes back in middle school. I'd had no plans to go out during the summer, so I hadn't bought a pair since finishing middle school. Well, no use regretting it now. I had nothing to do, so I decided to retreat into the shade of the

trees for the time being. A cool wind blew past me as if invited by the burbling water, and the sunshine filtering through the trees and down onto me felt nice. Normally, a moment like this would be rather boring, but when you're at my level, you can kill time doing anything.

Like bird-watching, for example. This place looked like a great spot to find some feathered friends. There was a wide variety flying around and twittering. But of course, I don't know anything about birds, so my venture ended in failure. Man, those things are obnoxious and loud.

Like playing marbles, for example. I started sniping targets with pebbles like a B-Daman. By the third rock, my fingers started to hurt from flicking them, so I stopped. Rocks are too hard, and my spirit is too soft.

Like bug watching, for example. Why are ants always so huge and black in the summer? I get the impression that they're way more powerful in the heat compared with the rest of the year. Maybe that's when they're in season. Well, they're still sour to eat, regardless. Source: me. Why do elementary school kids eat ants and paints? *Setsuko, that's not a marble! That's an ant!* Not that marbles are for eating, either.

But, like, kids sure are cruel. Playing with ants means stepping on them or pouring water into their nest or painstakingly frying them with a magnifying glass. Playing with potato bugs means rolling them up to use as BBs or burning them with sparklers to turn them white.

I mean, kids are capable of all kinds of cruelty.

X X X

I got pretty sick of observing ants, so I leaned back against the tree and zoned out, watching from afar as the others played in the water. Yuigahama and Komachi were actively frolicking around. Miura and Ebina were making loud splashes, too, and enjoying themselves. As for Miss Hiratsuka, she looked more like she was just keeping an eye on the group, but she would still occasionally yell "Take that!" and go on the offensive with a big wave.

Yukinoshita was the only one who didn't really know how to react to all the people bouncing around her. She just stood there, a little ways away from the rest. Loners don't understand such silly behavior. That's the reason they will often be informed that they are wet blankets. It's not necessarily because they're too embarrassed to join in. They're just under assault from so many thoughts, it's not so simple for them. They think, *Maybe I'll be bothering people*, or *Maybe that would be a bad idea*, or *Maybe, if I join in, I'll ruin everyone else's fun*.

But Yuigahama ignored all of that, going over to splash Yukinoshita. Indignant, Yukinoshita swung around, swiftly slicing the surface of the water. Water flew at Yuigahama like a shuriken, landing a clean hit on her forehead. Yuigahama sputtered, and immediately reinforcements arrived: Komachi, ready to go two-on-one.

Yukinoshita was serious now, and she could deal with both of them at once. Miura smirked and began firing off shots of water like a shower of Continuous Energy Bullets. Even Yukinoshita struggled to keep up with that. That was when Miss Hiratsuka showed up with a water gun to back her up.

Come on, it's not fair to bring weapons, geez. I guess I wasn't the only one to think so, as Ebina joined the fray to oppose her with another water gun. Before I knew it, the entire group had assembled to wage a watery war. *Well, I hope they all don't catch cold.*

Half nodding off as I watched them, I heard the scraping of footsteps on the path to my side. Turning toward the sound, I saw a familiar-looking girl. It was Rumi Tsurumi.

"Hey," I called out to her.

She nodded and came over to sit beside me. Neither of us spoke as we watched everyone playing in the river. The silence stretched on for a while, but eventually, as if Rumi had grown tired of waiting, she asked, "Hey. Why are you all alone?"

"I didn't bring swimwear. What about you?"

"Oh… We were supposed to have free time today. I finished breakfast and went back to our room, but no one was there."

Wow, nasty… I've also experienced something like that before. I'd fall asleep in class, and when I woke up, the classroom would be empty, and I'd think I was in a closed space or something. But it was just that everyone had moved to another classroom, and nobody had woken me up.

It's more startling than you might expect to suddenly end up alone. You might consider your classmates to be nothing more than background noise, but when they vanish all of a sudden, well, it's a shock. It's like if you're reading the latest volume of a manga you haven't read in a long time, one that used to have really dense artwork, and now the backgrounds are nothing but big white two-page spreads hitting you in the face. It's bewildering.

Rumi and I absently gazed at the river for a while. Yuigahama turned in our direction. She whispered something to Yukinoshita, and after a little conversation, the both of them emerged from the river. They went over to a blue tarp that had some towels on it, picked up a couple and dried themselves off, and then walked up to us. Still drying off her damp hair, Yuigahama squatted in front of us. "Um…would you like to play with us, Rumi?"

But Rumi curtly shook her head. What was more, she wouldn't even meet Yuigahama's eyes.

"O-oh…" Yuigahama drooped.

"I told you so," said Yukinoshita.

Well, that was just because refusing is the default response of the loner to an invitation. If you suddenly get invited to do something when you usually never are, it's best to assume that there's some hidden motive at play. People will ask you to come out on group dates just to embarrass you and make you the butt of jokes and stuff, you know. The other standard loner response is "If I can make it." If a loner responds with that one, there's about an 80 percent chance that they won't actually go. Source: me.

It looked like Rumi was afraid of Yukinoshita, as she turned back to me. "Hey, Hachiman."

"You're calling me by my first name…?" I asked.

"Huh? But that's your name, right?"

"Well, yes it is, but…" *The only one who's allowed to call me that is Totsuka, though…*

"Do you still have friends from elementary school, Hachiman?" asked Rumi.

"No, not really…," I replied. I hadn't had any relationships to be estranged from in the first place. "Well, I don't think you really need any. I doubt most people stay friends with people from elementary school anyway. Just forget about them. Once you graduate, you'll never see any of them ever again."

"Th-that's just you, Hikki!" said Yuigahama.

"I haven't seen anyone from elementary school since then, either," Yukinoshita responded immediately.

Yuigahama sighed in resignation and addressed the little girl. "Rumi, these people are just…unique, okay?"

"What's wrong with being unique?" I said. "In English, you'd say we're *special*. It makes us sound like we excel in some way, doesn't it?"

"Like the word *myou* in Japanese…" For some reason, Yukinoshita seemed to appreciate my remark. In English, the word *special* can also mean "the exception to a rule," so as a loner, calling myself *special* carries a positive connotation.

Rumi watched our exchange with a dubious look. It seemed she was not yet convinced by my theory.

All right, then I'll take this argument to the next level. "Yuigahama. How many people from your elementary school class do you still meet with now?" I asked.

Yuigahama put her index finger to her jaw and gazed up at the sky. "Hmm. It depends on how often you mean or, like, why we're getting together, but…if you mean meeting up purely to hang out, one or two, I guess."

"By the way," I continued, "How many people were in your year?"

"There were three classes of thirty kids."

"So ninety," I confirmed. "From the information you've given us, we can calculate that the percentage of people you're still friends with five years after elementary school is between three and six percent. Yuigahama is a total kiss-up, and even she can only manage that much."

"Wait, I wasn't k-k-ki…" Yuigahama turned beet red.

"Yuigahama, what he said has nothing to do with kissing." Yukinoshita brought her back to reality.

Ignoring their exchange, I continued. "And most can't manage to be that saccharine at all. They're about a quarter that sweet, at best. Like aspartame level. So you divide Yuigahama's range by four, and, uh…"

"Between zero-point-seventy-five and one-point-five," Yukinoshita instantly replied as I deliberated over the mental math. "Why don't you redo elementary school?"

Come on, are you the computer grandma or what? Also, if I were to redo elementary school, I'm pretty damn sure I'd just do the same things all over again, you know. "So if you take the average of those two numbers, it's about one percent," I continued. "Five years after completing elementary school, the percentage of friends you've kept is one percent. That's not even statistically significant. So you can round that down. You know the rule, round four down and five up, right? The difference between four and five is only one, but four still always gets rejected. Think of how little number four feels. When you think about poor number four, one is hardly worth your time, so you can just round down and erase it. QED, I'm right." Flawless logic.

Yukinoshita, however, was softly pressing her temple. "Your proof was founded on jumping from one supposition to another… This is a desecration of mathematics…"

"Even I can tell that was wrong, and I'm in elementary school," commented Rumi.

"Oh, I s— Huh? Uh, o-of course! That's not right!" For a moment, I had almost convinced Yuigahama. So close. I'd expect nothing less of the private school humanities type.

Well, the fun arithmetic lesson wasn't the point anyway. "The numbers don't matter," I said. "My point is, it's just a matter of perspective."

"Your proof was a pile of nonsense, but your conclusion somehow seems to be correct… How baffling…" Yukinoshita wore a complicated expression, half-exasperated and half-impressed.

"Hmm… I don't really agree, but maybe thinking to yourself that one percent is enough'll make you feel better. It is kind of exhausting to try to be friends with everyone." There was real feeling in Yuigahama's voice. She turned back to Rumi and gave the girl an encouraging smile. "So if you look at it that way, Rumi…"

Rumi weakly returned the smile, clutching her digital camera. "Yeah…that's not enough for my mother, though. She's always asking if I'm getting along with my friends. She got me this and told me to take lots of pictures during the field trip…"

So that was why she bought that. Well, I guess most people would feel like field trips are the kind of events you want to remember for the rest of your life. It wasn't odd for her mother to get carried away and splurge on a camera.

"I see...," said Yuigahama, sounding relieved. "Your mother is nice. She's worried about you."

But Yukinoshita's tone was glacial. "Is she? You don't think it's just a symbol of her desire for ownership, to exercise her authority and control her daughter?" Like thin ice underfoot, her question stirred up a rush of apprehension.

Yuigahama did not hide her shock. She looked like she had been slapped in the face. "What...? Th-there's no way that's true! And...you didn't have to say it like that."

"Yukinoshita, it's, like...practically a mother's job to get into your business. My mom nags me when I'm not out on a date or something on Christmas, and she comes into my room without asking to clean and organize my bookshelf. Moms wouldn't be so controlling if they didn't love you."

Yes, so when she neatly arranges my porno books on top of my desk, that's love, too. And the wordless pressure I feel afterward when I sit down in my usual seat for dinner is probably also love. If I don't make an attempt to believe that, I'd be in a dangerous place, mentally speaking.

Yukinoshita bit her lip hard and looked down at the ground between us and her. "Yes, normally, that is the case." When she lifted her head, her expression seemed kinder than usual. She turned to Rumi and quietly bowed her head. "I'm sorry. I was wrong. That was insensitive of me to say." It was a very sudden apology.

"Oh, it's okay...," Rumi replied, confused. "It sounded sort of complicated, and I didn't really get what you were saying anyway."

This had to be the first time I've ever seen Yukinoshita give a proper apology. Yuigahama was in wide-eyed shock herself. All at once, we fell completely quiet. Rumi was probably feeling awkward.

"Well, uh, how about this," I suggested. "Do you wanna take a picture of me, then? They're superrare items. Usually, this costs a microtransaction fee."

"No." Rumi refused instantly, her face serious.

I drooped a little. "…Oh."

But I was surprised when her serious look morphed into a broad grin. "When I'm in high school, maybe things will be different, and maybe what you just said will feel less creepy…," she said.

"At the very least, if you plan to stay as you are, nothing will change." Whoa there, Yukinoshita, dear. Even after an apology, she's not holding back.

"But your situation changes often enough," I said. "Until then, there's no need to force yourself to go along with the rest of them."

"But Rumi is having a hard time right now," Yuigahama said, giving the girl in question a look of concern. "So we have to do something…"

Rumi looked uncomfortable. "A hard time? More like…it just sort of sucks. I feel pathetic. When everyone ignores me, it's like I'm below them."

"Oh?" replied Yuigahama.

"It sucks. But there's nothing I can do about it now," said Rumi.

"Why not?" Yukinoshita asked.

Rumi seemed to be struggling, but she managed to put it properly into words. "They…abandoned me. I can't be friends with them anymore. Even if things went back to how they were before, this could happen again at any time. And if it's just going to be the same thing all over again, I think maybe it's best to end it now. I hate feeling like this, but…"

Oh, I get it. She'd already turned her back…on herself, and on everyone else. The whole idea that if you change yourself, the world will change—it's just not true. Your preexisting reputation and preexisting relationships don't flip from negative to positive just like that. People don't evaluate you based on additive or subtractive formulas. All they see is the picture painted by their own judgments and prejudices, not the way things actually are. They just see what they want to see. If some low-caste creep puts his all into something, people will giggle and be like, *Whoa, what a try-hard lo-o-o-ser*, and it's over. If you're not careful about how you draw attention to yourself, it'll just give them more to attack you with. If you're associated with a fairly complete and mature community, things are different, but when it comes to middle school at least, that environment is going to be there no matter what.

People want normies to act like normies. Loners are obligated to be loners, and nerds are coerced into acting like nerds. A high-caste person showing understanding to someone below them is seen as generous and refined, but the reverse isn't allowed.

Going along with the whole idea of *the world doesn't change, but you can change yourself* is an act of conformity, submission, acknowledgment of defeat; it's subordination of the self to the crappy, stinking, callous, and cruel world. It's nothing more than a big lie, self-deception swathed in lovely words.

An emotion bubbled up from deep in my heart. It felt like anger. "It sucks to feel pathetic?"

"...Yeah." Like she was holding back a sob, Rumi nodded. She looked frustrated, like she was ready to cry at any moment.

"...I hope that spooky-forest trek will be fun," I told her and then walked away. I had made up my mind.

A question had welled up within me, and I answered it myself.

Q: The world doesn't change. You can change yourself. Now then, how will you change?

A: You become the god of the new world.

Hayato Hayama

Birthday

September 28

Special skills:

Soccer, guitar

Hobbies:

Reading,
watching movies, indoor soccer,
guitar, marine sports

How I spend my weekends:

Getting out of the house, watching sports

7

In the end, **Rumi Tsurumi** chooses her own path.

They were calling it a spooky forest, but it was still just a school camping trip event. We obviously weren't going to employ any serious makeup or visual effects. It was the sort of simple setup that everyone vaguely remembers: making recordings of voices chanting Buddhist sutras, shaking trees under cover of night, putting on masks, chasing the kids around.

The forest at night was scary enough on its own, though. The stirring trees sounded like the voices of otherworldly beings, and when the wind blew, you felt the dead caress your cheeks.

That was how the forest felt around us as we performed preliminary inspection of the course, nailing down our plans for the evening as we went. We did a basic check over the whole thing and then left a stack of talismans printed on straw paper at the end on top of a thermometer screen decorated to look like a small wayside shrine. The kids' mission would be to take one of these back.

Though the course had already been prepared, we still checked over any potentially dangerous points to make sure the kids wouldn't get confused and end up lost. We consulted each other briefly as we proceeded, throwing out suggestions like *Let's put a person dressed as a ghost here*, or *Let's put a traffic cone here to make sure they don't go past this point*. I wasn't participating in the conversation, but I was mapping the whole thing out in my head. Mappy knows all about that. Mappy knows that road is a dead end.

When we came back to the starting line, Yukinoshita got the inevitable conversation started. "So what are we going to do?" she asked. That question was not in regards to the spooky-forest event itself. She was asking how we were going to help Rumi Tsurumi. All those who had been so active with their suggestions before now had nothing to say.

It was a difficult problem. Just paying lip service to the idea that everyone should be friends would have absolutely no effect, and more important, telling the kids something of that nature might temporarily smooth things over, but ultimately, the same thing would recur.

For example, let's say Hayama were to draw Rumi into the center of the group and use various social techniques to protect her. He was popular, so everyone might be friendly with her for a while. But Hayama wouldn't be able to stay with her 24/7. You had to strike at the root of the problem. But at this point, we had failed to come up with a clear answer.

Cautiously, Hayama spoke. "Perhaps all we can do is have Rumi talk to the other girls. We could create an environment for them to talk."

"They'll all probably still bully her anyway...," Yuigahama said, her gaze on the ground.

But Hayama didn't back down. "Then what if she talked to them one by one?"

"It'd be exactly the same. They might act nice at the time, but secretly, it would just start up again. Girls are way scarier than you realize, Hayato," Ebina said in a shiver-inducing tone. That made even Hayama fall silent.

"What, are you for real? That's *so* scary!" For some reason, that freaked out Miura. Well, she was the type to be straight about whatever was on her mind. Maybe being the queen for so long means you don't get involved in these shadowy politics.

Either way, being a normie sounds like a pain in the butt. So it's not just the good stuff you're supposed to share with your friends, but the bad stuff, too, huh? Well, I guess in this case, they're just sacrificing her on the altar of the status quo, though.

Something had to be done about that. "I have an idea," I announced.

"Forget it." Yukinoshita immediately rejected it.

"You jumped to that conclusion way too fast...," I said. "You'd really be bad at buying real estate." *Spend some more time deliberating over it, come on.* "Well, just listen. We've got this spooky-forest thing going on. This is a great opportunity to take advantage of."

"How would we do that?" Totsuka tilted his head.

I decided to ease in to my proposal in order to explain it as thoroughly as possible for Totsuka. "There's a certain something that happens very often during spooky-forest treks. You get my drift?" I said.

Everyone was slow on the uptake, though. I doubted Ebina was listening at all. Yuigahama was *hmm*ing in thought, but then she clapped her hands. "Oh! Everyone gets all jumpy and scared because of the *spasibo* effect? And that makes them feel closer?"

"I think you probably mean the placebo effect." Hayama smiled, but it didn't reach his eyes. They were too full of pity.

"...More important, the phenomenon you're referring to is the suspension bridge effect," Yukinoshita said, quietly lowering her gaze in grief. Suddenly the mood was grim, like this was a memorial service in remembrance of Yui Yuigahama.

"Wh-whatever! The important part is the idea!" Yuigahama rattled on, blushing.

"The idea's no good, either," I said. "Think about what often happens during spooky-forest treks."

"...Being startled and dying of fright, huh?" said Yukinoshita. "That wouldn't leave any physical evidence, it's true, and I believe you could explain it away by calling it an accident. But to go to such lengths... It's inhuman." The look she gave me was full of reproach.

"Wrong. *You're* the one with the inhuman ideas..." I cleared my throat and announced the correct answer. "What I'm getting at is that while you're busy trying to take photos of ghosts, you'll bump into a delinquent who's halfway through, and then he ends up chasing you around."

"That doesn't happen." Yukinoshita shut me down.

"Yeah, I don't think so," Hayama agreed.

"Shut up. Yes it does," I said.

Indeed, that gloomy girl who had been like, *I can sense spirits...* (for some reason, there's one like that in every class) had set the chain of events in motion. And then I'd been like, *Well, I can sense spirits, too, can't I? Or it'd be cool if I could.* And I had gone off to try to take photos of ghosts, and then it happened.

What I had ended up finding was not a wandering soul but rather a clique of delinquents. They had also apparently been in the middle of their trek, and when I encountered them with particularly poor timing, I had scared the crap out of them, resulting in some unjustified resentment on their part, and they had chased me around, and then, well... that's enough of this story.

Yukinoshita sighed in exasperation. "...This isn't building up to the worn-out platitude that plain flesh-and-blood humans are the scariest of all, is it?"

"Delinquents are scary, though!" Komachi was nodding vigorously. But...

"Close, but no cigar," I replied. "While it's true that humans are indeed the most frightening, the object of fear in this scenario is not the delinquents."

"Then what is?" Yukinoshita asked.

I paused for effect before I replied. "What's *really* scary are the people who are most familiar to you. You sort of trust them, so you don't expect them to betray you. It's terrifying because it's unexpected. In the case of these girls, well, I'd say friends are the scariest." I was explaining in a straightforward manner, but they still weren't getting it. "Let me be more specific." *It's not that complicated.* "People reveal their true nature in extreme situations. If they feel really, truly afraid, they'll do whatever they can to protect their own hides. People are incapable of considering others. They want to save themselves, even if it means making sacrifices. And once people have revealed the ugly side of themselves to one another, they can't be friends anymore. That's all you have to do to rip the group apart." I explained the plan dispassionately, but the reactions from the crowd were lacking. Nothing but grim silence.

"If they all become loners, there won't be any more fighting or conflict." My point was already made, but I still hammered it home.

X X X

"Wh-whoa...," said Yuigahama. By the time I was done, she was rather freaked out. Yukinoshita was glaring at me with her eyes so narrow they were practically slits.

"You're pretty twisted, Hikitani...," said Hayama. And he was the kind of guy who never said anything bad about anyone.

I sort of wanted to cry. I hadn't experienced a reaction as harsh as this since that time in elementary school when it was my turn to take care of the class crayfish, but then they cannibalized one another until all of them were dead, and then everyone blamed me for it at the class meeting.

Totsuka was the only one nodding with fascination. "You come up with so many ideas, Hachiman." Coming from anyone else, that would have sounded sarcastic, but Totsuka being Totsuka, I could honestly trust that the compliment was sincere. If it were anything else, I think I might have destroyed the world.

Yukinoshita deliberated for a while. "It's not like we have any other ideas... In this case, I don't think we have any other choice." Through process of elimination, she seemed to have reached a decision. This was what we had to work with. There wasn't likely much else we could try.

Hayama didn't seem happy about it, though. "...But that won't resolve the situation, will it?"

He was right. This wasn't the right answer. I knew full well that this was all wrong. "But it will cancel it out." I raised my head.

Hayama was looking me straight in the eye. His gaze was so direct, it was uncomfortable. I looked away. But I wasn't wrong.

When you have problems with your social relationships, if you destroy the bond, then you won't have anything to worry about anymore. You can avoid that downward spiral by cutting the whole thing off at the source. That's the best way to handle things.

Saying you can't run away—that's just the rationale of the strong.

The world is wrong, for forcing that mind-set on people. Claiming *It's not my fault, it's the world that's the problem* may sound like an excuse, but it's not entirely wrongheaded. It's not *always* your fault. There are many times when it's society, the world, your surroundings, someone else that's wrong. If no one else is going to recognize that, then I'll be the one to do it.

Hayama gave me a long, hard look. But then he broke into a smile. "So that's the way you see it… I think I'm starting to get why she'd look out for you."

I was just about to ask who the *she* he was referring to was, but he immediately got back on topic. "Okay. Let's go with that… But I'll be betting on the chance that they'll all come together to handle the situation. If this is about their true nature, I want to believe *that* is their true nature. I think they're all good kids at heart."

I was unable to reply to that effulgent smile. We were always in on it for different reasons, even when it was the exact same plan.

"What? I'm the one getting screwed with this plan!" complained Miura.

"Totally. It's too harsh for me, too," agreed Tobe.

"Come on, you guys." Hayama pacified them and then faced me again. "We'll go with your idea, Hikitani. I'll let you handle the *direction*." For some reason, he said the final word in English.

"…All right," I replied. Hayama's role in this would be an unpleasant one, but he'd agreed to do it anyway. So I had no choice but to respond to his spirit in kind.

So…what does *direction* mean in Japanese? What should I be doing right now?

X X X

When it was time to do the prep for the test of courage, Miss Hiratsuka called us all together in a room of the lodge and announced our mission. "They've requested that you tell some ghost stories in order to get the kids in the mood for the haunted forest."

Where there's a haunted anything, there's ghost stories. We'd get them worked up by telling some thrilling tales, and their ensuing fear might lead them to see ghosts. There's a saying: *A ghost seen is naught but leaves.* It means that people imagine the abnormal just because they're afraid.

You could even say that most supernatural phenomena are born from such false impressions and misconstructions. In other words, both the bowl of hot miso soup slowly gliding across the table and that sensation that there are still a few kernels of corn potage stuck in the pull-tab can are such errors. There's nothing supernatural about the world we live in.

"Do any of you have any special ghost stories?" she asked.

We all looked at one another.

Well, none of us are professionals like Storyteller Tamori, so we didn't have much. Aside from me, Tobe was the only one to raise his hand.

"Hmm," said Miss Hiratsuka. "Tobe…and Hikigaya, huh? There's a frightening combo. Tell me your stories."

If we were going to work the kids over for their haunted trek with spooky stories, then we'd be presenting in front of two classes of thirty, totaling sixty. We really couldn't afford to bomb our presentation. After borrowing one of the rooms in the lodge, we sat in a circle. We picked up some candles, too, to give it some atmosphere. Tobe and I both eyed each other silently to decide who would go first. I don't know if Tobe picked up on my cues or what, but he humbly raised his hand. "So, I'll go first…," he said.

The lights in the room were already off, and the only source of illumination was a few flickering and unreliable candles. A lukewarm draft blew in through where the window was open a crack, making the flames tremble and distorting the faint shadows they cast.

"This is about an older kid I know," Tobe began. "He was sort of like a street racer. One day, he was zipping through this pass all alone like usual, and he got pulled over by the police. He wasn't speeding at the time, which was strange. The policewoman came out of her cruiser and told him, 'You can't carry a passenger on your bike without a helmet… Huh? Where did that woman riding on the back go?'

"But this guy always rode alone. He never had any passengers. So… what on earth was it that she saw? A few days later…" Tobe wiped the sweat off his forehead and gulped. "He had a *dansu* with *baddo rakku*…"

He ruined it all with that ending. What's with the random English…?

The entire audience reacted with disappointment, but Tobe soldiered on. He's made of some sturdy stuff. "Now he's a dad with two kids. He stopped street racing, got a job, married the officer who stopped him that day, and now he's part of a happy family. These days he says his wife is scarier than any ghost."

"I didn't ask for weak comedy…," Miss Hiratsuka grumbled.

Heh, good grief. You can't call something like that a ghost story. I'll teach you the real meaning of fear.

"I'll go next, then," I said, pulling a candle in front of me. The flame flickered, and the candles cast an array of shadow clones across the wall. I'm gonna tell you all a real scary story now, believe it!

"This is a true story…" I began with the conventional line, and the chatter around me subsided. The sound of everyone breathing was particularly loud to my ears. "It happened when I was on a camping trip in elementary school. We were doing the same walk through the haunted forest that they do every year. Yes, it was a warm summer night…just like this one.

"We were supposed to split up into groups to go pick up talismans from the small shrine deep in the woods. Each team went in order, and finally, it was our turn. They were calling this a spooky forest, sure, but in reality, the teachers had just set it up. There were no *real* ghosts. We cowered at scarecrows and teachers draped in sheets, retrieved the talisman from the shrine, and made it back without a hitch. Nothing happened. It was just a good time, an opportunity to screech and scream. Or so I thought. But then Yamashita, a guy in my group, happened to say something.

"'Who grabbed the talisman?' he asked.

"That threw the group into an uproar.

"'Was it you?' they asked.

"'No, it wasn't me.'

"'Not me… Then who was it?' Not a single person in the group knew who had taken the talisman.

"Terror filled my heart. I was trembling so hard I could almost cry. Because…" I trailed off there, all eyes locked on me. Or perhaps the object of their focus was something else—the clouds of pitch-black darkness billowing out behind me. "…Nobody had noticed that I was the one who had taken the talisman…" I finished the story and blew out the candle.

In the dead silence of the room, I heard Yuigahama sigh. "That's just a loner story…"

"It would have been a lot more terrifying to hear you were friends with everyone in that group." Yukinoshita shot me a chilly glare. She was completely right, and there was nothing I could say to that.

"Good grief." Miss Hiratsuka exhaled a deep, deep sigh. "Are those pathetic attempts the best you kids can come up with?"

"Hey, come on," I replied. "You can't just ask an amateur to conjure up a scary story out of the blue. It's not gonna happen…"

"Hmm… It's a desirable skill for an adult, though. At drinking parties, people are going to want you to tell funny stories. It's always a good idea to polish those skills. It helps you grease the wheels of your professional relationships."

I was shocked. *I-it can't be…* "Wh-what did you say? I don't think that'd be possible for me. I think, for the sake of everyone out there in the workplace, it'd be best for me to never, ever get a job at all."

"What a perverse way to express your concern… Well, let me show you how it's done, then." Miss Hiratsuka lit the candle.

I suppose she did have the wisdom of age. Finally, we could hear a ghost story from an adult. The audience all turned expectant eyes toward Miss Hiratsuka, as if to say, *Tell us a story, one we don't know!* Trembling, trembling…

Miss Hiratsuka returned all those gazes with a bold smile and slowly began. "This is about someone I suppose I'd call a close friend. Her name was Haruka Kinoshita. But then, about five years ago, Haruka Kinoshita was no more… Right before she disappeared, she left me with a single phrase: *I'm going first.* Then she was gone. I never saw her again.

"But just a few days ago, I met a woman who looked somehow familiar. She seemed exhausted, but she wore a faint smile. It was the woman who had disappeared, or so I thought. I was about to call out to her, but then I saw a face behind her, grinning..." As she recounted her tale, Miss Hiratsuka's face blanched. It was as if the terror of that moment had returned. Her expression was so chilling, it sent shivers down our spines as well.

"...The baby on her back was already three years old. It was truly horrifying." Miss Hiratsuka blew out the candle before her, and the room went black.

I couldn't help but break the stone-cold silence of the room. "She just got married, changed her surname, and had a baby..."

Someone please marry this woman, seriously. Otherwise I'm going to feel so sorry for her, I'll marry her myself.

In the end, we just weren't any good at telling tales of fright, so we unanimously agreed that would play the *Ghost Stories* DVD that someone had left at the lodge.

X X X

While the kids were occupied with the DVD, we were steadily setting up their trek. As Yukinoshita's group was getting ready, Hayama called me over to discuss the details of our plan. We outlined the plan and its most important points and then started hammering out the details.

"It'd be best to make sure Rumi's group is going at the right time," Hayama said.

"Yeah. It'll probably take a while, so we should make them go last," I replied. "So do we fix the lottery draw?"

"No, that's not very practical, and it would take time. We'll just tell them when they have to go. Yeah...we can just say it's so the kids will never know what's coming. That it'll make it more exciting."

My briefing session with Hayama went extremely smoothly. I like to think my brain is made of the good stuff, but talking to him, I felt like he was one step ahead. Even delivering flimsy excuses, he seemed so cool, like everything was all well and good. It was weird.

"...All right, I'll let you handle that," I said.

"Roger. Who's going to lead them there?"

"I'll use traffic cones and stuff to herd them down the path toward the dead end," I explained. "You guys just have to be waiting back there."

"Got it. Also, about Tobe and Yumiko, I don't think either of them is capable of remembering overly detailed instructions."

Yeah, they seem like they'd be bad at memorization. "Just give them directions via cell phone. It wouldn't look off for them to be goofing around on their phones. In fact, the more time they spend doing that, the more realistic it'll be."

"I see..." Hayama's fingers danced over the surface of his tablet typing out the details. It really did make him look competent.

You know, though, talking is easy when it's about work. You don't have to try to come up with topics, and you don't have to agonize over how the other person might feel. It's nice; you're even allowed to be harsh when it's necessary for the task at hand.

"I guess that's about it," he said. "I'll tell Tobe and Yumiko."

"Thanks." They probably wouldn't listen to anything coming from me anyway.

"Then I'll see you later," he replied, finishing up the session, and we parted ways. He was going over to set things up with Miura and Tobe, and I would help Yukinoshita's group with their preparations.

There wasn't really much to set up, though, and it wasn't like we were gearing up for anything elaborate. We were basically just startling the kids as they walked around the woods at night. These events don't really focus on concept and detail like haunted houses do. It's more about the impact and making it into a game. Especially since these kids were just elementary schoolers. They'd have more fun if it felt more like a theme park experience as opposed to having some sort of cohesive narrative. Bluntly speaking, they'd have the most fun if we just sprang out at them from the darkness to scare them. During the spooky forest on my school trip back in elementary school, a bunch of unfamiliar old dudes were jumping out at me, then in another area voices were suddenly chanting sutras, and at the end, bedsheet ghosts were staggering around. It was total chaos.

Facilities that often host school camping trips, such as this one, always have the relevant creepy props on hand, and the teachers should have collected some things, too. And they did have stuff, but…when I saw what they had for us, I held my head in my hands.

"A demon costume…cat ears and a tail…a white *yukata*…a witch hat, robe, and cape…a priestess outfit…" This was going a little too far, even for a theme-park-style performance. This was more like Halloween.

Miss Hiratsuka had said the provider of the costumes was an elementary school teacher. There were no two ways about it: I was positive that the one responsible just wanted to see teenage girls in cosplay. It made me want to be a teacher…

First, there was Ebina's priestess outfit. Despite being a member of Miura's clique, she had an established reputation as the modest one, so traditional garb suited her. But in my opinion, the costume was less scary and more vaguely mystical. Maybe she would present a more ghastly picture if we had her stand out by the wayside shrine.

As I considered where each person might be stationed, I looked around to see how everyone else was doing. That was when I caught sight of Totsuka, tugging the brim of his pointy hat down over his eyes. He plucked at the sleeves and the hem of his robe, muttering in confusion. "Does a magician count as a monster…?"

"Well, if you're speaking as broadly as possible, I guess so," I said. He was clearly a witch girl, though. *Sharanran.*

"But it's not scary, is it?"

"No, it's scary. You're fine."

Yes, truly frightening. I'm about to head straight down the Totsuka route right now—terrifying. Phew…are you the one who cast that naughty spell on me? What am I even saying?

"Bro! Bro!"

Someone was tapping on my shoulder, though it was softer than a tap. When I turned around, a stuffed animal–esque cat paw was beckoning me. "What's that? A monster cat?" I asked.

"Probably…"

I think there was something like that in one of those big-time musi-

cals... That was what my little sister reminded me of, standing there. Komachi was covered in black fake fur, sprouting cat ears and a cat tail.

"I don't really get it, but it's cute, so whatever," I said. A pretty girl looks nice no matter what she wears. She'd probably even be cute in a mobile suit. Source: the Nobel Gundam in *G-Gundam*.

As Komachi waved her gigantic kitty paws, experimenting with the appropriate gestures, a ghostlike figure quietly materialized behind her.

"..." Without a word, the specter reached out to Komachi's kitty ears.

Smoosh, smoosh.

"U-um...Yukino?"

Pet, pet.

Yukinoshita grabbed the tail next.

Brush, brush.

Then she nodded. *What? What are you approving of here? Enough with that look on your face, like you're evaluating antiques on* Nandemo Kanteidan. *I feel like she's gonna bust out with a line like, "Oh, well done there."*

"...I think it's quite nice," she said. "It suits you."

"Thank you very much!" Komachi replied. "You look amazing, too, Yukino! Right, Bro?"

"Yeah," I said. "You look damn good in a kimono. Just like a *yuki-onna*. You look ready to kill a whole bunch of people."

"...Was that supposed to be a compliment?" Yukinoshita's eyebrows twitched upward.

A sudden chill slid down my spine. "Yeah, that's it, that icy feeling. Exactly like a deadly spirit of the snow. That outfit suits you, it really does." I complimented her as hard as I could.

Yukinoshita swept her hair off her shoulders and glowered at me. "That zombie outfit suits you, too, Hikigaya. The way your eyes are rotting is fit for Hollywood."

"I'm not wearing any makeup or anything, though..." I shot Yukinoshita a casual but leaden-eyed glare, but she gave as good as she got. I broke the eye contact before I could stop myself. Scary.

My gaze escaped to land on Yuigahama, who was fidgeting in a devil costume. She grinned broadly at the mirror, but then she suddenly shook her head as if she'd changed her mind, sighed, hung her head, and jumped straight into an excited series of poses, like a first-time cosplayer the night before a con.

"You're keeping yourself busy, I see," I said to her.

"Oh! Hikki..." Yuigahama wrapped her arms around herself as if to hide. Her expression betrayed some self-doubt. "...Hey..."

I waited for her to continue and held my eyes level, though they wanted to slip downward.

"U-um...what do you think?" she asked.

"If it looked terrible, I'd tell you, and I'd be making all sorts of jokes right now... It's too bad I can't."

"Huh? Um..." Yuigahama considered for a moment, but I guess she got my meaning, as she gave me a triumphant chuckle. "You could've just given me a straight compliment... Jerk!" Yuigahama cheerfully insulted me and then turned back to the mirror with even more pleasure than before.

Komachi must have been watching the whole thing, if her smug smile was any indication. "You're a *hinedere*, Bro."

Twisted on the outside, squishy on the inside—is that what she's trying to say? "Stop making up weird slang." But despite my protests, I had an indescribable feeling that it was futile.

That was when Hayama's group came back. Looking over at them, I could see that Miura and Tobe were ready to go. Miura wasn't even wearing a costume, but she was still scary. Ultimately, she was just a perpetual object of terror.

"Hayama," I called out to him.

He nodded at me and then spoke. "All right, let's go over this one last time."

It wasn't long before the spooky-forest trek would begin. It was going to leave a bitter aftertaste, no matter what, and we all knew that nothing good would come of it, but even so, none of us was able to stop it. The episode just continued along its course.

X X X

There was a bonfire burning at the starting point—for atmosphere, I guess. When the flames spread to the green wood on the pile, the fire crackled loudly, throwing off sparks.

"All right! Next up are...you guys!" When Komachi singled out a group, the children screeched and squealed. Clearly excited, they stood, and the entire group headed toward the starting point. We were already about thirty minutes into the test of courage. I estimated that about 70 percent of the kids had already started.

Hayama's idea of choosing the order of the groups on the spot instead of deciding beforehand was working well. I caught flashes of anxiety on the faces of the kids as they waited eagerly for their group's turn. Even Hayama breathed a sigh of relief as he saw it was successful. Then he immediately whispered something into Miura's and Tobe's ears. Maybe he was discussing the final stages of the plan.

"Once you're in, head to the shrine deep in the woods and get a talisman from the shrine there." Totsuka, in his witch costume, stood by the entrance to the forest as he explained the simple rules. He had been nervous at first, and he'd screwed up the lines a bunch, but once he sent off a few groups and got into a groove, he was doing just fine, as you can see.

It would probably be okay to leave this part to Komachi and Totsuka. Besides, Miss Hiratsuka was there, too, so there shouldn't be any major mishaps.

I covertly leaped into action to observe the kids' progress on their trek. While I was at it, I would also go check on how the other members of our team were doing. I walked hidden in the trees for a while, so as not to alert the children to my presence.

Yuigahama was stationed near the beginning of the trail. When the kids passed by her location, she jumped out at them from the shadows. "Grr! I'll eat you up!"

...What's with that scare? Is she trying to be Gachapin? Of course, the kids were not in the least bit scared at some stupid-looking girl jumping out at them. They ran away, laughing their heads off.

Once they were gone, Yuigahama's shoulders drooped, and she sniffled. "I kind of…feel like an idiot…"

Poor thing… I didn't know what to say to her, so I decided to just leave her there for the time being. Taking a shortcut through the trees, I circled around her and forged ahead. On my way, I heard the kids talking loudly. Their chatter consisted of comments like "Man, this is dull," or "This isn't scary at all" and uproarious laughter. I don't think they were actually scared. But when I made some rustling, their voices grew hushed all at once.

"What was that just now?"

"I saw something."

"There's nothing there…," I heard one of them say.

Nothing is scarier than the unknown. I quickly left the area before they caught sight of me.

Deep in the forest, the path was darker, and that alone was enough to make every hair on your body stand on end. Though it was summer, the evenings at high altitude are chilly. You couldn't be quite sure if it was just cold out or if the presence of some mysterious entity was giving you shivers.

Fickle moonlight and starlight illuminated the path. I continued on, following a bend in the trail. Ahead of me was a white shadow. The light filtering through the gaps between the tree branches highlighted her chalky skin, and the blowing wind made her outline undulate like something ethereal.

I couldn't speak. It wasn't because I was frightened. I was entranced, frozen in place by a crisp, terrifyingly icy beauty. Her gorgeousness seemed like a taboo, something forbidden to approach or even speak of, never mind touch.

I bet there were many other of her kind, in the past. Then people passed down tales, and somewhere along the line, their stories gave birth to actual supernatural beings. Seeing her evoked such speculations anyway.

Yukino Yukinoshita was simply standing there like a ghost, as if in a daze. Her body was enveloped in silvery moonlight and solemn, frigid wind. Time was frozen for no more than a few seconds before she realized someone was there and turned around. Her eyes landed on me in the shadow of the trees.

"Eek!" Yukinoshita jumped about a meter backward, startled to see me appear all of a sudden. "Hiki…gaya?" She blinked a few times and then breathed a sigh of relief.

Why did she have to freak out like that…? She made my heart skip a beat, too. "Hey," I greeted her.

"I thought you were a ghost… Your eyes look so dead."

What an uncute reaction. I let slip a sarcastic smile. "I thought there was no such thing as ghosts."

"Indeed, there isn't."

"You seemed pretty scared, though," I said.

Yukinoshita gave me a sharp, sullen glare before she started babbling. "Of course I wasn't scared. When you expect something to be there, your brain automatically creates images for your visual cortex, and it's a biological fact that those suppositions induce effects in the body. So there's no such thing as ghosts—to put it another way, if you believe there's no such thing, then it must be true. I'm positive."

That sounded suspiciously like an excuse…especially that *I'm positive* at the end.

"Anyway, how much longer will this be?" she asked.

"We're about seventy percent done. It's almost over."

"…I see. I have to stay here for a little while longer, huh?" She sighed. That was when we heard a rustling sound, a swaying in the undergrowth. Yukinoshita's shoulders twitched. *She really is scared, huh?*

Oh, crap. I guess the kids caught up with me. Standing out here, I'd be in full view. I immediately moved to hide in the shadow of the trees, but I was stopped by a firm tug on my shirt. When I turned around, I saw Yukinoshita grasping the hem.

"What…?" I asked.

"Huh? Um…" She looked confused. I guess the action had been unconscious on her part. When she realized what she'd done, she quickly let go and jerked her head away. "…Nothing. More important, don't you need to go hide right now?"

"Unfortunately, it's a little late for that." Before I'd had the chance to move, the kids had rounded the corner. The child in the front met my eyes. Running into a regular guy like me would absolutely destroy the mood. We'd gone to all that trouble to create this event, and I'd screwed it up.

Or so I thought. But as I watched, the children's eyes all went wide in fright.

"A z-zombie?!"

"No, that's a ghoul!"

"That look in his eyes! Run!" The kids sprinted away as fast as they could.

I gazed up at the starry sky with a vague desire to cry.

Yukinoshita smiled brightly and patted me on the shoulder. "Isn't that nice? You've made the children so happy. Your rotten eyes have turned this into a memorable event for them, see?"

"You're really bad at consoling people...," I said. Way to kick me while I'm down. "Anyway, I've got to get going."

"Yes, I'll see you later."

I left Yukinoshita behind and hurried on down the course. The kids had a head start, but if I could make my way along hidden in the trees again, I could probably come out ahead of them. Mostly ignoring the path, I pushed on toward the bonfire at the goal point.

At the minishrine at the goal, Ebina was waving a green tree branch. I guess she was using that in lieu of an actual sacred sakaki branch. "Reverence, reverence before the heavens!" she intoned.

She's even doing a chant, huh? Wow, she's sure set on performing this right. Y'know, since it's a rite. Wow, I'm an idiot.

Well, I guess it might be pretty scary to see a priestess suddenly pop out and catch you by surprise. Plus, that chanting was eerie.

Ebina noticed my approach and turned around. "Oh, Hikitani."

"Hey. You're looking pretty damn legit."

"I consume a lot of traditional occult stuff, too," she replied.

"Uh-huh..." What does she mean by that? Does she ship Seimei/Douman or something? That rabbit hole is too deep. I have no idea. Regular Ebina is way scarier than some straightforward priestess cosplay. Terrified, I left her with a casual "See you!" and fled as fast as I could.

X X X

After I looped around ahead of the kids and returned to the starting point, I saw there were only two—no, three groups left. Komachi designated the next group, and they were off. Once Hayama's crew had watched the kids leave, they set into action. "All right, Hikitani," he said. "We're gonna get going. We'll be counting on you to do your part."

"Roger." Our extremely brief briefing was now concluded, and I watched the Hayama trio leave and waited for it to be Rumi's group's turn. The bonfire sizzled, ashes dancing in the wind. Children's cries, somewhere between screams and exclamations of joy, rang out from deep in the woods.

As I waited, I observed how Rumi was doing. The girls around her were abuzz with chatter. Rumi alone had her lips pressed shut. The teacher was right in front of them, so the kids didn't openly exclude her. They just left her out in a way that would clearly distance her from the crowd. Rumi understood that, too, so she took another step away from them. Seeing her attempt to be considerate, I felt that malaise in my chest again.

Komachi pulled her cell phone from her pocket and checked the time. "...Okay! Next is...you!" One of the two remaining groups erupted into squeals. The final group let out sighs of part disappointment and part relief. Komachi and Totsuka prompted the second-to-last unit to embark. I watched them go and then covertly slipped away.

My destination was the fork in the mountain trail. That was the spot where one of the paths was blocked off by a traffic cone. Just as I had the last time, I stuck to the trees to avoid encountering the kids. The leaves, damp with night dew, were cold. As the hour grew deeper, the temperature seemed to be dropping, if slowly.

I swiftly bypassed Yuigahama's location and smoothly bypassed Yukinoshita's. I reached a point not far from the minishrine, where the path split into two: one that loops around the forest, and one that climbs up the mountain. I had done a bit of jogging, so I was panting a little. I slowed my breathing and then hid in the shadow of some nearby trees. It wasn't to do any scaring; it was just to hide. The second-to-last group walked by, their rowdy voices disappearing into the distance. After I was sure they were gone, I moved the traffic cone to block off the path that went to the minishrine and open the one that didn't.

Hayama, Miura, and Tobe were gathered along that way, which led up the mountain. I approached them with just one thing to tell them. "It's almost time. You guys take it from here."

"Roger," Hayama replied shortly, sitting down on a nearby rock. Miura and Tobe followed him as if they were waiting on him.

Assured that the three of them were now on standby, I went back to the fork in the path and disappeared into the trees again. I counted two, three minutes, waiting for Rumi's group to come. Right about then, they should have been departing.

With each passing hour, it felt like the darkness of the forest was deepening. Within the blackness, I silently closed my eyes and focused on listening. I could hear an owl hooting, branches rustling.

As I strained my ears, I twitched. I could hear voices. They sounded animated, and they were coming closer. Rumi's voice was not among them, but once the girls had come close enough for me to confirm visually, Rumi was definitely there. She was the only one with her lips pursed. But that would end tonight. The girl at the head of the group approached the fork. She glanced curiously at the path that was blocked off by a traffic cone but continued on down the open trail. The other members of the group followed her without question. Making sure to escape detection, I waited until they were all far enough ahead and made to follow them when I heard someone softly call my name.

"What's the situation, Hikigaya?" It was Yukinoshita. When I turned around, she and Yuigahama were both there. Rumi's group was the last one, so the two girls were done playing their roles as monsters.

"They're headed toward Hayama right now. I'm gonna go check it out. What about you two?"

Yukinoshita nodded. "I'm going, of course."

Yuigahama did the same. "Me too."

I nodded back at them, and then we slowly, quietly proceeded.

The girls were conversing in especially loud voices, as if in an attempt to drive away the darkness and the fear. As they strolled along, amusing themselves with their idle chitchat, someone cried, "Oh!"

Before them were three people. "Oh, it's you guys!" one girl said. When they recognized Hayama and crew, they ran up to the older kids.

"You're wearing totally normal clothes!"

"Weak!"

"At least try!"

"This whole spooky-forest thing isn't scary at all!"

"You're sure dumb for high schoolers!" The sight of familiar faces in normal clothing must have broken the tension of the event all at once. The kids, even more insouciant than before, complained at Hayama's group.

But when they approached, Tobe roughly shook them off and barked in a low, aggressive voice, "The hell? You think you can talk like that to us?"

"Ew, what's with that attitude?" Miura demanded. "It's not like we're your friends, you know."

The children immediately froze. "Huh…?" I could see their minds whirling around desperately in an attempt to process what they had just heard.

But Miura just kept going without sparing them a moment to process. "And, like, one of you guys was being totally nasty to us. Which one of you said that?" she asked, but none of the kids were capable of replying. They just looked at each other. Miura clicked her tongue as if their confusion irritated her. "I'm *asking* who said that. One of you did it, right? Who? Can't you even answer my question? Spit it out."

"I'm sorry…" One of the girls apologized in a frail-sounding voice.

Miura didn't care. She just spat, "What? I can't hear you."

"You kids try'na mess with us? Huh? C'mon." Tobe glared at the girls, and they shrank away.

But the queen bee was already behind them. "C'mon, Tobe, let them have it. It's supposed to be our job to teach them manners, right?"

The trio prevented the girls from escaping, slowly fencing them in. In only moments, Hayama, Miura, and Tobe had formed a triangle, trapping them inside.

There was Tobe, exuding a rough and violent air; Miura, every one of her words a sharp barb to hit them where it hurt; and Hayama with his unremitting cold stare, terrifying them with the unknown.

The kids had been so rambunctious before that this sudden turn in the mood felt particularly harsh. I'm sure they wanted to punch their past selves if they could for their stupidity, for getting carried away and fooling around. They had been having so much fun just a short while ago, and that was precisely what had slammed them down to rock bottom.

Tobe cracked his knuckles dramatically and clenched a fist. "Can I do it, Hayama? Can I let them have it?" At Hayama's name, the girls all looked to him. You could see a faint hope rising in them, that maybe the nicest one of the group might save them and intervene with a kind smile.

But the corner of Hayama's mouth rose in a sarcastic expression, and then came the line we had planned. "How about this? We'll let half of you go. The other half of you will stay here. You decide among yourselves who will stay," he said, and the coldness behind his voice was nearly cruel.

In deafening silence, the kids turned to share a glance. They were silently asking one another, wondering what to do. "...I'm really sorry," one girl said, even meeker than the first and nearly in tears.

But Hayama did not relent. "I don't want an apology. I said that half of you will stay here. Choose now." With every word, the girls' shoulders trembled.

"Hey, didn't you hear him? Or did you hear him and then ignore him?" Miura demanded, leaving the kids panicked.

"Hurry it up. Who're you gonna leave behind?" Tobe threatened, kicking at the ground.

"Tsurumi, you should stay behind...," said one girl.

"...Yeah, you be the one."

"..."

The girls whispered to one another quietly, deciding who to sacrifice. Rumi kept silent, neither acquiescing nor refusing. She'd probably been half expecting this herself. It was reasonable of her to assume she'd be pushed into this role.

I let out an involuntary sigh. So far, everything had progressed according to plan. All that was left was to see if they would play out the rest as I expected.

Beside me, Yukinoshita was doing the same thing. "So this is where we get to your goal, huh?"

"Yeah. We'll tear apart all the relationships around her," I replied at a low whisper.

"...But should we?" Yuigahama murmured softly.

"We should. Messed-up relationships like that are better off completely gone."

"Can you make them go away, though?" she wondered, uneasy.

My reply was uncertain. "Probably. If the girls are real friends like Hayama says, then their friendship will stick, and our plan ends. I doubt it'll be like that, though."

"Indeed," agreed Yukinoshita. "If tearing someone down makes you happy, if that's what gives you peace of mind, then you're only going to befriend like-minded people." She made her calm prediction of the future. No, as if she had already seen it happen.

When the kids shoved Rumi out in front, an expression of disgust briefly crossed Hayama's face, but he quickly hid that under a cold mask. "So you've come up with one. Come on, two more, now. Hurry up."

Another two. Even after picking out one, they still had to choose. Two more to be at fault, two more to shoulder the blame. The witch hunt commenced.

"...If Yuka hadn't said that before..."

"It's her fault."

"Yeah..." Once somebody mentioned a girl's name, other voices chimed in. One girl to send her to the guillotine, one to cut the rope, and one to eagerly await the result.

But still, no one willingly places themselves in a position of weakness. "No!" the girl in question cried. "Hitomi said that stuff first!"

"I didn't say anything! I didn't do anything!" insisted another girl, presumably Hitomi. "Mori was the one with the bad attitude. She's always like that. She's like that to teachers, too."

"What? Me? What I'm like to teachers has nothing to do with this.

You started it, and then it was Yuka," Mori fired back. "Why're you making this my fault?"

Their bickering was escalating, and it almost looked like they might end up grabbing one another by the collars any minute. Even from afar, the scene was so charged, I felt like the energy in the air would burn my throat.

"Let's just stop this and all say sorry…," one girl said. At last their emotions had all developed into a mix of fear and despair, but perhaps not hate, and they began crying. Either that, or they thought tears could get them some sympathy.

But their sobs had no effect on Miura's attitude at all. Quite the opposite: She was openly annoyed, taking the cell phone she'd been fiddling with and snapping it violently shut. Her fury spilled out of her like flames. "There's no one I hate more than girls who think they can solve everything just by crying. What're we gonna do with them, Hayato? They're still saying the same crap."

"…Two more. Hurry up and choose," Hayama repeated mechanically, stifling his sympathy.

Tobe started shadowboxing for emphasis. "C'mon, Hayato, it'd be faster to beat 'em all up."

"I'll give you all just thirty seconds," said Hayama. I guess he figured that things weren't going anywhere at this rate, so he set a time limit.

The time constraint put even more pressure on the girls. "They're not gonna forgive us, no matter how much we apologize," one girl said. "Should we call for the teachers?"

"Oh, you know what'll happen if you tattle. 'Cause we know what you look like," said Tobe, easily nixing that plan.

Now that they were out of options, the girls' talk petered out. Time passed in silence. The only one to speak was Hayama. "Twenty seconds," he said.

There was a brief pause, and then somebody in the group muttered, "…It really was Yuka."

"Let's leave Yuka," another one joined in, a little louder.

The voice that followed was rather calm. "…I think we should, too."

One of the girls—Yuka, no doubt—had a ghastly pale face. Quietly, she looked at the last girl, who hadn't said anything yet.

Under that gaze, the girl looked down and turned her head aside. "...Sorry. There's nothing we can do about it."

When Yuka heard that, her mouth quivered. It looked like she was completely unable to process what was happening.

Beside me, Yuigahama let out a stifled sigh. "There's nothing we can do about it, huh...?"

There really isn't. Nobody can resist the flow of the moment. Even if you understand that environment is causing suffering for someone else, there are some things that just won't work out. You can't fight the pressure to conform; you can't fight social norms. There are times when you are forced to do things you don't want to do. If "everyone" is saying it and "everyone" is doing it, and you don't join in, you won't be allowed to be a part of "everyone."

But there is no "everyone." "Everyone" doesn't say anything or punch anyone. "Everyone" doesn't get angry or laugh. "Everyone" is just an illusion created by the magic of the group, an apparition born before you realize what's going on, a ghost created to hide the malice of the individual. It's the incarnation of a trickster spirit who devours the ostracized and goes on to rain down curses on their "friends." In the past, it's made both of them, him and her, its victims.

That's why I hate it. I despise the world that forces "everyone" on you, that vulgar harmony based on scapegoating, the whole empty idea that paints over kindness and justice and transforms them into a vicious thing that grows more and more thorns with time. It's nothing more than a lie. You can't change the past, and you can't change the world. "Everyone" can't change what's already happened. But that doesn't mean you have to subordinate yourself to it. You can throw away the past; you can break the world and ruin it all.

"Ten, nine..." Hayama's countdown continued.

Rumi's eyes were closed, still and silent. She was tightly squeezing the digital camera hanging from her neck, as if it were a protective talisman. Perhaps in her head, she was praying or doing something like it.

"Eight, seven..."

I could hear the girls crying out in anger and sobbing. It looked as if the black forest were sucking up their hatred to deepen its own darkness. It was just about time. By now, they should have become well enough aware of their own malice and that of the girls around them. Now we just had to give them a cheerful "Gotcha! Sure scared you! ♪" and that would be enough. It was inevitable they'd be furious about it, but I could take the blame. And that was what I was thinking as I began to rise to my feet.

"Wait." Someone was tugging on the back of my shirt, pulling tight at my neck and strangling me.

"Ngkk! ...What?"

When I turned around, I saw that Yuigahama was watching Rumi intently. I picked up on her meaning and sat down again.

"Five, four, three..."

"Um..." Rumi raised her hands, cutting off Hayama.

Hayama's countdown stopped. He, Miura, and Tobe all focused on Rumi as if to ask, *What?*

That was when it happened. An intense flash enveloped the area. There was a continuous mechanical *snap, snap* as a torrent of light overwhelmed the black night and dyed everything white.

"Can you run? This way. Hurry."

As the world flickered before my eyes, I heard Rumi's voice and then the sound of footsteps, like people running by me.

It took me a moment to grasp what had happened. "That light just now... That was a camera flash." I rubbed my eyes as they finally adjusted to the darkness again. I guess Rumi had used the digital camera hanging from her neck. It had been so unexpected, it was as if a stun grenade had hit us. Hayama, Tobe, and Miura were all frozen in place.

"I guess this means she saved them all," said Yukinoshita. Very quietly, she added, "I can't believe it..."

Looking somewhat pleased, Yuigahama said to me, "I guess they really were friends, huh?"

"No way," I replied. "If you can't be friends without tearing someone down, it's not the real thing."

"Oh yeah..." Yuigahama lowered her eyes in mild disappointment.

Even so, I could say one thing. "...But if you know it's fake and still want to reach out...then, that's probably the real thing, I bet."

Yukinoshita nodded grudgingly. "...Yes, perhaps that is true."

"Not like I really know," I added.

"Why do you have to be like that? You're so apathetic...," Yuigahama said wearily.

Can't do anything about that, though. I honestly don't know.

"But you know," said Yuigahama, "I hope it's the real thing." And she smiled.

"'Nobody in this world fits the classic mold of the villain. Normally, everyone is good or at least ordinary. But in the right circumstances, they may change suddenly, and this is what makes them so frightening. One must always be on one's guard.'" The passage that I had memorized suddenly came to mind, so I recited it.

"What're you talking about...? You're freaking me out." Yuigahama eyed me suspiciously. How rude.

But Yukinoshita hummed and gave me a small nod. "Souseki Natsume?"

"Yeah," I replied. "That's what he wrote. But when you think about it, it also means no one fits the classic mold of the saint, either. And under the right circumstances, you might suddenly change into a saint sometimes. Probably."

Yuigahama tilted her head. "Hmm? So what you're saying is that, ultimately, you can't say if it's the real thing?"

"That's what I'm saying. Everyone's got their own perspective, but you can't know. 'The truth is in the grove,' as they say."

"'In a Grove'? That's Ryuunosuke Akutagawa, though...," remarked Yukinoshita. My pointless interposition of our old standby, banter on Japanese literature, only elicited an exasperated sigh from her, and Yuigahama was tilting her head with confusion. *I guess I should have used Souseki for my summary after all...*

While I was busy desperately trying to come up with some witty Souseki reference, Hayama's trio came toward us.

"Nice work there," Hayama called out to me.

"Yeah, you too," I replied. I thanked Tobe and Miura for helping out, too. Without them, it never would have happened in the first place. They were the ones who deserved the credit.

"I'm never doing anything like this again… My eyes still hurt," complained Tobe.

"Hey, are we done now?" asked Miura.

"Can we leave cleanup to you guys? I'm a little tired, too." Hayama sighed deeply. He looked seriously exhausted. Unsurprising—he's usually a pretty good guy, so playing the villain must have been a strain.

"Yeah, we'll manage," I said. "There's not much left to do anyway."

"Thanks." Hayama gave a faint smile and then left with Miura and Tobe in tow to head back to their rooms.

"We're going to go get changed, too," said Yukinoshita.

"Yeah, of course. It's hard to do stuff in these," said Yuigahama.

"Okay," I replied. "See you, then." I split with the two girls and started toward the plaza. I could clearly see the brightly blazing campfire from here.

X X X

The children were singing a song as they circled the towering flames. It was a let's-be-friends-forever sort of song. Personally, it triggered some old trauma for me. Komachi, Totsuka, and Ebina had gone back to get changed, and I was alone, staring vacantly at the fire. When the ditty was over, it was finally time for the ever-so-thrilling and exciting folk dance. Watching it from my outside vantage point, even such a detestable event as this one was somehow beautiful. It was weird.

The members of Rumi's clique were all miserable, though. Well, they had all only just brutally exposed their nastiness to one another, so if you asked me, this was expected. All the girls were ignoring one another, but they occasionally glanced in Rumi's direction. *I think maybe from now on, they'll slowly start including her.*

I didn't have anything in particular to do, so I sought out Miss Hiratsuka. I found her chatting together with the elementary school teachers. When I approached, she noticed me and dropped out of the conversation to come over toward me. "Good work on the haunted forest," she said. "You can go back now. It doesn't look like there's much left to do, and it can probably be done tomorrow anyway. Did you manage to resolve the issue?"

"Oh, that... Well, I dunno." I was unable to give her an answer.

Yukinoshita, apparently done changing, approached us. "All he did was make a group of children cry and form rifts in their relationships."

"I'm sensing some bad faith in that interpretation," I said.

"It's true, though, isn't it?"

"Well, yeah, but..." I couldn't argue with her. Frankly speaking, she was right, and I was stumped.

Miss Hiratsuka tilted her head, unsure of how to react. "I don't really get what happened, but...based on what I'm seeing over there, they don't seem totally isolated from one another. More like just separated...? Well, that's good enough. It's very like you kids." Miss Hiratsuka cracked a smile as she watched the children do the folk dance and then returned to her former position.

Only me and Yukinoshita were left. "Hikigaya..." She said my name as if she were having some difficulty. "For whose sake did you want to resolve this?"

"I did it for Rumi-Rumi, of course," I replied, shrugging. I mean, it wasn't like anyone asked me to do it. I'd just undertaken a single project: to fix Rumi Tsurumi's social situation. I had never intended to do anything at all for anyone else. Maybe certain people were projecting and bringing their own backgrounds into it, but I wasn't going to start developing conjectures about that. I didn't feel like I did anything.

"...I see. Well, that's fine, then." Yukinoshita left it at that, asking no further questions as she turned her eyes toward the campfire in the center of the plaza. The folk dance was just coming to a close, and everyone was getting ready to go back.

The kids walked on down the path, right by us. I found myself looking straight at Rumi. Her eyes caught mine, but she immediately looked away in an utterly automatic reaction. When she passed by me, she didn't glance my way at all.

"No rewards forthcoming, hmm?" Yukinoshita quipped.

"It's not like I did anything actually good. If you just say it like it is, we threatened some kids, destroyed their friendships, and used people to do it… It was the worst way to go about it. And there's no reason she should thank me."

"Indeed so… But things do get easier when there's no longer a whole group to gang up on you. Besides, she reached her conclusion of her own free will. You could call what you did dirty or a mistake, but you're the one who set the stage for her actions." Yukinoshita told it like it was straight out, without hiding a thing. "That's why even if you receive no accolades for it, I think you're allowed to glean at least one good thing from it." Unusually enough, the smile on Yukinoshita's face was not condescending, sharp, or sarcastic. It was gentle.

But it only lasted a moment, and then she whirled around toward Yuigahama approaching us with a bucket and some sparklers. Komachi and Totsuka grabbed Miss Hiratsuka to steal her lighter and immediately set about playing with the fireworks. Miss Hiratsuka looked to be enjoying herself. How nice.

"Yukinon, sorry I took so long!" said Yuigahama. "Here, I've got sparklers."

"I must pass. You two go ahead. I'll watch you from here," Yukinoshita replied.

"What? But I bought all this stuff…"

"I'm too tired to do any more fooling around," Yukinoshita said to pacify her. "Be careful with those." And then she sat down on a bench a little ways away.

"Are you my grandma…?" I muttered.

Yuigahama and I borrowed Miss Hiratsuka's lighter, too, and used it to get a candle going for igniting the sparklers. Apparently, these were part of a bundle that Yuigahama had bought at the convenience store right before the camping trip. She had split half of them with Komachi.

When lit, the sparkler sizzled and shot a jet of green flame. *Whoa, that's pretty cool… I wonder how you're supposed to play with these, though.*

I think it was supposed to be different from the frying-potato-bugs thing. Do you just watch them burn? I can imagine how you might play with bottle rockets, though. They're used for, like, bombing and stuff. I've read that before in *Kooky Trio.*

"Yukinon! Look, look!" Yuigahama held four of the sprays in each hand, wildly swinging her arms around. *Is that supposed to be Vega style or what? This stuff is dangerous, so you probably shouldn't be doing this at home.*

Yuigahama danced around and drew sweeping streaks of light in the air. Since Komachi and Totsuka were flailing around with their fireworks, too, I figured this was what you were supposed to do with them.

But burning them all up in such a dramatic show meant the spray-type sparklers ran out pretty much immediately, and then it was time for the regular sparklers. I surrounded the stick with my body as best I could to protect it from the wind and then lit it. Yuigahama crouched down daintily across from me and gently encircled her sparkler with her body, just as I had, and slowly lit it. The sparklers popped and crackled, emitting a ball of orange light. It was so quiet that it made all that previous flailing around seem odd by comparison.

"...This'll work out for those girls, right?" Yuigahama said.

"I'm not the one who decides that," I replied. "So I can't say anything."

"But now they'll stop with the random ostracizing."

"They lost their friends in exchange, though," I said, and as I did, a fragment of sparkler ash fell to the ground. When the molten-orange light hit the ground, its brilliance rapidly faded away.

"Here," said Yuigahama, handing me another one. "...But, like, don't you think this is a relief for them? It's hard on you, being pressured into all that stuff. This is coming from me, and I'm always letting myself be pressured by everything, so you know it's true."

Source: Gahama, huh? She makes a convincing argument. Maybe I can believe that. I brought the sparkler I'd been fiddling with toward the candle. It sizzled in a faint plume of smoke, and the tip of the stick erupted into a globe-shaped spray.

Yuigahama's sparkler burned out with a poof. As if she'd been

waiting for that moment, she whispered, "Hey, Hikki. We did it all, didn't we?"

"Did what?"

"The stuff we talked about when we ran into each other that time. We didn't have a barbecue, but we made curry. We didn't go to the pool, but we played in the water. And we weren't sleeping in tents or anything, but we did get to stay at a campground. And we were the ones doing the scaring, but we still did a haunted forest."

"You're saying all that stuff counts?" I felt like our experience was substantially different from what she had suggested.

But Yuigahama just tossed her dead sparkler into the bucket and took out another one. "It's close enough! And...we're lighting fireworks together right now."

"I guess."

"All my ideas came true. So...you should make the two of us hanging out together come true, too." Yuigahama stopped there.

It was as if my gaze were magnetically drawn toward her. Our eyes met, and she smiled. Our sparklers crackled and bloomed.

Still, I had only one response. "...Yeah, whatever, sometime."

X X X

We cleaned up the fireworks, and after that, things were the same as the previous night. I took a bath in the indoor bathroom in the manager's building and then proceeded down the path to the bungalow as the night wind blew by. I was the last to bathe that day, so I'd been able to take my time.

When I got back to the bungalow, the lights were already off, and the other guys were probably all asleep. There was a futon spread out in the corner of the room for me—by Totsuka, no doubt—and when I slipped underneath the blanket, I let out a sigh. ...*I want him to be my bride.*

"Hikitani..."

"Hayama? Did I wake you up?"

"No. I just had trouble falling asleep."

No wonder. Who'd have sweet dreams after being dragged into all that stuff? I had just been watching from the shadows, and the guilt did get to me. "Sorry for forcing such a crappy role on you," I apologized.

"It's okay. I don't really feel that bad about it. It just sort of reminded me of the past… A long time ago, I saw something similar, and I didn't do a thing." Hayama spoke with no trace of scorn or pity. He was just reminiscing.

I don't know anything about his or Yukinoshita's pasts, so I had nothing to say to that. All I could do was roll over in place of some non-committal conversational noise.

"If only Yukinoshita had turned out like her sister," he said.

Oh yeah, their families know each other, so he's always known Haruno. But though we were acquainted with her, my opinion on the matter was different from his. "Oh no…," I said. "It's a good thing she didn't turn out like that. Just imagining a friendly Yukinoshita is terrifying."

Hayama laughed. "That's true." It was dark, and I couldn't see, but from the tone of his voice, I could tell he was smiling. Then his voice suddenly dropped low. I could faintly hear him breathing. "…Hey, I wonder how things would have gone if you'd been at my elementary school, Hikitani."

My reply was instantaneous. "Duh. There'd just have been another loner at your school."

"Maybe."

"Definitely," I said, my voice brimming with confidence.

In the darkness, I could hear an indistinct, stifled chuckle. He cleared his throat, pretending it hadn't happened. "I think a lot of things would have ended differently. But still…" He paused as if choosing his words. "I don't think I would have been able to be friends with you, Hikigaya."

……His unexpected remark made my mind go momentarily blank. To think that Hayama, the guy who could get along with anyone, would make such a claim. I paused briefly, then responded in a deliberately reproachful tone. "…That's mean. I'm a little shocked."

"I'm joking. Good night."

"Yeah, night."

Perhaps that was the very first time I recognized who Hayato Hayama really was…and he recognized who Hachiman Hikigaya was. His tone had been kind, but a harsh undercurrent had lurked beneath it. I had a gut feeling that what he had told me was the unvarnished truth.

8

With **Yukino Yukinoshita** aboard, the car drives away.

In the car on the way back, the ride was quiet.

The occupants of the seats behind me had been annihilated. They'd all conked out within thirty minutes of departure, as is common on car trips. Up in the front passenger seat, I felt like I might nod off, too, if I didn't concentrate. But I'd feel bad for Miss Hiratsuka if I fell asleep right then, so I made an effort to stay awake.

The highway was empty. It felt kind of surreal, since it was vacation time for students like us, but for the rest of the world, it was a normal weekday. It wasn't even the Bon festival yet, so there was no reason for the highway going into Chiba city to be busy. I'd just have to put up with another two or three hours, and we'd be there.

"I plan to drop all of you off at the school. Are you okay with that?" asked Miss Hiratsuka. "It's just a little too much work to take each and every one of you around to your homes." It sounded like she was just deciding how we would get home.

"I think that's fine," I replied, and she gave me a nod and a *hmm* in return. She was probably tired, too, so I sensed that it would be best for her if this trip ended as soon as possible.

Still facing forward, Miss Hiratsuka quietly commented, "This time around…you crossed a rather dangerous bridge. If you had made even one wrong step, it could have become a problem." I didn't remember telling her all the details of what had happened, but she'd apparently learned it from someone. She was most likely talking about the Rumi Tsurumi incident.

"Yeah, I'm sorry," I apologized.

"I'm not criticizing you. I'm sure it was unavoidable. In fact, I think you did quite well, considering the time constraints," she said.

"It was a horrible way of going about things, though."

"Yeah, you're awful."

"Why are you evaluating my character here…? I thought we were talking about my methods?"

"Only a horrible person would think of a plan like that. But maybe it's precisely because you're so low that you can approach someone else at rock bottom. That's a valuable talent."

"What a mean way to compliment me…" I drooped.

Miss Hiratsuka, on the other hand, was humming along cheerfully. "Now then, how will we work out the points this time?"

"This is a total victory for Hachiman, right?" I said. This one was all me: planning, design, and production… Though I have serious doubts that what I did was ultimately helpful, it was only appropriate that I be evaluated based on my ambition, interest, and attitude.

"Hmm. But if Yukinoshita had not made the decision to undertake the project in the first place, you probably wouldn't have gone into action. And if Yuigahama hadn't talked everyone into it, you wouldn't have found a reason to act in the first place."

"Ugh. So we're all tied at number one, huh…?" *Man, so close!* I thought.

But then she smirked back at me, and I had an ominous suspicion. "How long have you been under the delusion…that you're all tied at number one?" she said.

"That again?"

"You originally tried to skip out of this. So minus one point for that, and if Yukinoshita and Yuigahama have one point each, you're at zero."

"I had a feeling this would happen…"

"But anyway, good work." Suddenly, her hand reached over from the driver's seat. Her other hand still on the wheel, Miss Hiratsuka patted me on the head.

"It's embarrassing for you to treat me like a kid," I said. "Please stop."

"Don't be shy, come on!" Miss Hiratsuka seemed to relish teasing me. She stubbornly persisted in her head patting.

"Oh, no, I don't mean me. I thought *you* might be embarrassed. Treating a high schooler like a kid really makes you look old and—"

"Hikigaya. You may sleep now." She knife-handed me square in the neck, and my consciousness plunged into a black tunnel.

X X X

Someone was shaking me roughly. "Hikigaya. We're here. Wake up."

"Mm…" When I opened my eyes, before me was a familiar sight. It was my school. The time looked to be sometime past noon. I must have been exhausted; I'd slept like a rock, deeply enough that I didn't remember falling asleep, and now that I was awake, I felt refreshed. "Sorry," I said. "I must have fallen asleep at some point."

"Hmm?" It was Miss Hiratsuka. "……Oh yeah. Don't worry about it. You were probably tired. Come on, out of the van," she prompted, being uncharacteristically kind.

I stepped out of the vehicle with the thick air of high summer clinging to my skin. The atmosphere gets like this around here, close to the sea. It had only been two or three days since we had left, but I had missed it.

After some stretching and yawning out on the street, we unloaded our bags from the van and drowsily prepared to go home. The reflected heat from the asphalt was seething hot. We all checked to make sure we hadn't forgotten anything and then formed a sloppy line, like we felt we should.

Miss Hiratsuka observed us with satisfaction. "Good work, everyone. This trip isn't over until you're at home, so take care on the way back. You're now free to go." She was looking pleased with herself for some reason. She'd probably been planning to end the trip with this classic teacher-student exchange since even before we'd left…

"So, Bro, how are we getting home?" Komachi asked me.

"I guess we'll take the bus to the Keiyo Line," I said. "We'll do some shopping on the way back."

"Aye-aye, sir!" she replied cheerfully with a crisp salute. Then she turned to Yukinoshita. "Since we're taking the Keiyo Line, will you be coming with us, Yukino?"

"Oh, all right… Partway, then." Yukinoshita nodded.

Yuigahama and Totsuka looked at each other. "I guess Sai-chan and me are taking the bus, then," said Yuigahama.

"Yeah, I guess so. See you…," said Totsuka.

We were all saying our good-byes, heading our separate ways home. That was when a jet-black limo pulled up beside us with the smooth, low purr of an engine, slowly slinking past. In the left-hand driver's seat sat a middle-aged man with silver-gray hair peeking out from underneath the hat of his driver's uniform. The rear passenger-seat windows were tinted to obscure the interior.

"What an expensive-looking car…," I commented. There was some kind of flying golden fish ornament on the front, and the hood had been polished to a shine, not a single smear on it. *I feel like I've seen that before…* As I examined the car more closely, the stylish driver stepped out, gave us a sharp bow, and briskly opened the rear door.

A woman emerged from the car, the kind who would make you feel the comfort of a cool autumn day, even at the height of summer. "Hey there, Yukino-chan!" Haruno Yukinoshita was adorned in a bright white sundress as she stepped gracefully from the car.

"It's my sister…" Yukinoshita trailed off.

"Huh? Yukinon? …Your sister?" Yuigahama blinked rapidly, comparing Yukino and Haruno Yukinoshita.

"Wow! You two look a lot alike…," Komachi murmured, and Totsuka nodded vigorously. The pair were on opposite ends of the spectrum, but they closely resembled each other, like Nega and Posi.

"Yuki, you were told to come back home for summer vacation, but you didn't," said Haruno. "I was so worried, I came to pick you up!"

"How did she know where we were…?" I quietly asked Yukinoshita. "Frankly, I'm terrified now…"

"She probably tracked me down through the GPS in my cell phone," replied Yukinoshita. "Good grief. She's always trouble."

Haruno cut in. "Oh, it's you, Hikigaya! Ooh, so you were hanging out together after all. Hmm? You're on a date! You're on a date, aren't you?! I'm so jealous! Oh, to be young!"

"Not this again...," I groaned. "I told you, we're not dating."

She was prodding me with her elbow. This girl was the most obnoxious person ever. I gave her my you're-bothering-me look, but she didn't back down. In fact, she escalated and practically glued her body to mine. She was annoying, and soft, and in the way, and nice smelling, and I frankly wanted her to get lost.

"U-um! Hikki doesn't like that." Yuigahama tugged my arm, pulling me away from Haruno.

The older woman stopped immediately. She surveyed Yuigahama with curiosity, but I also caught a sharp glint in her eyes. She put on a calm smile and then faced Yuigahama. "Hmm, so this is a new character, huh? Are you...Hikigaya's girlfriend?"

"N-no! Nothing like that!" Yuigahama stuttered.

"Oh, that's good," Haruno replied. "I was just thinking, whatever would I do if you were in Yukino-chan's way? I'm Haruno Yukinoshita, her sister."

"Oh, nice to meet you... I'm Yui Yuigahama. Yukinon and me are friends."

"Friends, huh...?" Haruno was grinning broadly, but her tone was ice-cold. "So Yukino-chan has a proper friend, huh? How nice. That's a relief." Her words were soft, and her tone was soft, but the atmosphere enshrouding her suggested if you were to touch her, thorns would burst out from underneath. "Oh, but you're not allowed to touch Hikigaya. That belongs to Yuki."

"No he doesn't."

"Seriously, no."

Yukinoshita and I responded practically in unison.

"Look! You're perfectly in sync!" Haruno chirped with pleased laughter. Was this teasing for fun, or was it just part of her act?

"That's enough, Haruno." This time, it was Miss Hiratsuka who spoke.

Haruno's laugh immediately broke off. "It's been a long time, Shizuka-chan."

"Don't call me that." Miss Hiratsuka jerked her head away. I guess that embarrassed her.

I was surprised the two of them were acquainted, though. "You know her, Miss Hiratsuka?" I asked.

"She's a former student."

"Does that mean—?" I attempted to probe for the real meaning behind Miss Hiratsuka's all-too-brief answer, but Haruno cut me off.

"Well, we can do some catching up another time, right? All right, Yukino-chan. Let's get going."

But Yukinoshita showed no indication of moving. She was practically ignoring her sister.

"Come on. Our mother is waiting," Haruno said.

Yukinoshita had maintained her arrogant attitude up until that point, but at that word, she twitched. She showed the slightest hesitation. Then she breathed a resigned sigh and turned to me and Komachi. "Komachi. I appreciate your invitation, but I must offer my apologies. I will not be able to go with you." The way Yukinoshita spoke was stiff, formal, and somehow distant.

Komachi's reply was bewildered. "Um, o-okay… Well, if your family is waiting, then…"

Yukinoshita gave a clear smile and then, in a voice so soft it seemed to become entirely inaudible, she whispered, "…Good-bye." Haruno prodded her back, and she disappeared into the car.

"See you, Hikigaya. Bye-bye!" Haruno gave me a flighty wave, climbed into the car, and said to the driver, "Tsuzuki, let's go."

The driver bowed and quietly closed the door. Without a glance our way, he slid into the driver's seat. I guess that initial bow had not been directed at us but at Yukinoshita.

I couldn't see what was inside the car beyond the tinted windows. But I got the feeling that Yukinoshita was sitting ramrod straight, as usual, facing front, with only her eyes turned toward the window to the side.

The limo started its quiet engine, and the car smoothly drove out. It departed in a long, straight line and then disappeared around a corner.

I watched it go, stunned. Yuigahama gave my sleeve a gentle tug. "Hey…that car…"

"Well, those chauffeured rental limos all look about the same. And I was in a lot of pain, of course, so I don't remember everything about that car," I said, but I wasn't being sincere.

The truth was, the moment I saw that limo, I knew.

I did not see Yukino Yukinoshita again that summer.

Reference:
Natsume, Souseki. *Kokoro.*

Afterword

Hello. This is Wataru Watari.

As I write a story set in the middle of summer during the middle of winter, I feel quite acutely that this was why I became a light-novel writer. So anyway, how are you all doing this season? I'm doing well.

And so, the story finally breaks into summer. When you think summer, you think of the season that youth shines brightest. Summer wear, swimwear, sheer bras! Just after I wrote that, I realized that, oh yeah, my mom is reading this book, too… So anyway, summer. It's so important for high school romantic comedies, you'll end up waiting in the summer.

I've always been more miserable in this season than any other time—I really hate it—it was a painful, miserable chapter of my life. I always just wanted to be a representative for the JSDF (Japan Secluded Defense Forces), if I could, staying at home to make sure my house is safe. It wouldn't even be weird to call me a soldier of ancient Japan, protecting my assigned area. I'd love it if they would include a *Jitaku no Moribito: Guardian of the House* in the Moribito series. That's how much I hate summer.

I mean, Marine Day? That's just discriminatory. Some people *don't* go to the ocean in summer. I think they should take that into consideration and make a "House Day" and make *that* a national holiday. Actually, I really just want more days off. People talk about "summer vacation" or whatever, but adults don't get one. Once you get a full-time job, summer vacation is just, like, three days. Are you kidding me? That's just the Bon holiday! And I got so excited about it, too! "Vacation time!" I said. "I can have so much time off! Yay, summer break! Wataru loves this vacation!" I deserve an apology here.

So anyway, this has been Volume 4 of *My Youth Romantic Comedy Is Wrong, as I Expected*. Please look forward to more of Hachiman Hikigaya's summer vacation in the next book. Below are my acknowledgments. In English, you say *special thanks*, and in German, uh…*danke schoen*?

Holy Ponkan⑧: I only wrote this book because I wanted to see you draw swimsuits for it. Thank you for the illustration book, too. Thank you so much. The swimsuits are the best!!

Mr. Hoshino, my editor: we would be just chatting casually about making a drama CD or a limited-edition illustration book, and then you made that stuff happen in reality. I was blown away. Are you Shenlong or what? Thank you so much.

Mr. Kenji Inoue: Thank you for your comments on the ad wrap, despite the fact that we've never met. Exhausted as I am by deadline after deadline, your words have been very encouraging to me.

All my writer friends: Thank you very much for getting together while I was busy drinking and making up an alibi for me as my deadlines were looming.

And to all my readers: I feel like I can keep going thanks to your support. There have been rough times, but I do love this job. Thank you, honestly, so much. I hope you will continue to stick with me.

All right, I think that's about enough. I will set my pen down here.

On a certain day in February, in a certain place in Chiba, while drinking warm MAX Coffee,

Wataru Watari

Translation Notes

On Souseki Natsume's *Kokoro*

P. 2 **Souseki Natsume** (1867–1916) was one of the most prominent Japanese novelists of the modern era, the most famous of his books being *Kokoro* (meaning heart, mind, or spirit). It explores the relationship between the anonymous narrator and his older friend, a man known only as "Sensei" (teacher). While the book does explore themes of isolation, Hikigaya's interpretation of the book is particularly misanthropically simplistic. That said, the book is pretty heavy reading for a kid in eighth grade.

P. 3 The **Meiji period** was from 1868 to 1912, and it encompassed a time of revolution. Japan went from being under the rule of the shogunate, the military government, to the rule of the emperor. It was a time of fast-paced modernization and militarization. *Kokoro* was published in 1914, and one of the major themes was the arrival of modernity.

Chapter 1 ··· This is how **Hachiman Hikigaya** spends his summer vacation.

P. 5 **"...Friend/Zero."** Reference to *Fate/Zero*, the light novel by Gen Urobuchi that was a sequel to his visual novel *Fate/stay night*. There is also a manga and anime adaptation.

P. 8 “***Crush devils!***” Hachiman is referencing a particular ad for the video game *Idolmaster 2*, a game centered on managing your pop idol group. It features the well-known voice actor Shigeru Chiba. He looks at the default name for the group Namco Angels, decides he doesn’t like the name, and declares he’ll call them Crush Devils.

P. 9 **“…I had no idea why she was suddenly writing her draft on that grid paper.”** This is referring to the kind of paper pictured on pages 2–3. Hachiman wasn’t using it correctly—the purpose of the paper is to keep your characters a uniform size, writing one character per box. In Japanese schools, all essays are handwritten on this sort of paper.

P. 9 **“…they got a famous manga artist to draw the cover for the special edition.”** Shueisha printed an edition of *Kokoro* with cover art by Takeshi Obata, the artist behind *Death Note*, *Bakuman*, and *Hikaru no Go*.

P. 9 **“And what the hell is with calling year-end parties ‘forgetting-it-all parties’ anyway?”** In Japanese, the term for “year-end party” is *bounenkai*, meaning “forgetting-it-all party.” They’re ubiquitous in business settings and usually involve heavy drinking.

P. 10 ***Mu*** is a monthly magazine focusing on occult subjects, like UFO cover-ups, astrology, and ESP.

P. 10 **“As proof, Hokkaido has an extremely short summer vacation and longer winter vacation…”** Hokkaido is the northernmost island of the four main islands of Japan. Summers are cooler than Honshu.

P. 11 **“No, don’t call me a *hikki* for that. Well, I guess you could.”** In the Japanese, Hachiman uses the word *hikki*, a shortened version of the word *hikikomori*, or a total shut-in who never leaves the house. This is also why Hachiman hates Yui’s nickname for him.

P. 11 The **Summer Sonic** Music Festival is a two- to three-day music festival held simultaneously in Chiba and Osaka, with both Japanese and international guests, including big-name performers.

P. 12 **"Shall I tell you what's lacking? ...You're far too slow!"** This is a monologue from Straight Cougar, an Alter user from the *shonen* anime *S-CRY-ed* whose power is superspeed.

P. 12 ***Beauty Looking Back*** is the name of a famous ukiyo-e print by the artist Moronobu Hishikawa (1618–1694) of a woman turning to look over her shoulder. It has come to be used more generally to refer to this particular pose in art and photography.

P. 15 The **Potsdam Declaration** was issued in 1945 by Allied nations as a call for Japan's unconditional surrender. Prime Minister Kantarou Suzuki's response was to treat the declaration with silent contempt.

P. 16 **Ryotaro Shiba** is a prolific and wildly popular writer of historical fiction and nonfiction, his most famous work in the West being *The Last Shogun*.

P. 16 **"...I'd recommend the Delfinian War, the Twelve Kingdoms, or the Moribito series."** Record of the Delfinian War is an eighteen-volume series of fantasy novels by the prolific author Sunako Kayata. The plot is standard fare involving taking back the throne to a kingdom and a visitor from another world turned hero. The Twelve Kingdoms series by Fuyumi Ono is another fantasy series that involves visitors from another world entering a fantasy world based on ancient China. These novels are available in English, as is the forty-five-episode anime adaptation. The Moribito series by Nahoko Uehashi has a twenty-six-episode anime adaptation and stars a warrior named Balsa who, in her journey, happens to save a prince's life and so becomes his bodyguard.

P. 17 Orestes Cucuas **Destrade** is a former pro baseball player.

P. 20 **"Do you know about thermal expansion?"** Hikigaya is referencing an Internet meme that originated from a line in Volume 17 of *A Certain Magical Index*. There is a scene where a character drops a gun into a cup of hot tea, claiming that thermal expansion will now cause the gun to stop functioning. The Internet reacted to this with incredulity and mockery.

P. 20 **Saburo** Ohmura is a pro baseball player with the Chiba Lotte Marines.

P. 20 **Chiiba-kun** is the mascot of Chiba prefecture. He's a red dog with a very pointy nose. His design was based on the shape of Chiba prefecture, giving his nose that distinctive pointed shape.

P. 22 **"There's Ojaga Pond…that old abandoned telecommunication place."** Ojaga Pond is a reservoir in Togane. There is a legend that a woman killed herself there by jumping over the falls and still continues to haunt the place. The statue of Kannon at Tokyo Bay is so tall, it was also a popular spot to commit suicide until they built barriers to prevent people from doing so. There is also an extremely creepy tunnel that leads up to it. The university Hachiman refers to is Chiba University, and there was in fact an execution ground there in the Edo period. The old telecommunications place he's referring to is the Kamigawa Radio Station, which was used by the Japan public telephone corporation to conduct secret military tests in World War II. It's a very creepy-looking, old concrete building.

Chapter 2 … No matter what you do, you can't escape **Shizuka Hiratsuka**.

P. 25 ***Pet Encyclopedia*** is a short, five-minute show that does highlights on real peoples' pets.

P. 25 ***Summer Vacation Kids' Anime Festa*** is a summer programming slot for children's anime like *Doraemon* that would normally air on weekend mornings and such. During the summer, it will run on weekdays.

P. 25 **"No, not an angel sanctuary."** Hachiman is referencing the gothic angels-and-demons manga *Angel Sanctuary* by Kaori Yuki.

P. 25 **"Yes, I am free... I am...*we* are Gundam."** This is a reference to Freedom Gundam, a mecha from the anime *Mobile Suit Gundam SEED*. The phrase "I am Gundam" is the catchphrase of Setsuna F. Seiei, a Gundam pilot in *Mobile Suit Gundam 00*. He says it so often and in such seriousness, it's a popular target for parody among fans.

P. 28 **"...the category error of the light-novel world is Gagaga Bunko."** Gagaga is the imprint that publishes the original Japanese editions of this series. It's also known for publishing material that doesn't really "count" as a light novel, despite its being a light-novel label. The designation of "light novel" is fairly arbitrary in the first place, but generally speaking, they are dialogue heavy, character driven, light on prose, and otaku oriented.

P. 28 **"...the end was that it was never-ending. It's Golden Experience Requiem."** Golden Experience Requiem is a Stand power in *JoJo's Bizarre Adventure* by Hirohiko Araki. This Stand's power is to "turn anything to zero." When killed by this Stand, it will result in an infinite death loop, and thus, "the end that is never-ending."

P. 29 **"*I should have had about eighty thousand points, though. 'Cause I'm Hachiman.*"** This is a pun. *Hachiman* can mean "eighty thousand" in Japanese.

P. 30 **"Oh, it wasn't Shelley—it was Vermouth, wasn't it?"** Hachiman and Komachi are talking about the kids' detective manga *Detective Conan* (or *Case Closed*) by Gosho Aoyama. Shelley is a character who formerly worked for the antagonist, the Black Organization, and Vermouth is their agent, so you could conceivably get their character types mixed up.

P. 31 **"Oh...my cell reception is unstable... I do like reading those books, though!"** SoftBank is a major Japanese conglomerate that is most well-known for their cell phone network. They are known for being the cheapest of the big three cell networks (the other two being Docomo and au), and also the least reliable. Their CEO and founder, Masayoshi Son, is of Korean ethnicity, the second richest man in Japan as of 2015, and a known philanthropist. He's also going bald. The name Masayoshi (a common Japanese name for a boy) is written with the characters for "justice." SoftBank is also involved in various publishing ventures, including digital publishing. Its publishing subsidiary is SB Creative Corp., which in turn owns GA Publishing, a light-novel label.

P. 31 **"Sorta like Kitaro's antenna."** Kitaro is the protagonist of the classic 1960s manga *GeGeGe no Kitaro* by Shigeru Mizuki. The story revolves around spirit monsters from folklore. One of Kitaro's special powers is his antenna, which can detect spirit activity.

P. 32 **"...I don't need love, summer."** *Ai Nante Irane Yo, Natsu* (literally "I don't need love, summer") is the name of a 2002 romance TV drama.

P. 35 **"In English, you would say his *smile* could *cure* me with *pretty*."** Hachiman is referencing *Smile Pretty Cure!* the ninth installment of the magical girl anime franchise Pretty Cure.

P. 36 **Comiket** is the massive biannual fan comic market hosted at the Tokyo Big Sight.

P. 36 The **Sword of Promised Victory** is the name of Saber's sword in the visual novel *Fate/stay night*.

P. 37 **"How long have you been under the delusion...that we were headed to Chiba Station?"** This is playing with a dramatic line from Aizen in Volume 45 of the manga *Bleach* by Tite Kubo. The original line goes, "How long have you been under the delusion that I *haven't* been using Kyouka Suigetsu?"

P. 37 **"You thought our destination was Chiba Station? Too bad! It's Chiba Village!"** This is a twist on a Japanese Internet meme not unlike Rickrolling. Someone creates a tempting link that appears to be one thing, but when clicked, it leads to an image of Sayaka, a character from the anime *Magical Girl Madoka Magica*, with the text "Too bad! It's Sayaka-chan!"

P. 38 **"The daily grind marches on, aside from during the Bon festival."** The Bon festival is an annual commemoration of the dead. It's generally regarded by most Japanese people as one of the major holidays, and workers often take time off to go home and spend the time with family.

Chapter 3 ··· **Hayato Hayama** is socially adept with everyone.

P. 42 **"Your memory is on par with an MO disk."** MO is short for "magneto-optical disk." It was a form of media storage somewhat like the MiniDisc, and it never really took off outside Japan. It was most often used in corporate settings rather than in home computers. Visually, it looks like a floppy disk but has higher memory capacity.

P. 43 **"I know about MDs, but…"** The MiniDisc (MD) was a competitor to the cassette tape that, like MO, did not really take off outside Japan, though it was not quite as obscure as MO. Eventually, it was crushed by compact discs.

P. 45 **"…the type of people you'd see biting into midsummer fruit."** This references the title of a sappy love song about young summer love by the Southern All Stars (an old rock group that formed in the 1970s) called "Manatsu no Kajitsu" (Midsummer fruit).

P. 45 **"They were the kind who would have a barbecue or something on the sandbar of a river…"** Hachiman is referring to a well-publicized incident in 1999 when a group of people had a picnic on the sandbar of the Kurokura River. The water came rushing in, and they had to be rescued.

P. 45 **"Ebina, the intense *fujoshi*"** ***Fujoshi*** literally means "rotten woman" and refers to women who enjoy BL manga and fantasizing about sexual or romantic relationships between men. The Japanese counterpart of the slash fangirl.

P. 50 **"It's like the call-and-response at school graduation ceremonies."** At school graduation ceremonies, the whole class recites a sort of call-and-response chant together. One student will lead the chant, beginning with phrases such as "The field trip!" and the entire class responds in unison, "Left us with so many memories." Often, these lines are exactly the same across schools.

P. 51 **"Man, elementary schoolers are the best! ...Being one, I mean."** This is a quote from Subaru, the protagonist of the loli light-novel series called *Ro-Kyu-Bu!* by Sagu Aoyama. Subaru is a teenage lolicon and coach for a sixth-grade all-girls basketball team.

P. 52 **"You sound like 'A Night at Fifteen'..."** "Juugo no Yoru" (A night at fifteen) was Yutaka Ozaki's debut single in 1983. The lyrics are about teenage malaise and rebellion against the stifling, strict, and unfair nature of school and society. It was based on Ozaki's experiences as a teen.

P. 56 **"Just as Stand users are drawn to one another..."** In Hirohiko Araki's long-running manga *JoJo's Bizarre Adventure*, a "Stand" is a kind of superpower, and Stand users are drawn to each other by fate. This is the central conceit of the series, as the members of the Joestar family and their allies are drawn to the villain, Dio Brando, as they all share these powers.

P. 62 **Yamanashi** prefecture is located in central Japan near Tokyo. *Yamanashi* also means "wild pear."

P. 63 **"Well, Tottori and Shimane do kinda feel the same..."** Tottori and Shimane are neighbouring prefectures in southern Honshu. They are the least populous and second-least populous prefectures in Japan, respectively.

Chapter 4 ··· Out of nowhere, **Hina Ebina** begins proselytizing.

P. 70 ***"'It's nothing, it's nothing.' Are you the opening song of* Azuki-chan*?"*** *Azuki-chan* is a *shoujo* manga by Yasushi Akimoto and Chika Kimura that ran from 1993 to 1997. The story focuses on the normal everyday life and relationships of an elementary school girl. In the opening song of the anime adaptation, the first line of the chorus is "*Nandemonai, nandemonai*" (It's nothing, it's nothing).

P. 72 **"'What the heck is a book boy…?' It's true that I do like books, but it's not like I eat them or anything."** Hachiman is referencing the Book Girl light-novel series by Mizuki Nomura. The protagonist is a spirit who eats stories by consuming the paper they are printed on.

P. 73 **"You can do, like, konjak noodles and daikon and stuff… I'm like, is this hot pot or what?"** *Shirataki* are clear noodles made from konjak. They're typically tied up into tiny little bundles in soup. They don't get mushy, no matter how long you boil them. *Shirataki,* daikon (a sort of turnip), fried tofu, and *chikuwa* (a tube made of fish paste) are all typical ingredients for hot pot. You don't normally see them in Japanese curry.

P. 74 **Pixiv** is a popular site for users to upload their art to share and display. It's like the Japanese equivalent of DeviantArt.

P. 74 **"Hikki knows all about that. I know that bay leaves come from bay laurels."** This is in reference to an Internet meme. The original is "Moppii knows all about that. Moppii knows everyone loves her." Created by 2ch, Moppii is a cute blob character, a "witch who watches over threads regarding sales of anime products." She was originally based on the character Houki Shinonono from the Infinite Stratos series, but she took on a life of her own as a meme.

P. 74 **"Laurier…doesn't mean pads…"** Laurier is a well-known brand of menstrual pads in Japan.

P. 74 **"They've evolved. Warp digivolved."** In the Digimon franchise, the term *warp digivolve* is used to describe a digimon skipping a stage in monster evolution, going straight from rookie to ultimate level.

P. 77 **"What a Cinderella story. A Super Dimensional Cinderella."** Super Dimensional Cinderella is the pop star Ranka Lee's nickname in the *Macross F* anime.

P. 77 **"...you could even call it a Reality Marble."** Reality Marble (literally "innate bounded field") is a concept particular to Type-Moon's Fate series. It involves an individual turning himself or herself into an entire world or reality.

P. 78 **"Her nickname from now on is Rumi-Rumi. Is this *Nadesico*?"** In the 1996–1997 anime *Martian Successor Nadesico*, Ruri Hoshino is an aloof and arrogant twelve-year-old girl whose catchphrase is "bunch of fools." Her nickname is Ruri-Ruri.

P. 81 **"Why is it that the more you say *absolutely do not tell anyone*, the more they spread it around? It's like, are you Ostrich Club?"** This is a popular gag in Japanese comedy. It originated in a segment of the variety comedy show *Super Jockey* (1983–1999) that involves people climbing into a tank of extremely hot water. Ryuuhei Uejima of the comedy team Ostrich Club begins by climbing over the tank, grasping the sides with his hands and feet, saying "Don't push me...don't push me...absolutely do not push me!" This scene was in fact staged, of course, and "don't push me" was code for "I'm still getting ready, don't push me yet," while "absolutely do not push me" was the signal to push him in. The reveal of that fact lead to the phrase "Absolutely do not _____" actually meaning "Please do _____" in comedy shows and on the Internet.

P. 85 Nestlé **Milo** is a chocolate-and-malt powder that's something like hot chocolate mix or Ovaltine. It's popular in Asia and Australia but not typically sold in the United States aside from Asian grocery stores.

P. 93 **"There's no such thing as a girl who hates *yaoi*!"** This is a quote from Kanako Ohno, a character from the manga *Genshiken* by Shimoku Kio. *Genshiken* is about a college otaku club.

P. 95 **"It's a *geas*, an evil law."** The term *geas* originates in Irish folklore, meaning a sort of vow or spell that certain individuals are compelled to follow. The term was spelled as *geass* in the anime series *Code Geass*, which began its original run in 2006. In the series, a geass is a special power the main character is endowed with that enables him to give orders through magic force that others are compelled to obey.

P. 96 **"*You've got guts, kid! You're a little firefighter.*"** This is a quote from the manga *Firefighter! Daigo of Company M* by Masahito Soda. As a child, the protagonist runs back into a burning building to save a dog, and the firefighter who rescues him says that line to him, inspiring him to become a firefighter.

P. 96 **"Is this Medoroa? This is so bad, even the Great Demon Lord Vearn would be in trouble."** In *Dragon Quest: The Adventure of Dai*, a manga spin-off of the Dragon Quest video game series, Medoroa is a combination of the two most powerful fire and ice spells. Vearn is the main villain of the series.

P. 98 The **Three Kingdoms era** (220–280) is an era of Chinese history that is particularly popular in historical fiction, likely owing to the Chinese literary classic *Romance of the Three Kingdoms*. The **shogunate era** is a broad term covering the Kamakura, Muromachi, and Edo eras of Japanese history, from 1192 up until the Meiji revolution of the nineteenth century. Basically, it means the era of the samurai class system and the military government. Both of these eras are popular settings for historically based BL.

P. 98 **Ikebukuro** is a commercial district in Tokyo. It's also the site of "Otome Road," or more bluntly, "Fujoshi Street," a small cluster of otaku merchandise, *doujinshi*, and manga shops, with even a butler café or two, that bends toward feminine tastes, in contrast with Akihabara, which is more stereotypically associated with male interests.

Chapter 5 ··· All alone, **Yukino Yukinoshita** gazes up at the night sky.

P. 99 The **Gáe Bulg** is a mythical spear in Irish mythology, but Hachiman is most likely familiar with it as a recurring weapon in the Final Fantasy series or the Lancer's weapon in *Fate/stay night*, localized as Gae Bolg.

P. 100 **"Hawawa! Master, the enemy is here! >.< "** This is a quote from Shokatsuryou Koumei in the erotic visual novel *Koihime Musou*. The story is loosely based on *Romance of the Three Kingdoms*, except the entire cast is moe girls. She has a habit of saying "*Hawawa!*" earning her the name of the "Hawawa strategist."

P. 100 **"And time resumes."** In Hirohiko Araki's *JoJo's Bizarre Adventure*, the villain, Dio Brando, has the power to briefly stop time. His iconic line when he activates his powers is "THE WORLD! Time, stop!" and when his ability is at its limit, he says, "And time resumes."

P. 100 **"I got my underwear snugly Pilder-On..."** This refers to an Internet meme that originated from the classic 1970s mecha anime *Mazinger Z*. A Pilder is a vehicle that serves as the command center for a giant robot. "Pilder On" is what they say when it docks into the main unit. The Internet applies this to various scenarios, like a cute animal landing on the head of a character and presumably "taking control" of the "main unit."

P. 103 ***I Don't Like You at All, Big Brother!*** is the title of a faux-incest (not related by blood) manga by Kouichi Kusano. Of course, the character who is saying that *is* in love with her big brother.

P. 103 **"A combination worthy of despair, like a Potara-fused Goku and Vegeta."** In the *Dragon Ball* series by Akira Toriyama, the Potara earrings are one means of fusing two people together in order to create a being who combines both their powers. Vegito is the combination of Goku and Vegeta into one ultrapowerful entity, via said earrings.

P. 105 ***Grander Musashi*** is a kids' fishing manga by Takashi Teshirogi that ran from 1996 to 2000. The titular character, Musashi Kazama, travels the world with his friends looking for legendary fishing lures, or "legenders," that have the power to attract more fish.

P. 108 **"Oh, so she wasn't doing the *At the Mercy of the Sky* thing? So was this the *Heaven's Lost Property* thing, then?"** *Sora no Manimani* (At the mercy of the sky) is a manga by Mami Kashiwabara. Running from 2005 to 2011, it was a drama about a high school astronomy club, with a twelve-episode anime adaptation. *Sora no Otoshimono* (Heaven's lost property) is a manga (2007–2014) by Suu Minazuki about an "Angeloid" fallen from heaven, with an associated anime, game, and light novel.

P. 109 **"Never mind a *Date* with defeat, she's a *Nobunaga* with defeat."** Date Masamune was a Sengoku-era (1467–1603) daimyo, famed as an outstanding tactician. Oda Nobunaga was the general famed for uniting Japan and ending the era. He was also known as a brutal and merciless man who even called *himself* the "Lord of Six Hells."

P. 109 **"Like some kind of legendary end-of-century leader."** This is a reference to the comedy manga *Seikimatsu Leader Den Takeshi* (End of century leader-legend Takeshi) by Mitsutoshi Shimabukuro. The main character is a "born leader"—born with a beard, his first word was *leader*.

P. 109 **"He was probably raised on classic manga from *Shonen Jump* magazine."** *Weekly Shounen Jump* is the most popular manga serialization mangazine in Japan, serializing many of the popular adventure, action, and sports titles, like *Naruto*, *Bleach*, *One Piece*, *Slam Dunk*, *Death Note*, *Gintama*, and the older arcs of *JoJo's Bizarre Adventure*. Aside from certain odd outliers, most of the titles have themes revolving around the "Jump triangle" of friendship, competition, and hard work. They're generally about good, old-fashioned heroes saving the world and achieving their dreams.

P. 111 ***"I want to know defeat."*** "I want to know defeat. What is defeat?" was a line often said by the professional competitive 2D fighting gamer Daigo Umehara and then popularized to a meme level by 2ch. He may have originally gotten the line from Keisuke Itagaki's martial arts manga *Grappler Baki*, but it's not certain.

P. 114 A ***yamato nadeshiko*** is the traditional ideal woman.

Chapter 6 ··· Unfortunately, **Hachiman Hikigaya** did not bring a swimsuit.

P. 117 ***Horizon in the Middle of Nowhere*** is a light-novel series by Minoru Kawakami. It's a science fiction story that really has nothing to do with the sort of lines that Hachiman is talking about crossing.

P. 121 **"I wasn't doing any alchemy or anything; it's just the polite thing to do before a meal."** In Hiromu Arakawa's manga *Fullmetal Alchemist*, certain individuals, including the protagonist, perform alchemy by creating a circle with their arms, putting their two palms together.

P. 122 **"The overflowing helping she handed me was like something out of *Manga Japanese Folk Tales*."** *Manga Nihon Mukashibanashi* (Manga Japanese folk tales) is a series of animated shorts from the 1970s featuring classic fairy tales like "Momotaro." The part Hachiman refers to is a scene where a man eats from a bowl of rice piled abnormally high. This is such a popular scene that a "folktale serving" has become shorthand to mean a "giant serving of rice."

P. 122 **"Ohhh! Are they gonna make a circle and hold hands and go 'Bentora bentora'?"** The "dance" that Komachi is talking about originates from a 1964 interview with the American UFO "expert" George Van Tassel, who claimed to be telepathically communicating with aliens. He describes communicating with aliens by speaking their language. *Bentora* is supposed to be an alien word meaning "spaceship." The popular idea is that four or five people should get together, join hands in a circle, and chant "Bentora bentora" to summon aliens. While this interview faded into obscurity in the West, it gained a foothold in Japanese pop culture, and though George Van Tassel himself is largely forgotten, the idea that "Bentora bentora" summons aliens persists among occult fanatics.

P. 122 **"Did you mean to say 'Oklahoma Mixer'?"** The Oklahoma Mixer is in fact a real folk dance from Oklahoma, but you'd be hard-pressed to find an Oklahoman who has actually heard of it. It's extremely well-known in Japan, though, as a "classic American folk dance" that's taught to elementary school children, a practice that most likely originated during the occupation. It involves couples joining hands and dancing in a circle.

P. 126 ***"'Wasseroi!' ...Come on, that's never happened to me in a bathroom stall..."*** This is a reference to the gag manga *Pyu to Fuku! Jaguar* (Make it toot, Jaguar) by Kyosuke Usata. There's a scene where the protagonist cries "Wasseroi" while watching a toilet flush, calling it a "toilet festival." *Wasseroi* is an essentially meaningless cry like "yay!" that's typically associated with celebrations or festivals.

P. 126 ***Splash Star*** is a spin-off in the Pretty Cure magical girl anime franchise.

P. 127 **"Yukino Yukinoshita was, as her name suggested, the embodiment of snow."** *Yukino Yukinoshita* means "saxifrage flower of the snow." A saxifrage flower, in Japanese, is written with the characters meaning "under the snow."

P. 128 **"I'll splatter your guts!"** This is Tokiko Tsumura's catchphrase in the *shonen* battle manga *Busou Renkin* (Arms Alchemy) by Nobuhiro Watsuki.

P. 132 **B-Daman** are a line of toys by Takara. They're little plastic humanoid robots that shoot marbles—as one would expect, since *biidama* means "marble." They're meant to be used in competitive games.

P. 132 **"*That's not a marble! That's an ant!*"** This is playing with a line from the film *Grave of the Fireflies*, in which Seita tells his little sister, Setsuko, "That's not a candy drop! That's a marble!" This is a particularly dramatic scene, right before Setsuko's death of starvation, but the Internet picked it up and turned it into a rather dark meme, since *hajiki* means both "flat marble" and "pistol," leading to the obvious joke of "Setsuko, that's not a candy drop! That's a gun!" The meme spun on from there, leading to jokes in the pattern of "That's not an ____, it's an ____," made all the more iconic by Seita's particular regional accent.

P. 133 **Continuous Energy Bullets** are a form of ki attack in the *Dragon Ball* series by Akira Toriyama.

P. 133 **"...when I woke up, the classroom would be empty, and I'd think I was in a closed space or something."** In the Haruhi Suzumiya light-novel series, "closed space" is an alternate dimension that overlaps reality; it is characterized by gray skies and isolation.

P. 136 **"*Come on, are you the computer grandma or what?*"** "Computer Grandma" is an NHK children's song from the 1980s. It's basically a song about how Computer Grandma can do anything and everything. It's part of a TV program called *Minna no Uta* (Our songs), in which they play children's songs with short animated videos repeatedly in between children's shows. Generally, the same songs will continue for months, so they're highly memorable.

P. 139 **"A: You become the god of the new world."** This is a rather infamous quote from Light Yagami of the manga *Death Note* by Tsugumi Ohba and Takeshi Obata. Light's idea of changing the world involves killing a lot of people.

Chapter 7 ··· In the end, **Rumi Tsurumi** chooses her own path.

P. 147 **"There's nothing supernatural about the world we live in."** This is a quote from Akihiko Chuuzenji the protagonist of the popular Kyogokudo series of mystery novels by Natsuhiko Kyogoku. Chuuzenji solves mysteries with seemingly supernatural elements, but he does not believe in the supernatural himself, judging the root of each incident to be purely psychological.

P. 147 **Storyteller Tamori** is a Japanese television icon who has been around for decades, known for his trademark sunglasses. One of his many television roles was as host of a series called *Yo ni mo Kimyou na Monogatari* (*Tales of the Unusual*), which consisted largely of creepy paranormal stories somewhat in the vein of *The Twilight Zone.*

P. 148 **"He had a *dansu* with *baddo rakku*..."** This is an iconic quote from Haruki Wanibuchi, a character from the 1990s delinquent / street racer manga *Kaze Densetsu: Bukkomi no Taku* (Wind legend: Taku of the biker gang) by Hiroto Saki and Juuzou Tokoro. In this chapter, Wanibuchi, a gang leader, drifts to evade some pursuers, who end up crashing into a truck. He comments that his pursuers "had a *dance* with *bad luck*," emphasizing that he didn't engage in any violence himself, and it was all an accident.

P. 149 **"...*Tell us a story, one we don't know!* Trembling, trembling..."** This is a line from the song "Grow Up," the opening theme song of the 2000–2001 anime *Gakkou no Kaidan* (literally "school ghost stories"), localized in English under the title *Ghost Stories*. The English version is infamous for having a completely rewritten comedic script, but the original Japanese show was standard fare.

P. 152 **"He was clearly a witch girl, though. *Sharanran.*"** *Majokko Megu-chan* (Little Meg the witch girl) was an early magical-girl anime from the 1970s, and it was highly influential on later titles like *Sailor Moon*. The opening theme song begins with the nonsense line "*sharanran*."

P. 153 **"Source: the Nobel Gundam in *G-Gundam*."** The Nobel Gundam in *G-Gundam* is the only Gundam in the Gundam Fight to be piloted by a woman and, as such, is heavily decorated in tertiary sexual characteristics, with a design that makes the giant robot look as if it is wearing high heels and a schoolgirl uniform and has long blonde hair.

P. 153 **"*Enough with that look on your face, like you're evaluating antiques on* Nandemo Kanteidan. *I feel like she's gonna bust out with a line like, 'Oh, well done there.'*"** *Nandemo Kanteidan* (The Evaluate-Anything Team) is a variety show that began running in 1994. In each episode, experts evaluate antiques, collector's items, and such. Seinosuke Nakajima, a regular on the show, is famous for saying, "Oh, well done there."

P. 153 A ***yuki-onna***, which literally means "snow woman," is a type of spirit in Japanese mythology. While her traits and method of killing vary from tale to tale, she is generally described as having pale white skin and long black hair; sometimes she is wearing a white kimono or is nude. She appears in winter, often in snowstorms, and causes people to freeze to death.

P. 156 **Gachapin** is a green bucktoothed dinosaur with a sleepy-looking face and was originally the costar of a variety show for small children called *Hirake! Ponkikki* along with his companion, Mukku. He's sort of like

Barney the Dinosaur. His role has gradually expanded to be a general Fuji TV station mascot celebrity, making cameos on a wide variety of shows.

P. 159 A **sakaki** is a sort of flowering evergreen tree native to certain parts of Asia. It's considered sacred in the Shinto faith and is used for a number of ritual practices.

P. 159 **"Does she ship Seimei/Douman or something?"** An *onmyouji* is a traditional Japanese practitioner of the occult, and this is a popular subject in anime and manga. Abe no Seimei and Ashiya Douman were prominent *onmyouji* of the Heian period (794–1185); they were also rivals.

P. 168 **"In a Grove"** is a short story by Ryuunosuke Akutagawa (1892–1927) that features a variety of different characters telling the same story from different perspectives, and the inspiration for Akira Kurosawa's film *Rashomon*. In Japanese, "in a grove" has become an idiom to describe a situation in which everyone's story is different and the truth is unknown.

P. 172 **"I've read that before in *Kooky Trio*."** *Zukkoke Sannin-gumi* (Kooky trio) is a series of children's adventure stories about three boys. The series spans over fifty volumes.

P. 172 **"*Is that supposed to be Vega style or what?*"** Vega is a character in the Street Fighter series of video games who wields claw weapons (imagine Wolverine's claws).

Chapter 8 … With **Yukino Yukinoshita** aboard, the car drives away.

P. 180 **"The pair were on opposite ends of the spectrum, but they closely resembled each other, like Nega and Posi."** Nega and Posi are two cat mascot characters from the 1980s *shoujo* anime *Creamy Mami, the Magic Angel.* The two cats look exactly the same except for their swapped blue and pink color palettes, but as their names imply, they are like negative and positive, with completely opposite personalities.

Afterword

P. 185 ***Waiting in the Summer*** is the name of a 2012 high school romantic comedy anime.

P. 185 **JSDF** actually stands for "Japan Self-Defense Forces."

P. 185 **Marine Day**, the third Monday in July, is a national holiday in Japan. The purpose of the holiday is to consider the importance of the ocean to Japan, as an island nation.

P. 186 **Shenlong** is the dragon that grants wishes to those who gather all the dragon balls in Akira Toriyama's manga *Dragon Ball Z.* It was based on the Chinese myth of a spiritual dragon by the same name.